A DISH SERVED COLD

FOR MY FAMILY

George Colkitto

A DISH SERVED COLD

RYMOUR

© George Colkitto 2021

ISBN 978-1-8384052-7-4

Published by Rymour Books
45 Needless Road
PERTH
PH2 0LE

http://www.rymour.co.uk

cover and book design by Ian Spring
printed by Imprint Digital, Exeter, Devon

A CIP record for this book
is available from the British Library

All rights reserved. No part of this publication may be reproduced, stored in a retrieval system, or transmitted, in any form or by any means, electronic, mechanical, photocopying, recording or otherwise, without the prior permission of the copyright holder or holders. This book is sold subject to the condition that it shall not by way of trade or otherwise be circulated without the publisher's prior consent in any form of binding or cover other than that in which it is produced.

The paper used in this book is approved
by the Forest Stewardship Council

GEORGE COLKITTO is an ex-tax inspector, chartered accountant and bookshop proprietor. He writes both poetry and prose which have featured in many magazines and anthologies and he has won several literary prizes. He is the author of the Sebastian Symes series of Victorian detective novellas, featuring Sebastian Symes and Major Ritson, contemporaries of Sherlock Holmes. This is his first full-length crime novel.

CHAPTER ONE

Shuggie pushed half a scotch pie to the side and placed his knife and fork delicately on his plate. For a big man he picked at his food, rarely eating everything. There were only the two customers in Jimmy's Café, Shuggie and his mate Razor. When they entered there were a few late breakfasters lingering in the warmth; regular customers who were not put off by the peeling green paint on the walls, the chipped formica tables and red flooring worn thin in places to show the grey backing. Shortly after the newcomers arrived the lingerers slipped quietly away. Most kept away from Shuggie and Razor, if they had the choice.

Razor leant forward. There were those who thought that he was called Razor for his penchant for slashing anyone whom Shuggie wanted cut up. Now as he gazed at the half pie, his thin angular frame, head like a hatchet with long Roman nose protruding from his sallow face, hair shaved to leave a grey stubble, the reason for the name was clear. 'You leavin' that, big man?'

Shuggie smiled. 'Aye. On you go. How you're no' a fat lard I'll never know.'

Razor whipped the remains of the pie on to his plate. 'An' the chips?'

Shuggie nodded as Razor stabbed the three scraggy left-overs and popped them into his mouth, bits of chip spluttering out as he muttered a reply. 'Know me. I can eat what I want and nae bother.'

'Well get it over quick. We've business to see to. Yon daft ponce, in the wee steakhouse place, pays up today.'

'You sure? Been a bit reluctant last few weeks.'

Shuggie leant back, the chair creaking under the strain, placed two huge hands behind his mop of black curls and grinned. 'I thought that. I went round yesterday and reminded him about last week when he was stroppy. Any more trouble this time I wouldn't just give him a wee gentle tap to encourage him to be civil. This time would be serious' The chair grated across the tiles of Jimmy's Corner Café. 'Right swallow that and were off '

For a big man Shuggie moved with speed. As Razor stuffed the last of the pie into his mouth, Shuggie was half way to the door pulling on the thin black leather gloves he always wore when on a job. With a dismissive wave to the eponymous Jimmy behind the counter he let Razor dive after him as the door swung shut.

Jimmy wiped his brow with the dirty dish towel draped over his shoulder and fingered the fading bruise under his left eye. It was the remainder of one of Shuggie's gentle taps. Still it was his own fault. Him thinking Shuggie might pay for his grub and for Razor's. They went back twenty-three or so years, him and Shuggie; back to first day in Primary School. Shuggie towered over everyone but was a quiet soul, bullied in fact. Jimmy had taken him under his wing. So he thought it worth the ask being an old school mate and all that. Shuggie had pointed out, Jimmy was lucky not to have to pay them to keep his place open. Jimmy looked at the empty café. Maybe he should chuck it.

At the posher end of Paisley, Colin Ingleby was thinking the same as he counted twenty pound notes on to the marble surface of the bar at Gerry's Steak House Restaurant and put two hundred pounds into a white envelope. Should be brown, he thought.

Outside it was a bright spring day. The sort of day that usually made Colin feel alive but today he did not want to go and stand at his restaurant's doorway and drink in the view across to the ancient Abbey. In the good times he would watch as couples met at the Cross before strolling down to lunch. These were not the good times and he knew the only people he would see approaching were not welcome. He fingered the cut across the bridge of his nose. There were bruises fading under each eye. He cursed Shuggie Cameron.

Colin used to like looking in mirrors but today he tried to avoid the image in the one behind the bar. He knew a tired man would be staring back, with bruises hiding dark shadows, with frown lines which grew deeper each day. He had lost the swagger of his youth when he was the teen heartthrob of the Academy; playing rugby, star outside half of the first fifteen. At one time Old Grunger, the Sports Master at Balfour Academy had thought he would play for the district, perhaps make the national under eighteens although at five ten and one hundred and seventy pounds he was a little light for the top flight. The knee injury, which gave him a slight limp, had finished all that; tap tackled by his cousin in a bounce game. His waist had gained a few pounds but he could still glide between tables balancing a tray on outstretched arm, occasionally dreaming he had sold a dummy to an English full-back as he planted the glasses on the white table-covers to the cheers of a Murrayfield crowd. But burdened with money worries it was a while since he had be able to lose himself in day dreams.

He looked at his watch. They'd be any minute. His hands shook as he sealed the envelope. He picked up his mobile and looked again at yesterday's text message from Geraldine. 'Forget it, loser you are on your own.' It had been a faint hope that she might come back, would understand why he wasn't going to the police. Shuggie had pointed out, when he arranged 'security' for the restaurant, that side-kick Razor had a nephew who was a sergeant in the local nick; any reporting of the meeting would merely increase the cost in money and... The rest was unsaid but Colin understood.

It cut no ice with Geraldine. 'If you pay him I'm off,' she'd said. He had paid and she had moaned and then last week he had said he would stop. He meant to but his nerve failed him when he had to face Shuggie and Razor. She had shout and gone and he still got hit.

On the wall beside the mirror was a large photograph of Gerry. He'd named the place for her and her dark-eyed gaze welcomed every customer. He would need to get that down. He wasn't having her staring down on him every day. If he kept going maybe he should change the place's name. Did he want to come to work every day in a restaurant called Gerry's Steak House? Did he want to come to work period?

He stuffed the envelope into his trouser pocket as Shuggie and Razor walked in. In a sudden rush of anger and fear and hate, he picked up the meat cleaver which he'd brought from the kitchen. It had been a last minute thought to take it from the rack of knives and bring it through to the counter, insurance against Shuggie hitting him. Without waiting for them to speak he pointed it at them and shouted, 'Fuck off, Cameron. I'm not paying you again. Now get out.'

For an instant, Razor was taken aback by the vehemence of the welcome then was all set to teach this mad bastard a lesson he would not forget. 'Come on then punk. Make my day.' He moved forward as he spoke but, to his surprise, Shuggie pulled him back.

'Leave it,' Shuggie said.

Colin was shaking. He could feel the blood throbbing in the veins at his forehead. His head was swimming and he feared he would faint if the confrontation lasted any time. He slashed the air with the cleaver.

'I said fuck off. I'm not paying.'

Shuggie and Razor turned and left. Colin laid the cleaver on the cold marble and then grabbed it as the door swung back open. Shuggie looked in smiling.

'In future remember your manners. It's Mr Cameron to you. And that was a bad move. Now its three hundred but we'll give you a month free for the repairs.'

He was gone before Colin had said 'What repairs?'

Paul Elroy McNeil read the letter again. He had been convinced the original contact was a con. How many people had received fake e-mails from scammers saying that they had an unknown great uncle who wanted to leave them a fortune in his will? Or some namesake in Africa who just needed a bank account to transfer millions out of the country? First step in ripping them off. But in his case it had been true. There was a great uncle Tony and now he had in his hand the letter, from Geland, Sushter and Liebermann, of Chicago, with news that it would soon be dead great uncle Tony and rich Paul Elroy McNeil.

As he looked up from the letter he caught sight of his face reflected in the large window of his flat which had a view out over the river at the Mill Waterfall and on to the Town Hall and the Abbey steeple. He ran his fingers through a mop of slightly greying blond hair; time to visit Cut Above and get it re-tinted. Sandra, his girlfriend was sure to remark that if he let all the colour grow out there would be nothing left to distinguish him from his loser of a cousin, Colin Ingleby. At times she was so bloody annoying. Surely she could see that Colin was at least fifteen pounds heavier and had that limp; stupid bastard doing a cartilage, just when they would both have made the Districts. It would have made the papers, cousins playing in the District Fifteen at stand-off and inside centre. With Colin in the side he would be a natural for inside centre, despite Old Grunger's opinion that the two of them were not in the same league. Idiot couldn't see that it was a double act and that Colin would be nothing without him alongside. All that went out the window when the tosser fell over his own feet.

He tapped the letter against his other hand, saying aloud, 'This time Colin it's me who's the star.'

Paul was certain of his good fortune for he had checked on the lawyers and on his benefactor, Tony McNeil Simpster, his grandfather's half-brother. It was genuine and he would inherit Simpster's fortune. Mind you he would keep quiet about it, for no-one needed to know that the source of that wealth was a bit iffy. The old boy was ninety, his life on a shaky hook which had become even shakier, so that the inheritance would be soon; an inheritance that would transform Paul's future.

His creditors would have to be kept at bay for a few more months. Perhaps the bank would extend his overdraft when they saw the letter? It had been a hard few months at his work. Things at Yellow Brick Road, Scotland's leading estate agency, at least that was what they advertised, were becoming difficult. Sales in general had dropped off and Paul was suffering more than most. The old charm seemed to be slipping and he was under pressure in the office. Moreover there was that drawer of urgent bills he had hidden from Sandra but with this in the offing he would put those on one of his credit cards. He might open his own agency. He surveyed the open plan lounge kitchen diner, turned back to the view over the river, the thick white shag-pile carpet cosseting his steps. Thank God for great uncle Tony.

Actually it was amazing that Tony Simpster had lived to ninety, given he had been shot twice in 1946 and spent the fifties in a state penitentiary. Since then Tony had been on the right side of the law, or rather, Paul thought, he had avoided being caught.

Paul texted Sandra, *Steak Gerry's tonight 8.00,* then wondered about booking. There was no way they would not get a table, for the restaurant would be empty on a Tuesday. He could tell Sandra he did it to cheer Colin up as it would let the restaurant know there would be customers that night. Colin was going through a bad patch and would be pleased to get the business. He did not need to say to Sandra that it would be a bitter sweet thought for Colin would know that Gerry had spoken to him about the break-up. Booking would say that ahead would be an evening of Paul's quips. He decided to text; *Table for 2 at 8.00*. He added, *Put best champagne on ice*, laughed as he typed *best champagne*. That would really wind Colin up. Would he tell him about the millions to come? Not yet. There was plenty to wind Colin up about with the business struggling and Gerry gone.

Colin was always down when he saw Paul. It wasn't just that it remained him of their days on the rugby field. He hated to be reminded of the days when he was top of the class, the one all the teachers said would make a success, not like Paul, the class skiver. Well the skiver had almost made it as estate agent. The skiver had a riverside flat. The skiver had the Merc. All secure now the money was coming. The skiver was shacked up with the lovely Sandra, who, tonight, would look as stunning as ever and so little digs about Geraldine having gone would hit home.

He fiddled with his Rolex, fake but he knew Colin thought it was real. Tonight he could make a few jibes about the restaurant being quiet, flaunt his success. Yea he would keep the bit about the millions until they were in his hand.

Sandra's phone vibrated. She had it on silent while filming was in progress. She nearly missed it for Sam Browne contrived to squeeze between her and the props table, at that moment, so that he pressed tightly into her.

'I'm sure you could make this bigger,' he said in those deep sonorous tones so beloved by his fans. All heads turned and she felt her face redden. 'The nose' he said 'the nose' as if suddenly realising the double entendre. 'You lot have a bad mind.'

He placed his hands on her hips as if to ease past but they lingered a little longer than was necessary and slid down her buttocks as he moved away

There was laughter from most of the males, cast and crew, but little from the women. They knew, only too well, about his wandering hands and lewd comments. Sandra wondered how the fans would react if they saw him in real life, an ageing lecher with halitosis, but no doubt they would believe in him in his latest role as a romantic Cyrano de Bergerac. The world was full of fakes.

Pushing back her dyed blonde hair she wished she had punched Browne, split those pale rouged lips or bloodied his nose or kneed him in the crotch. Any of those would have satisfied her but ended this job, probably ended her career. Make-up artists who assaulted the star were not in great demand.

She read Paul's text. 'Bugger', she thought, 'a bad day goes worse'. She would need to rush back to the flat after work, change and then spend an evening watching him wind up his cousin, Colin. Poor bloke could do without that with Gerry having left him. She had heard that chefs did terrible things to peoples' food if the customer upset them. She tried not to dwell on that, when out with Paul, but always ordered a different dish from him so that the staff would know which plate was his.

Tonight Paul would niggle Colin about Gerry but the boot might soon be on the other foot. This relationship was doomed and some day she would let Paul know what she really thought of him. She had been drawn to him by his looks but also by the trappings of success but once the initial lust had worn off, she realised the wealth was fake and so was Paul. It was time to go but where to and how was the problem, so it had drifted into these long months. She was a fool to stay. When they started going out she thought he had money, what with the flat and flash car, but when she had moved in, there was the reality of debts and more debts. Actually at the moment she would be a fool to go for if this inheritance was real and was going to make him rich then she was getting a share of that before she blew him away.

Sandra saw that Sam Browne had finished the last scene as a young Cyrano, well as young as they had been able to achieve with make-up, and would be coming over for the next prosthetic. She took it from the box and, on impulse, spread the inside with rouge. He wanted his nose bigger, she would make it look it. Before she could undo her prank Browne was in the chair and had picked up the prosthetic.

'Time for you to get your hands on me girl.'

She steeled herself to touch him. He deserved more than a joke. As she fitted it to Sam it occurred to her that it was possible that the joke would backfire and cost her the job but at least, when he took it off, his beery nose would show its true colour. Anyway it was too late now for regrets. The deed was done.

CHAPTER TWO

In Gerry's Steak House only Paul and Sandra remained from the sparse Tuesday evening's customers. Colin could hear Stefan, his chef, in the kitchen clearing up. He slipped from the shadows taking the champagne bottle from the ice bucket on the bar and topped up Sandra's glass with the last of the wine. Christ, he thought, surely bloody Paul and Sandra would go home soon. The other diners, all four of them had left just after nine. It was a faint hope. Paul tapped his arm as he poured.

'Let's have another bottle,' said Paul, 'and you must join us.'

Colin shook his head. He'd had enough of Paul's none-to-subtle comments. 'Things to do. Have to clear up in the kitchen.'

Paul was stretched out over his chair, jacket long ago discarded and three buttons on his shirt undone, showing his hairy chest. Having drunk most of the first bottle of champagne and a fair bit of the second, along with the two brandies after the meal, he was in a garrulous mood.

'You need to relax. Enjoy life a bit more. No wonder Gerry got fed up with you. You've been like a wet rag all night.'

'Who said Gerry was fed up?' Colin snapped back. 'She wants a break from…' 'there was a dramatic pause before he added coldly … 'customers like you.'

He knew he should not have said this but Paul was a bastard; hints all evening about how well things were going for him, the champagne was to celebrate good news, which for the moment had to remain secret. Commiserations about Geraldine mixed with comments such as maybe Colin could replace her with a looker like his Sandra.

Paul laughed. 'OK. I'm out of line. So why not get drunk at my expense. Bring another bottle. Let's all get blootered.'

It was Sandra placing a hand on Colin's arm and saying, 'Please do. I would like that,' swung it. There was something in her eyes and tone made him nod.

He went through to the back. Stefan had finished cleaning the range and was about to start washing down the worktops. Colin opened the back door and took Stefan's coat from the hooks alongside it.

'Leave that', he said. 'That's the last of the customers gone. I'll get that in the morning.'

He did not want to admit to Stefan that he was being friendly to Paul and that they were about to start a late drinking session. It would start an argument for Stefan hated Paul. This was partly from the many sarcastic comments Paul made about Stephan's cooking, but mainly because he thought Paul was a racist. Paul insisted in calling him 'Magnetic', because he was a Pole. Tomorrow was Wednesday, the restaurant did not open till the evening, he could have a long lie, recover from the session with Paul and Sandra and still finish the kitchen before Stephan came in to work.

'See you tomorrow at 4.00pm,' he said as he ushered Stefan out into the darkness of the rear yard.

He nipped up to his small flat above the restaurant. Hidden in the depths of the fridge, he had a really expensive bottle of champagne. He had been keeping it for his own special occasion but, with Gerry gone, that was not going to happen any time soon. He flicked on the kitchen light, pulled out the contents of the fridge and retrieved the bottle from its hideaway at the back. He threw the scattered contents back in and, lifting the bottle, patted the label. Tonight he would drink as much of Paul's money as he could.

In the rear car park of Gerry's Steak House, Razor stirred at the sound of the kitchen door opening. The shaft of light sliced through the dark and silhouetted in the doorway he saw Colin Ingleby and Stefan, his chef. From the deep shadows by the bins he heard their conversation, smiled about what they would be seeing by 4.00 tomorrow. Shortly after Stefan left, the lights in the upstairs flat came on briefly and then went off.

Razor checked his watch, settled back; last customer gone, Ingleby off to bed, give it an hour, Shuggie had said, which would make sure Ingleby was asleep, and then he could go to work, have the place trashed before Ingleby could react. So an hour it would be. Taking a pouch of tobacco from his pocket he adjusted his position, so that he could see his fingers, in that small area of brightness where the street light angled over the car park wall, rolled a cigarette and lit up.

A cat wondered in, glanced up at him and walked on. After it had passed, he heard a scurry among the litter in the far corner and the shadowy shape of a rat moved quickly away, disappeared into the back alley. Razor watched it go and then let his thoughts wander with the faint trail of smoke rising as he exhaled. He finished his fag, flicked the dout to the ground and checked his watch again. Christ, it was only fifteen minutes since the lights went out. He rolled another fag, turned over a beer crate as a seat and wedged himself in the angle between yard wall and building. Here he was out of the breeze that was beginning to gain strength.

A car horn blared, a screech of brakes and the cat from earlier shot over the wall by his head. 'Jesus' he said under his breath, his heart hammering. He checked the time. It was nearly 2.00am. 'Bugger, must have fallen asleep.'

Standing rather stiffly he placed the beer crate back where he had found it, picked up the rucksack he had left by the bins. On his way round to the front of the restaurant he took a loose brick from the alleyway wall. The street was deserted and here, it was in relative darkness. Glass from the broken street-light, broken by Razor that afternoon, lay in the gutter. He was a little surprised to see from a glimmer in the window of the restaurant that a candle was burning somewhere inside. Careless, he thought sarcastically, that could cause a fire. Shuggie and he would need to have a word with Ingleby about that; when they were looking after the place, they would not tolerate unauthorised fires.

Razor moved into the doorway of Gerry's Steak House, took two bottles from his rucksack, placed them by the door and lit the fuses. It only took a few seconds for him to smash the glazed door with the brick and lob both fire-bombs, now well alight, through the broken pane. There was a satisfying whoosh of flame as he turned and walked away.

The scene round the table was one of disarray. A large amount of drink had been consumed.

Earlier, during the banter, Colin threw the ring given to him by Geraldine onto the table, saying, 'So much for that Luckenbooth design, my and Gerry's initials engraved inside. Symbol of eternal love, she said.'

Paul picked it up from the table and put it on and admired it in the candlelight. 'Looks pretty good. How about I keep it and have it re-engraved for Sandra and me.'

Colin tried to grab it back as Paul added. 'Two hearts entwined, kissing. Maybe you were a lousy kisser, Colin. Maybe it was not your lack of business success that drove Geraldine away but your prowess as a lover.'

Sandra was so totally pissed and so totally pissed off with Paul that she offered to adjudicate; somewhat to Paul's surprise and Colin's delight. This was the last straw for her in a horrible evening. She had been correct about the rouge trick on Sam Browne not ending well for her. Browne had gone ballistic and insisted that she be fired on the spot. Faced with a ranting star, the director had ordered her from the set and tomorrow, in the afternoon, she saw the clock on the restaurant wall said it was nearly 1.00 am., today, she faced a disciplinary meeting.

When she got home to the flat, Paul was so absorbed in his letter, his news, about going to Gerry's to gloat at his good fortune against Colin's failures, that he had no time for her tale of woe. And now it was all about how she was 'his Sandra' like a bloody possession.

Now was her turn for revenge.

She seized Colin in a passionate embrace and kissed him. She intended to say he was marvellous whatever happened but actually Colin was. Whether it was the drink, her fragile state, Paul watching, or chemistry, in that kiss her feelings for Colin changed. Moreover she sensed in him a similar response. The embrace became softer, lingered until Paul shouted.

'OK. Cut it out you two. I shouldn't have said you were rubbish, Colin.'

Sandra broke away, winked at Colin and, turning to Paul, said, 'Rubbish. He's bloody good.'

By now Paul was out of his seat and prizing them apart.

Colin pushed him away. 'Perhaps you should take lessons,' he said, 'watch'.

He pulled Sandra towards him. Before he could kiss her Paul swung him round and punched.

As both were very drunk, it might have ended OK, for Paul's timing was terrible and Colin was falling, from being spun round, when the blow struck, but as Colin over balanced he struck his nose on the table, opening up the cut already there from Shuggie's 'wee tap'. He began to bleed profusely. Sandra grabbed Paul's handkerchief from the top pocket of his jacket, which lying on the adjacent table was the nearest thing to hand. She started to staunch the flow. Blood splattered Paul' shirt as he grabbed it back. He was not having his best silk hankie ruined on Colin. He shoved a napkin from the table into Sandra's hand. 'Ruin one of his,' he said falling back on to the seat.

Sandra guided Colin to the bar where she soaked the napkin in icy water from the champagne bucket and pressed the wet cloth to his nose. It took several minutes for the bleeding to stop.

When the upper pane of the glass door shattered, they froze in surprise. It seemed to Colin that time slowed as he saw the two burning bottles arc into the dining room. Sandra screamed. The contents spread over the floor, flames catching on the table cloths and wooden tables. Colin, in some strange reflex action began to put on the jacket lying beside him. With it half on and half off, he realised the speed with which the flames were catching hold. He caught a glimpse of Paul still slouched in his seat as the fire reached him and shouted, 'For Christ sake, Paul, run.' He saw Paul stir, rise and start towards them before thickening smoke blocked his view. He grabbed Sandra by the arm and throwing the jacket over their heads hustled her out into the kitchen.

Paul did not follow them. Left alone in the aftermath of the punch, he had carried on drinking, sullenly watching Sandra's ministrations, until he fell into a stupor. He did not stir when the glass in the door shattered, nor when the first petrol bomb broke on the floor by the door, not even when the second landed near his table.

He half heard some shout from Colin about 'run' and began to stir but he was too slow, too drunk. A sheet of smoke and flames cut him off. He glimpsed the swing door into the kitchen open as Colin and Sandra escaped. Smoke caught in his throat and he stumbled and fell.

Close to the floor the air was cooler and he could see. Christ, there was no way to the door for there were flames everywhere. He was going to die. Instinct made him roll away from the fire, back into an alcove where seating had been built to form a booth. The fire had not reached as far. He lay gasping with fear. It was only a matter of time.

There was a gap under the bench seating, narrow but he could slide under. Like an animal seeking shelter he burrowed beneath it, curled into a ball and pushed back as far as he could go against the wall.

What he thought was solid was an illusion, thin plasterboard over an old entrance to the restaurant cellar. When he felt the wall flex, Paul braced is feet against the bench and pushed. The plasterboard gave way and he fell, passing from heat into cold dampness, the seconds it took to fall ten feet seemed endless and flashing through his mind was the realisation that this was the end.

The landing stunned him. Winded, bruises, hands and face stinging where they had been scorched by the heat, Paul stirred, testing each limb to see that it was not broken. He was lying in a pile of... what? It stank. He heard squeaks, rats. Paul gathered his thoughts. He was not dead. He was in the cellar. The Fire Brigade would come and he would be OK.

His eyes were becoming accustomed to the dark and he could make out shadowy shapes. He was on mound of what seemed to be boxes, covered by tarpaulin. Whatever had been stored was ruined now but it had broken his fall. He was lucky to be alive.

He began to giggle hysterically. What were the chances, about to inherit millions, go for a celebration meal and die in a fire? The giggles stopped. Hang on; what were the chances of that? This wasn't chance. Someone had tried to kill him. He should have foreseen it. Great uncle Tony, gangster of Chicago, there must be people out there thought they should inherit, not some bum in Scotland. Someone wanted him dead. Perhaps at this very minute waiting outside to make sure he was dead. Did he want them to see where he went? If he slipped away he could disappear until he had the money and then what could they do? Smoke was beginning to filter down from above, a rat scurried past his feet. Bugger the future; he might die in this shit hole if he couldn't get out.

Paul slid down the tarpaulin, feeling ahead with out-stretched arms. Reaching the cellar floor he stood up gingerly. His body ached and for a moment he thought of giving up. A crash from above as something collapsed onto the restaurant floor spurred him on. Through the gloom he thought could make out a wall ahead and a patch of faint grey. Shuffling in that direction his right foot hit a loose brick, then more bricks made him stumble. He fell against the cellar wall. Close up the grey patch was a gap in the wall round a pipe which went through to the adjacent property. He peered into another cellar. Here, three glass grills in the pavement above let in a little light from the street. The old brick work was loose and easily pulled away to make the gap into a hole large enough to squeeze through.

By the light from the above Paul could see that on the far side was a wooden door. He picked his way across to it through some old pipes. It was locked but the wood was rotten and when he kicked against it the lock gave way to reveal a stone stair. Fortunately the door at the top was not locked for it was solid. He opened it slowly. Green and white tiles of a tenement close shone in the light of a bare bulb, almost blinding him after the darkness. No-one was around. He tiptoed out the back door.

Paul was heading for the lane, staying tight against the wall between the tenement's back green and the restaurant yard, so that he was hidden, when he heard Colin and Sandra over the wall.

'Do you think he's dead?' Sandra whispered.

'Dead! Shit, look at the place. There's flames coming from the kitchens now. He hadn't a chance. We'd better get away. I'll explain later but I don't want to be found at the moment.'

In the brief silence that followed Paul imagined Sandra's tear filled eyes and was about to call out he was OK when she spoke.

'Come back to Paul's. I need to think.'

Paul was shocked by the calmness in her voice and lent against the rough bricks. Of course. They had to be in on it. One or both. Who else knew he would be here? No-one. And they'd fixed it to leave him alone. Christ the bloody punch missed the bastard and yet they made a meal of it to get over to the bar. He slapped his forehead, froze when the slap sounded to him like a cannon shot but there was no questioning voice from the other side of the wall. Christ he was an idiot. He had to get away. But where? He was in shirt sleeves, dirty from the cellars and stinking of smoke and God knows what. He felt his pockets, loose change in one, no wallet that was in his jacket back in the restaurant. On his belt was his bunch of keys. He could get into his flat but going there was no good as Sandra would be there and she wanted him dead.

A thought struck him and he quickly checked the bundle of keys. Yes, it was there; the key to one of the penthouse flats on the top floor of Mill Tower, the floor above his. Three days before he had been showing it to a potential buyer who said he would be back with his partner for a second viewing. He had kept the key in case of the phone call. Well that was what he had told the office and it was half true but in reality he wanted to get back in on his own to lust after the opulence and dream of his inheritance and owning a place like it. He clasped hands and thanked God. It could not be better. He could keep an eye on Sandra, he knew no-one would check on it, and Graham McCluskey, the owner had kitted it out so that it looked as if it was occupied.

Thank God for Graham McCluskey who believed in holding out for a premium price and believed in dressing his properties appropriately, even putting clothes in the wardrobes, towels and toiletries in the bathroom, tins and stuff in the kitchen. Who had left the sale in his hands.

Paul smiled, how often he had cursed the man when unwillingness to drop the selling price threatened a deal and the commission. McCluskey had a reputation as a hard man so Paul never argued with him but he was a good client even if he was an awkward one. Now, it was worth all the delayed and lost fees. He could hide there for days.

CHAPTER THREE

Sam Browne ran his fingers through his unusually black hair and grimaced as Shuggie made himself comfortable on the white leather sofa, pulling the matching footstool across and swinging his size ten boots on to it. Sam knew that there would be more scratches, marks which no amount of leather polish would rub off. He consoled himself with the thought that it was a necessary price to pay for Shuggie's services, for Shuggie was good at what Sam required. He still had doubts about Razor, but that was another price he had to pay to have his enforcer, for Shuggie wanted Razor. According to Shuggie, Razor saved the cost of three more heavies. He scared punters so much that the two of them could handle everything. Shuggie was a believer in the fewer people involved the fewer problems.

The leather suit was the least of his worries. He poured two whiskies and handed one to Shuggie. Ingleby refusing to pay could start a trend if they did not dealt with him quickly, but how deep into this protection racket did he want to be. This was going further than he had thought when McCluskey put the squeeze on him.

'You're sure Razor will handle it OK?' he asked.

'Look,' replied Shuggie, 'its dead simple. The restaurant will be empty. Windows put in, a quick trash of the bar. Ingleby will get a hell of a fright. He'll be putty from now on and we send out a message, not to mess with us.'

'What if Ingleby comes down. Can we trust Razor. We don't want him dead or a cabbage?' asked Sam.

Shuggie shook his head. 'He's up in his flat. There's a back fire escape. He's basically a coward and will not seek confrontation. It'll be fine. And if not…' There was along silence and Shuggie seemed to drift, lose concentration until Sam moved uneasily. Shuggie looked through him coldly, 'tough, things happen. Razor will see it doesn't get out-of-hand.'

Under the fake tan Sam blanched but he was not an actor for nothing and knew what this required was a non-committal shrug. Inside he was in turmoil. This was becoming darker by the day. Six months he had been running protection for McCluskey, the bastard, but he had to pay for the cocaine somehow and if that tape ever got out that was the career gone. Penthouse flat and a couple of blondes he could laugh off, but him folding a twenty pound note to sniff up the lines on the coffee table, that was curtains for him on TV, at least for a few years. He looked at his reflection in the huge mirror on the wall behind Shuggie. He was holding up pretty well but even he would concede that he did not have a few years. Shit he had to keep this going. He muttered aloud, 'that bastard McCluskey'

Shuggie stared at Sam, eyes narrowing. 'Did you say, McCluskey? What's he got to do with it?' His feet dragged across the leather of the stool as he stiffened on the couch, veins in his neck bulging.

Sam could not believe he had said it aloud. McCluskey had said never to mention his name and certainly never to Shuggie. He was about to die… twice'

He thought quickly. He could pretend he hadn't said that name, said someone else, but who, and why now. No he had to admit it but he had to have a reason other than the real one. He gained time by taking a slurp of whisky.

'Yea. I was thinking that any sign I'm, we're, getting soft, McCluskey'll be right in there, taking over.'

Shuggie gave a harsh chuckle. 'Don't you worry about McCluskey, while you pay me, he'll never get a look in.' He stopped to pick up his glass. 'And he knows it.'

Sam raised his glass to Shuggie, 'That bastard McCluskey, and Colin Ingleby, whose goose is cooked.'

Shuggie stared at him quizzically for a moment then seemed to relax on the settee. 'Yea, like that. To cooking their goose. ' They clinked glasses and drank.

Sam breathed out. The moment had passed; Shuggie had no idea McCluskey was involved. He failed to note the brief smile flick across Shuggie's face as he recognised Sam's attempt at deception, betrayed by the slight sweat on Sam's brow, the twitch in the corner of his left eye, the tightness in his lips, as he lied. Sam thought that he was a consummate liar but Shuggie was well versed in spotting the signs. He had wondered if McCluskey was somewhere on the scene and now he knew, and Shuggie had a score to settle.

In the rear yard of the Steak House, Colin cradled Sandra in his arms, watched the flames licking under the kitchen door. There was no way that Paul would survive. It was pure chance he and Sandra had got out.

He realised that despite the shock of the night's events he liked the feel of Sandra's body next to his, but that was not why moments ago he had pulled her even closer and was holding her tightly against his chest. With her face pressed into the jacket she could not speak and he was certain he had heard a noise over the wall. Someone was waiting for them.

It had come to him as they ran through kitchen that those bastards wanted him dead. He had been thinking of that as they stood watching the flames spread and he had decided to slip away for a while and go into hiding. When they found Paul's body there was a chance they would think it was him. Anyone in those flames would be unrecognisable. The ring from Gerry would still be on Paul's finger and Gerry would recognise it. He might be able to disappear until the heat died down and miraculously resurrect to claim the insurance money. Now he was certain of it. Someone was creeping around on the other side of the wall and he had to keep Sandra quiet. As he moved slowly away from the wall, he saw that Sandra was about to speak. He held a finger to her lips. She looked puzzled but stayed silent.

The lane was deserted. Colin heard a faint clinking, as if someone was rattling a bunch of keys from the neighbouring yard. Whoever it was could not see them and he hurried Sandra the few yards to the street and turned into the maze of narrow lanes. Behind him he heard the sirens of the approaching fire engine. When Sandra looked up at him and pointed back to the main road he shook his head and hustled her on.

It was only half a mile to Paul's flat but it took them over forty minutes. Colin stopped whenever he thought that he saw anyone about. He also wanted to make sure that they were not being followed. He had an impression that as they left the yard he had heard muffled footsteps and twice he thought he saw something white move in the shadows, wondered if he could make out a man hiding, but he must be wrong because fleeting as the view was, it reminded him of Paul.

Sandra wept for most of the journey, between sobs muttering that she had cursed Paul throughout the meal for his selfishness and that when the fight broke out she had wished him dead. She repeated over and over 'It's my fault.'

CHAPTER FOUR

In the north bound London to Glasgow train, Hunter Dunbar the third, shifted stiffly in his sleeper berth, pulling the blanket tighter, cursing the chill. He had not felt warm since he took a taxi from Heathrow Airport to Euston.

He consoled himself with the thought he would be home in a couple of days. Liebermann had said this had to be a quick job; not that he would have hung about. When Sol Simpster said he wanted someone hit, Hunter did it fast. There was regular business for an efficient killer and Hunter took pride in his reputation. He wondered if his parents had a premonition when he was born, looked at him and saw no tiny defenceless infant but a jungle predator, said he has to be called Hunter. He had overheard a comment in a Chicago bar, 'Keep out of his way. The guy's a nutter. Even his mother said he was a psycho.' Perhaps this time he would get past the lawyer to meet Simpster. From what Liebermann had let slip, this hit was high on Simpster's list.

Hunter checked the time. They would arrive at Glasgow in an hour. With any luck he could be on the train back tonight. A few hours in London and then back tomorrow to his own bed in Chicago, curled up warm with Chantelle. These Scots hicks wouldn't know what had happened. Some guy McCluskey was to meet him from the train, local small-timer. Hunter shivered, pulled the blanket over his head, drifted into a doze, hoping McCluskey was clued up enough to get this show moving.

Glasgow Central Station was beginning to buzz with early commuters as the passengers from the night sleeper filed down Platform one. Hunter Dunbar could see over their heads to the barrier, adjusted his black hat to a rakish angle. Suddenly he quickened his stride pushing between two fat ladies, overtaking a young man in business suit.

Sam Browne was at the gate holding a large white card with McCluskey emblazoned in bold black. Hunter hurried past the ticket collector and stooped beside Browne pretending to adjust his shoe. He whispered angrily.

'Don't look down, McCluskey.'

Sam involuntarily did so.

'I said, don't look down', Dunbar growled. 'Wait a few moments, then go outside. I'll find you.'

Dunbar straightened and shouldered his way off without looking back.

Sam waited as instructed before following across the station concourse towards the main entrance. Outside he wandered towards the statue of a fireman which was at the corner. From there he could also see the exit to Hope Street. At the corner he turned to look the length of the street. From behind a hand grabbed the sign angrily from under his arm.

'You fuckin thick bastard. I said I would be wearing a black hat and at six-four you couldn't miss me. Want to tell the fuckin' world I'm in town. Look you stupid bastard there's CCTV all over this bloody place and you walk round with your name in lights. What sort of zombie are you, McCluskey?'

It had been after midnight that Sam received McCluskey's call as he sat drinking. He was running his fingers over the fresh scratches on the foot-stool where Shuggie's boots had scared the leather. He needed whisky to dull his nerves. The phone had jerked him from his reverie. He had no choice but to agree when McCluskey called. So he had been up at six to meet an American gangster from the night train and pretending to be McCluskey. He'd had film roles with fewer possible twists. Still all he had to do was hand over a brown envelope and take the guy to the penthouse in the old mill.

Sam bristled as Dunbar berated him. He was not used to looking up at people, was conscious of the dark bags under his eyes and that his grey roots were showing. He had to be on set later this morning.

There was menace in this American. McCluskey had said that the man was dangerous, and if McCluskey thought that then this was a man to get shot of as soon as possible. Had McCluskey said about a hat; he could not remember, but given the whiskies it was possible. He decided best to ignore the rant. Keep it brief. Why couldn't McCluskey deal with his own problems?

'Misunderstanding,' he muttered. 'Sorry, sooner were gone the better.' He thrust the envelop into Hunter's hand. He was glad that he'd checked and all it contained was a photograph of a man called Paul Leroy McNeil and an address for him in the Heritage Mill. It was a bit of a shock when he first looked for he thought that it was Colin Ingleby until he saw the name. Bloody similar looking though. He could relax for it did not matter if the transfer was caught on camera. You could not be prosecuted for handing over a photograph. 'Car's down here,' he said heading off.

Paul lay naked on the bed on the penthouse mezzanine. There were clothes in the wardrobe and some things in drawers, as he had remembered, but when he crept into the flat the previous evening, he could not find anything like pyjamas or underwear. His soot and blood stained clothes lay on the floor where he had dropped them. He had been too exhausted to turn down the bed and slept where he fell, spread-eagled on the black silk quilt.

He woke with a start when he heard voices in the hall, rolling to the floor as the door to the open plan lounge opened. He peered through the gap under the smoked glass balustrade to the mezzanine. A long thick giant of a man carrying a hold-all and black hat stepped in followed by a half-familiar face.

'This place secure, McCluskey?' The tall man, from his accent American, walked to the window, 'now that's a view. These old churches are quaint, ain't they.'

'The Abbey is twelfth century,' said Sam Browne. 'Yes, only you and Mc... ' Sam stuttered into a chocked cough, 'only you and I have a key.'

'Twelfth century. You don't say. Gee that's old.'

'There's a bedroom through here, en-suite,' Sam showed Dunbar into the room off the lounge.

Paul realised how lucky he was to have chosen the mezzanine last night. His fixation with owning a flat like this and sleeping on the mezzanine had brought him straight up the spiral stair without a moments hesitation. With the two men gone he gathered his clothes but before he could put on any Sam and Hunter were back. He slid back down to watch the scene below.

'So McCluskey, You say this is Heritage Mill, the actual block where the Paul McNeil guy lives.'

'That's my information. A flat on the floor below I think. Sorry don't know the number and could not see the name on that board in the entrance.'

Paul placed the face to the voice. An actor in one of the TV soaps. Did local fête openings. Had looked at a couple of properties as investments. Something Browne. Why did this American keep calling him McCluskey? He was nothing like McCluskey. And how come he had a key? And more importantly why was a big bugger of an American interested in him?

'Yea, no problem, I'll find the number. Just checking we were in the same block. I'll tell Liebermann you guys came good.'

Sam pointed to a carrier bag he had left by the door as they came in. 'There's stuff in there for you, eggs, bacon, coffee etc. Enough to get you started.'

'Fine. That's all I'll need. Won't be here long,' Hunter picked up the carrier, 'I've got your mobile number. I'll ring when I want you.'

Paul felt the cold morning air from the corridor outside as Sam left. There was no warmth in the polished pine floor and he realised he was shivering. He lay getting colder as Hunter rustled up bacon and eggs, cursing the open plan living of the penthouse which a few days earlier he had been extolling as one of its attractions. He did not dare move even though the American whistled tunelessly as he slurped coffee and made his breakfast, then sat at the breakfast bar with its view over the falls to the Abbey. When he finished eating the man took a photograph from a brown envelope and sat for ages looking at it and then at the view and then back to studying it.

It seemed like hours before the American clattered the mug down, had a final look at the photograph, and went through to the bedroom. Even then Paul lay unmoving and frozen for several minutes, afraid he would return. It was only when he heard faint snoring that he decided he could risk escape. He could barely feel his body and what could be felt, ached. He wondered if anything was broken from the fall through the restaurant floor. He had to grasp the balustrade to pull himself up. It creaked alarmingly as he levered his full weight upright.

In the bedroom, Hunter Dunbar jerked awake, alert. He slipped to the floor eyes fixed on the door. He knew there was someone in the flat, sensed that the noise that woke him had caused them to freeze. Kept his breath shallow

Paul began to relax. There was no sound from the bedroom. He let go of the balustrade without thinking and, as it adjusted to the release of pressure, it creaked once more. Before he could react the bedroom door burst open.

Don't move, Buddy.' He saw the American was pointing a gun. 'Who the fuck are you?'

CHAPTER FIVE

Jimmy's Café had its usual band of early morning customers. Workmen rushing a filled roll, the lonely needing another voice, the insomniac finding a reason to be up and about. There was extra chatter this morning about the police buzzing around the town centre and the smoke hanging above it. The buzz of conversation drowned out the music on the radio. The noise dropped to a murmur when a traffic report cut in as customers listened for updates about the road in the town centre which the police had closed due to a major fire. Jimmy was able to enlighten those who had missed the seven o'clock news.

'That fancy restaurant in Shawl Place. Burnt to the ground, they say. Buildings either side are being shored up to make them safe. Canny get near for Fire tenders and polis. Couple of the taxi blokes heard a bobby say it could be arson. That owner who lives up stairs. Well he canny be found. Me, my guess, insurance job gone wrong. Ask yerself how many failing hotels, pubs, eateries catch fire. Damn, I'd bloody do it if I could afford insurance. This burns down I wouldnae get tuppence.'

A flurry of rude replies stopped when a blast of cold air drew the customers' attention to the café door. Razor entered and the chill in the café was as much from his arrival as from the icy draft, but when Shuggie did not appear, the customers relaxed a little. Razor was a mean mad bastard drunk, or when he took offence, or was acting on the orders of a boss, but Shuggie was a quiet menace; unpredictable. He could be considerate and kind or cold and hard. Best thing was to avoid. No Shuggie and they could continue to eat, as long as they kept their heads down. As Razor scanned the café two men quickly rose to vacate his favourite corner table.

Razor nodded to Jimmy and sat waiting. Other orders were ignored until Jimmy filled a plate and placed it with exaggerated deference on the table. A minor act of defiance which gave him some satisfaction and allowed him to swagger back behind the counter. Razor was too busy tucking in to notice any slight.

Razor cleared the plate in a flurry of laden forks and bulging cheeks. He had just taken a slice of bread to wipe up last traces of egg yolk, when the café again filled with cold air. He saw Shuggie standing in the doorway and waved to the chair opposite. Shuggie dismissed the invitation with a shake of the head and a jerk of his thumb to the street. Razor stuffed the bread into his mouth. He scrambled out, metal chair clattering on the table leg, plate skidding, dangerously near to falling, as he hurried to catch up with the departing Shuggie.

'Hey Big Man, what's the rush. Ye no havin' breakfast?'

Shuggie walked on a few steps then stopped. 'I said a warning. Widows mashed. Trash the place. When the fuck did I say fire. I never use fire, you little shit. Christ you've destroyed the place. And what about Ingleby? Did he get out?'

Razor wilted under Shuggie's stare. 'I thought you'd be pleased. Just a bit of a fire and ye know it scares the punters. No-one's was ever gonna mess with us efter this.'

'A bit of a fire! For fuck's sake the place is a ruin.'
Shuggie came closer. His breath moving Razor's fringe. 'What about Ingleby?'

'I don't know. I mean I dinna hang about. Chucked in the two Molatov cocktails, saw the flames catch and I wis off. He wis upstairs. I checked. I did. He must o' got out.'

Shuggie turned away heading towards the town centre. 'Well he's not been seen. Odd that for a man whose house is a smoking pile of rubble. You would expect him to be seen. He's not in a hospital. I'm thinking you've cremated him.'

Razor stood stunned by Shuggie's anger then hurried after him. They walked side by side in silence until, as they passed a gap site between disused church and ornamental flower beds, Razor touched Shuggie's arm. 'See, Big Man, it happens, don't it. Fire, its a dodgy thing. Maist times I get it right. Yon pub that was there. Remember, The Cricketers, it burnt doon. That wis eight year ago. That's the last time I got it wrang.'

Shuggie swung round mid-stride. 'The Cricketers was you. I thought it was McCluskey.'

The vehemence of the response took Razor aback. 'Aye, well it wis. I wis with him.'

Razor saw Shuggie grimace and heard his sharp exhale. 'A girl died. Fuck man, you killed… ' The sentenced died.

He rarely gave a thought to what Shuggie was feeling, indeed Shuggie was a closed book when it came to feelings. It was as if he had none. Today the veins stood out on his temples. His fists clenched and unclenched, knuckles showing white. The restaurant fire seemed to have struck some nerve. And now the reaction about a dead girl. Razor did not like it. Why would Shuggie care about a barmaid? Mind you she was McCluskey's ex and Shuggie hated McCluskey. His throat tightened, causing him to squeak as he pleaded.

'We dinna know she wis there. McCluskey said the pub would be empty. It wis midnight on a Sunday. We dinna know she wid leave McCluskey to be wie that man in the pub. Had taken tae kippin' in the back.'.

'And you started the fire.'

'The two o' us. Not just me. McCluskey. But listen, the lass died but it wis an accident.'

Shuggie stood immobile, jaws tight clenched. Razor searched for words; anything to have the moment pass.

'Look how it turned out. It made McCluskey. Fair shook the punters. That's how McCluskey's empire grew fast. It'll be the same for you. Your reputation will be made if McNeil is dead. Dinna dump me. Ye know that's what McCluskey did. The bastard got rid o' me. Said if I ever said a word he'd… Shite. Big Man. Dinna mention whit I said or I'm deid.'

The few seconds of silence that followed seemed to Razor to be hours. A man waiting to be condemned he watched Shuggie. McCluskey would have no hesitation. Cross him and it was death. At least Shuggie was calmer. 'Please Big Man.'

Shuggie gave a nod, 'No worries, Razor. Away back have another coffee,' and he was off, continuing up the hill past the College, bleary-eyed students parting before him. Razor did not hear him mutter, 'No worries, you're dead already.'

CHAPTER SIX

Sandra woke, sunlight blinding her, panicking. That was a shot. Her dream was no dream. She and Paul were being chased through the streets by a mad gunman. Slowly her vision adjusted to the light. She was in bed. There was Paul comfortably beside her. But she had heard a shot. She was sure of it. Either that or she now dreamt in sound and that had never happened before. And the night was coming back. That was not Paul, the man whose hand rested on her left breast was Colin Ingleby. Paul was a frazzled crisp back in the restaurant. She closed her eyes, sank into the pillow.

She should be upset but was not. She rather liked that it was not Paul beside her. Perhaps the fire had done her a favour. Perhaps Colin would feel that he too had found a soul-mate. She wondered if this was shock, glanced at the head next to hers, sleeping, handsome despite the bruises beginning to spread round the eyes, the sticking plaster over the split nose. She kissed the bristle shadow on a strong chin. A girl could dream. The thought brought her back to the shot. Come on girl, a car back firing on the road by the falls, who would be shooting in Heritage Mill?

Colin's eyelids flickered and he stirred, his fingers moving gently over her breast and on to the curve of her neck. She rolled closer her hands reaching to embrace him. He whispered, 'Gerry', but she did not mind. Gerry was the woman from the past; today was a beginning. 'It's Sandra' she said, lips touching each bruised eye. 'Sandra... and we're safe. Go back to sleep.'

She slipped out of bed, put on a dressing gown and went through to the kitchen. Colin would wake to a feast. They would need to think and a full stomach, Sandra believed, helped thinking. She was certain Colin would be a kindred spirit. In the kitchen, lying by the window was a letter to Paul from Chicago lawyers which she began to read. Colin came through not to the aroma of bacon but too see Sandra lost in thought.

'You, OK. You've been crying. You been thinking about Paul?' He placed a comforting hand on her shoulder. 'I don't know what to say.'

Sandra held out the letter, 'Not Paul, read that,' but carried on speaking as he tried to concentrate on the print. 'Shit, shit, shit. Seventeen million dollars, how much is a million dollars, six-fifty, seven hundred thousand pounds, isn't it. It has to be something like that. So it's about twelve million pound. Jesus. What I could do with twelve million.'

Colin managed to scan the page and get the gist of Sandra's rant. 'But it's Paul's inheritance. And he's not got it yet. And won't now he's dead.'

Sandra dropped her head into her hands, pulled at her blonde locks in anguish, 'But he would get it soon if he hadn't bloody died last night. And if he had that money he would spend, and it was us you know, a couple. OK, I might have begun to hate his selfishness, his bloody ego but I mean twelve million; bugger I would have lived with him for a while more. Damn it, I would have married him for the divorce settlement.'

She stopped with a gasp. 'Oh Colin. Sorry. It was the shock. You've lost everything and here am I spouting. And he was your cousin. God I sound as selfish as him. It's the thought of that money and it's gone.'

He went to her side, took both hands in his, thinking how beautiful she was when vulnerable, tears welling in her soft brown eyes. Last night had torn a burden from him. The restaurant had been failing for months he just could not see a way out. Now it was gone and there was insurance, not a lot but he could find somewhere to live. Gerry was gone and it was clear she was not coming back. She had loved the idea of the restaurant, of being the owner' partner, of wealth. It was a mirage and when that went so did she. He gathered Sandra to his chest and kissed her hair. 'I think I may have found much more than I have lost.

Sam Browne was drinking whisky. It was early, even for him, and he was to be on set at ten. Sam had few rules when it came to pleasures. His reputation as a hell-raiser was earned over years of excess but he prided himself that On set he was professional, turned up on time and always sober. Hunter Dunbar unsettled him. Why did McCluskey want to remain hidden? Why have the American believe that Sam was McCluskey? His hand shook as he drank.

He sat staring at the fresh scratches on the leather footstool, pictured Shuggie reacting to McCluskey's name. Yes, that was who the American reminded him of, Shuggie. They had that same way of looking at you, like the way a dog's eyes changed before it attacked. At least he was free of the man for now. He rinsed his glass, popped a mint into his mouth and started to read the day's script changes.

His mobile phone bleeped. His scheduled eight-thirty reminder for the shoot. Sam smiled. That stuck-up Sandra whats-her-name would be fired. He slicked back his hair, wondered if the new girl would be a past conquest or fresh territory to be explored. He was running through a list of possibilities when his mobile phone rang. No contact name came up so he decided to ignore it. In the silence which followed he found that he could not concentrate on the script so he gathered up his hat and jacket, tied his red scarf in a carefully crafted knot and headed off.

His Mercedes drop-top coupé was not new but its age was concealed by the personal number-plate. Time for posing, he thought, an image of him sweeping into the reserved parking space at the shoot. Perhaps Alice would be the new make-up girl. Alice had a soft spot for him and would be willing company for later. If he ignored the strange squeaking when she was excited it would be a pleasant diversion for the evening.

He fired up the engine and listening to the satisfying burble as he activated the electric roof.and pulled away from the roadside. It was one of those sunny days which lifted his spirits. Despite the sun the wind was a little cold and Sam wondered if he should travel with the top down then dismissed the thought with a laugh. Time to enjoy this life, his life, McCluskey, the American, they were part of another world.

It was as if the Fates read his thoughts for at that moment his phone rang.. The same unknown number. He was about to ignore it a second time when he realised it would be the American. Bugger he'd only left him an hour or so ago what could the man want now.

'McCluskey. Where you been? You better get your arse over here.' Hunter Dunbar sounded annoyed. 'How the hell was the hit here in your flat?'

Sam remained silent trying to grasp the conversation. The hit! What hit? Who had he hit? And, as it wasn't his flat, how would he know?

'Shit McCluskey you better start fuckin' talking. I've a naked dead man bleeding all over your mezzanine floor.'

Sam could feel pressure in his head, blood thumping in his ears. He'd been worried about Shuggie and Razor getting him involved in murder and now this bloody American. That bastard McCluskey.

He nearly went through a red traffic light and braked hard as he replied, 'What naked dead man? I don't know… anything.'

'It's the guy McNeil. Listen it don't matter how he was here. Saved me fuckin' time in finding him. But he's naked and dead and no ID and fuckin' faceless. I need him found and I need him identified fast as McNeil. So get your arse over here.'

'Did you say faceless?' Sam thought he had misheard the American. The accent was harder to follow on the mobile and he he was trying to cope with the fact that he was in deep, deep, trouble.

'Yea. Bastard turned and ducked. Ain't got no face.'

Sam thought about hanging up. It was McCluskey's flat. He did not care if they found a body there. He had no intention of getting close and personal with a body or with a mad American. He was about to shut down the phone when he remembered the scene at the railway station. He was an idiot standing with a big card saying McCluskey and McCluskey would say he had given Sam the keys to his flat. He had to do something. Shuggie. He'd send Shuggie.

'Look I'm driving. Can't come now. Impossible. I'll send Shuggie Cameron. He's good. He'll sort it. Big guy, dark curly hair, with you soon.' Sam made various squeaks and swishing noises which he hoped sounded like interference. 'Bugger losing signal.' He hung up.

It was when he said Shuggie's name that it struck him; how did he explain this? tell him to go to McCluskey's flat; to meet an American; with a body to dispose of? But he had to think of something.

The river at the old mill was in flood. An overnight storm in the hills south of Glasgow had swollen the river and it roared and surged over the rocks The weir was buried under a wall of water. As ever, some mad youths were on the banks beneath, dancing in the spray. Shuggie recognised the two Wilson boys. If they went in that would be a dent in the supply of drugs for a while. It look like they had had a good night sampling the goods.

When he left Razor, Shuggie had intended to head for the burnt-out restaurant to see if he could pick up any information about McNeil, but, with confirmation that McCluskey had torched the Cricketers, he had been drawn inexorably to the bridge overlooking the falls. As he grasped the metal rail his hands shook. From here he could see the windows of the Old Mill where Mel used to work. Mel who died in that fire. And now he knew it was started by Razor and McCluskey. Razor might not have known she was in the pub but McCluskey bloody well did. Shuggie's knuckles stretched the skin to breaking as he gripped the rail tighter. He spoke quietly to himself.

'Christ Mel. Why didn't you stay working in the mills. You and ambition. Or was it for me? All it got you was bastard Graham McCluskey and then that no-hoper Robbie Stanton and bloody murdered.'

Shuggie walked down past the tannery to sit close by the river. Spray from the falls drifted between the trees, settled on his cheeks, hid his tears as he remembered his big sister, Melanie. She would have been twenty-nine. Just twenty-nine. He could do with her now to keep him right. She always had.

He wiped his face. Recalled Mel with her arm round his shoulders, sitting here as she told him she was going out with McCluskey and he had asked if was because of him. Frightened she was doing it to stop the bullying. He could remember every word, had gone over them so often in his head.

CHAPTER SEVEN

Shuggie loved the roar of the water flooding over the weir. It had started when he was a child, that day, nearly twenty-five years back, when he had stood here with his Dad and Mel; felt the pavement shake under his feet and spray wetting his face, like soft rain. He remembered his Dad had to drag him away. As a teenager he came here when the river was in spate to listen to the roar. The power of the water as it leapt over the weir and ripped round the rocks, which formed the natural barrier the engineers had reinforced to create the Mill lade, seemed to him like the turmoil in his own life.

'Bloody Razor,' he muttered to himself, ' why tell me now. Christ you've had years to let that slip. Bugger, I could've told Browne to stuff the collection work, gone after McCluskey and far away from the memories. Now I've probably done for that poor bastard Ingleby. OK I didn't throw the petrol bombs but I let it happen. Should have realised what a fuck up Razor would make of it. Fuck am I as bad as McCluskey.' Shuggie kicked the ground, thought back to Mel and him, this spot, the day it started to go wrong.

No it went further back than that, as far back as he could recall. Back to when they all lived on the same street; the McCluskey boys, Graham; four years older than him and one years older than Mel and Billy; two months older that Shuggie.

Shuggie had always been big. His mother often spoke of her difficult labour, of the big baby, of the first day at nursery when he was a head taller than the other three-year olds. How she never bought clothes for his age but for older kids.

But though he was big, he was quiet and shy, and some said slow. He was the butt of jokes in Primary and had hoped the move to Secondary would let him hide within an increased pool of pupils. It was a false hope for a large shy boy with a reputation carried over from his primary. He could not escape the enmity of William McCluskey, youngest of the McCluskey clan. Billy was the opposite of Shuggie, medium build but wiry and hard. From the first he saw in Shuggie a target to be made fun of and he took that from their home street to Primary School. He was not going to let that stop now they had moved on to Secondary. The bullying moved from names and jokes to violence and humiliation as the years progressed.

Wasn't so bad when Mel was there. She was beautiful. It was hard to imagine she was Shuggie's big sister, for where Shuggie was large and awkward, she was delicate and sexy. She had a dancer's walk, moved as if on a cushion of air. Long dark hair, sensuous curves and an upturn smile, made her an object of desire for most of the males in the school, from the lecher of a gym teacher to first-years. No-one wanted to ruin their chances with Mel by openly bullying her brother.

When she left the torment got worse. He had tried to keep it secret from Mel and succeeded for about a year but she could see him retreat into a silent hulk. He had come here to the falls nearly every day after school, waiting for the trickle of workers from the new businesses set up in the Business Centre to tell him Mel would be there shortly. Stood watching for her smile and wave. He could not tell her that he needed her protection for the walk home. Billy McCluskey was impotent when Mel was around, for his older brother Graham had her down as the prize catch; what Graham wanted he usually got and Billy dare not get in the way.

The opening bars of Dance Macabre broke into Shuggie's thoughts. He flicked open his mobile phone., caller ID came up; Sam Browne. It was unusual for Browne to ring this early and Shuggie's first reaction was that something had happened about the fire. As he answered he realised it couldn't be that. Browne would be well down the queue if any news broke. Only Shuggie and Razor had ever been seen in the Restaurant, not Sam Browne. No matter, as from the opening words he knew that he needed all his wits.

Sam Browne, speaking in a high pitched croak, hardly recognised his own voice. All his training said to relax his throat and project a strong man in total control but, as he was shaking uncontrollably in a side street near the studio, he was not in control and found words choking in his throat.

Immediately he hung up on the American he had swung out of traffic into this quiet spot. How the hell was he to get Shuggie to go to McCluskey's. He ran through various openings but none had a chance. Bugger there was only one way and that was the truth. Shuggie might decide to beat his head in when he heard but… What had he to loose? It was that or head for the hills. No way was he going to meet Hunter Dunbar and a dead man.

'Shuggie, I'm in big trouble. I need your help with a dead man. Look there's no easy way to say this. I know you and McCluskey have history. But McCluskey's involved. I think you've had your suspicions. I work for McCluskey.' Sam stopped. How often did he have to say the bloody name. It was like he had a death wish. He waited for Shuggie to hang up or explode. The cold silence was worse. It was seconds but seemed interminable to Brown before Shuggie spoke.

'You better tell me McCluskey's the dead man.'

'Listen Shuggie. I had no choice. I owe McCluskey big. I mean big.

I gamble… badly. Hit a bit of drugs. Can't help it. He let me keep going said it was no problem and then came back…'

Shuggie laughed, 'and you believed him.'

' …came back and said pay now or… look there will be no work for me if… I have a scar or broken nose or… Shit, Shuggie I'm too old to have plastic surgery. I had to do it. I need help. You've got to help me.' There was silence. 'Listen, McClusky got me to meet some mad American, Hunter Dunbar. I was to say I was McCluskey. And now the bastard has killed a guy. And wants me to get rid of the body. Shit Shuggie. I can't. I'm an actor. I can play tough. But with dead men, killers I'm way out of my league. I'm begging you, Shuggie, get me out of this.' Still there was silence. 'Christ, say something. Say you'll help.'

'You work for McCluskey and want me to help.'

'I'll tell you everything. Just listen… please… please, Shuggie. I'll give you anything you want.'

CHAPTER EIGHT

It was the dead man being in McCluskey's flat that had swung it. Shuggie ignored the lift and took the stairs to the penthouse. He forced the leather gloves tighter into his fingers as he climbed, wondering about this killer he was about to meet. He wanted to arrive hot and dishevelled. To look like an idiot who climbed umpteen flights. He wanted to give the impression of man who was slow and thick. Hunter Dunbar sounded to be dangerous and it would do no harm to have him underrate Shuggie.

He had been inclined to let Browne stew in his trouble but this could be the opportunity he had been waiting for and Brown would be deeper in debt to him than he was to McCluskey. There had to be mileage in a dead man.

Dunbar answered the bell so quickly Shuggie guessed he had been hovering near the door, fleetingly wondered if the American was not as cool as Browne suggested. The cold dark eyes that bore into him made Shuggie glad he had adopted his thick Scotsman persona. Dunbar was indeed a man you had to beware.

A big brown hand yanked him in the door and pressed him to the wall, a pistol pressed under his chin. 'Who the fuck are you.'

'Shuggie Cameron.' he twisted his head to relieve the pressure on his throat. 'Mr McCluskey sent me.'

'How come you got in without buzzing. Thought this fuckin' building was meant to be Class.'

'Had the code. Door code.' Shuggie felt Dunbar tighten his grip. 'Got it from Mr McCluskey.'

'Fuckin' amateurs. Does he give it out to anyone. No wonder

McNeil got in here, McCluskey probably gave him keys to the fuckin' apartment.' He released his grip and returned the pistol to its shoulder holster. 'You're lucky I'm not trigger happy or you'd be dead too.'

Shuggie mumbled 'thanks' keeping his eyes down, as if looking at the floor, but taking in the designer suit, the expensive shoes. Dunbar liked to live well. It was telling on him though. Shuggie could see that this big man was used to violence. He took in the thickening on the knuckles, the index finger on his right hand slightly bent where it had been broken, the scar tissue from old fights under the right eye. But Dunbar's body was showing more than wear and tear. It was getting slack. The shirt was tight, buttons straining, the suit had been re-tailored to accommodate a spreading gut. The grip which had held Shuggie betrayed the slight shake of too many nights of heavy drinking.

Shuggie relaxed a little. He backed himself to take this man. He was sure that he could have when Dunbar was in his prime, though it would have been a fair match. Now it would still be a hard fight but Shuggie was happy that Dunbar was no match for him if it came to the crunch. Also Shuggie would make certain of a big advantage. He would play the dullard,. So while he knew this man was dangerous, everything Shuggie did would create the impression of a slow mind, emphasise that Shuggie was just hired help, muscle with no brain.

'Mr McCluskey says I've to help you clear up some mess.'

Dunbar grinned. 'Yea, could say.'

He indicated for Shuggie to follow and they went through into early morning sun. Shuggie blinked in the brightness of the double height living room after the dark of the hall. As his eyes focused he could see on the mezzanine floor a bare foot protruding beneath the glass of panels of the balustrade. He could smell death, a whiff of cordite and smoke. The smoke was a surprise for as far as he could see there was no fire-place.

'Seen a body before?' asked the American as they headed up the stairs.

'Aye. I can handle bodies.'

'Good you'll need to handle this one. You OK with blood?'

It was a bit late to ask for the mezzanine was indeed a mess to be cleared and most of it was blood, mixed with some hair and brains. Shuggie pretended to shrink back from it. 'Christ.' Then when Dunbar glowered. 'Aye. I'm OK with blood but you might have mentioned it sooner. Given a bit more a warning.'

Shuggie was pleased to see that, despite the deep polish on the hard wood floor, blood had seeped into the grain. He doubted if that could be fixed so it would be a whole new floor. And the walls would need redone. The bullet hole was an easy fix but blood splatters spread over a wide area. McCluskey would have quite a bill. And no matter what he did Shuggie was sure that forensics would be able to show that a man had died here. One day he would make sure that the police knew that and when they came there would be proof.

He should thank Sam Browne. Well, maybe he would go a little easier on him but Sam would have to pay for the lies.

'What do you want me to do?'

'We need this guy dressed and found. But first I need you to go to his flat and get identification.'

'How he ended up here, butt naked.'

Dunbar shrugged. 'Anyway my lucky day. But there's nothing in these clothes says he's Paul McNeil. They're not goin' to identify from his face.'

Shuggie nodded. 'Aye' well that's right enough.'

'The guys in Chicago need McNeil found and registered dead

fuckin' yesterday. No delay. No mix up. He lived in this building. So you find out where. Get in. Get some ID. And get back here. I'll get him dressed.'

'How do I get into his flat?' asked Shuggie.

'With these..' Dunbar handed Shuggie a bundle of keys on a ring. 'That was all he had on him.'

Shuggie recognised the key-ring immediately, Gerry's Steak bar. He look back at the corpse. On the right hand was a ring. He knew that ring. Had seen it yesterday morning when Colin Ingleby had refused to pay protection. Now he realised the smell of smoke came from the clothes and the body. This man had been near a fire. It was stronger here mixed with stench of blood and death as the body warmed in the sunlight. And if he was not mistaken there was charring on those trousers and smoke stains on the shirt. No wonder Ingleby was missing. He must have come here from the restaurant. Razor hadn't killed him after all. He had not died in the fire. This cold American had blown his brains out. But why was Dunbar certain that the body was some man called Paul McNeil and who had sent an American all the way to Paisley to kill him? Where did McCluskey fit in?

It was as he was leaving that Shuggie saw the photograph on the table by the window.

'You get a great view of the town,' he said, going over to stand beside the table. He pretended to be interested in the view as he squinted at the photograph. It looked like Ingleby. Or someone very like Colin Ingleby. Bit younger and thinner. He was wondering what excuse would let him pick it up for a closer examination without antagonising the American when Dunbar cut into his thoughts.

'Get movin'. This is no time for day-dreamin'.'

−53−

Shuggie was cursing as he came out of the lift. He had gone down to the foyer to discover that Paul McNeil's flat was just one floor below McCluskey's. He checked the L-shaped landing for signs of life. It was good fortune that, of the four doors, the one he wanted was hidden on the short leg of the L. He jangled through the bundle of keys. There were a couple that looked likely but he decided against trying them. If the body was Ingleby then McNeil was might be at home. Bursting straight in would not be a good plan.

Shuggie rang the bell. There was no answer but he could make out faint voices from behind the door. He rang again and this time held the button.

An attractive blonde opened the door. She pulled a short Chinese print dressing gown tighter when she saw Shuggie . Her eyes were red as if she had been crying and there were shadows round them. He guessed that she had not slept well. The same smell of smoke as in the penthouse drifted out from the flat.

'Yes.' She said tetchily. 'We heard you ring the first time.'

Behind her a man appeared. Shuggie knew that face. He never forgot a face and certainly not ones he had punched recently. Though this one was a surprise as he thought that the owner of it lay dead upstairs.

Colin Ingleby was only there for an instant. Recognising Shuggie, he ducked away and disappeared back into the house.

'Hi Colin, I've come for a chat,' Shuggie said, putting his foot in the door. 'I think you better invite me in.'

The young woman moved into the doorway to block his entry. Shuggie admired her pluck. He never hit a woman but as she was about eight stone and five foot four tall it was a futile gesture. He smiled down at her. 'I did ask politely.'

She was about to make some reply when Ingleby reappeared,

sighed and placed an arm on her shoulder and eased her aside.

'No Sandra. Its no good. I know this bastard. He'll get in if he wants in. I don't want you hurt. It's me he wants. We might as well do it the easy way.'

Sandra looked confused and muttered, 'What the...' as Shuggie stepped inside and closed the door.

'Wise man Colin. Now you and...Sandra... nice to meet you Sandra... can tell me what the fuck is going on. How about a coffee?'

Colin and Sandra hesitated for a moment and then headed along the hall to the living room. Shuggie hung back. He needed to check that these were the only people here. A quick scan of the rooms at this end showed that they were empty. Sandra came back from the lounge as he opened the final door. She pulled angrily at his sleeve.

'Do you mind. That's our bedroom. Private.'

He shrugged her away, ignored her 'You can 't just walk in here and...' checked the room and the en-suite. Again both were empty. The bed had been slept in. It looked as if Ingleby and Sandra had share it last night. Their clothes, reeking of smoke, lay discarded on the floor.

'Colin. Colin. Do something.' Sandra glanced out to the living room door but Colin did not appear. 'Look. I don't know who you are but I think you should leave.'

Shuggie shook his head. 'Let's get that coffee. You and Colin have some talking to do.'

Colin barely moved as they joined him. Slumped on a black leather settee he did not look up as his words came out in a rush.

'Sorry Sandra. it's me. I screw up everything. Listen Mr Cameron, it's me who you want. Let's get away from here. You do what you want to me but Sandra doesn't need to be part of this. Christ knows how you found me so quick. I just came here cause I thought it was safe. I'm sorry I didn't pay up yesterday. Christ, was it only yesterday. I shouldn't have argued. I know that. I'll pay when I can. I'll pay double. I'll… ' He half stood, rising from the settee like a rusted automaton, and fell back under Shuggie's cold stare and shake of the head.

'Pull yourself together and shut your face. I need to think. And where's that coffee?'

Shuggie crossed to the breakfast bar that separated kitchen and living space. As he watched Sandra set up the all-singing-all-dancing, state-of-the-art coffee machine and busied herself putting out mugs, the heading on the letter lying on the worktop caught his eye. Chicago. McNeil had correspondence from Chicago.

He shifted his position so that he could read without being noticed. Grunted 'milk, two sugars,' to Sandra's enquiry. Asked for a choccy biscuit to gain time so that he could read it again as Sandra pulled down a tin and produced a packet of Penguin.

'Now. We'll sit and Colin, and you, will tell me about last night. About you at the restaurant when it caught fire and… '

Colin found some life. 'Caught fire. When you torched it you bastard.'

' … and how do you know Paul McNeil.'

'Know him.' Colin began shouting. 'He's my cousin. Was my cousin. You fuckin' murdered him. He never got out.'

Sandra sat beside Colin as he spoke and he placed a protective arm round her shoulders to draw her close. She nestled against him, stared at Shuggie.

'He did it? Colin, was it him? Who is this man?'

'Scum. Fuckin' lowlife scum. Protection racket. Been taking money from me for months. That's why Gerry left me. And I lost it yesterday. Told him to fuck off. I didn't pay and bloody Paul did.

—56—

Last night. The fuckin' fire. It was him ... or probably not him. Some other bastard would do it for him. He likes to hit people. See them suffer. Well Mr fuckin' Cameron, I'm suffering.'

'You killed Paul.' Sandra repeated quietly. 'You killed Paul.'

Shuggie sat down on the matching settee, facing them from the other side of a low coffee table, leant in closer. 'No. I did not. Paul did not die in the fire.' He spoke slowly emphasising each word. 'I thought you had, Colin, when you were missing. It is your body they are searching the building for. But now I know that no-one died in the fire. I'm glad of that. I never want anyone to die in a fire.'

Colin laughed, 'Aye, pull the other one.'

Sandra met Shuggie's gaze. 'Paul, didn't die? But we were there. We saw the flames. He couldn't have got out.'

'Well he did. He was similar to Colin, wasn't he? They'd almost pass for twins.' Sandra nodded. 'I've just seen him in the flat upstairs.'

'Oh, thank God. he's alive. But why is he upstairs?' Sandra stopped speaking her hand flying to her mouth. 'Did he see me and Colin? Did he see us come here? What did he say to you?'

'He didn't say anything. He couldn't say anything. He's dead.'

'Dead. What do you mean dead. You said he was alive.' Shuggie shook his head. 'You bastard,' she screamed. 'You said he was alive.' She would have hurled herself across the coffee table if Colin had not tightened his arm round her shoulders and held her back.

Shuggie let her calm a little before replying. 'No. I said he didn't die in the fire. He was shot in a flat upstairs.'

Sandra stopped struggling with Colin, eyes blinking rapidly as she remembered being woken from her nightmares. She had not imagined it. She had heard a gun being fired.

'Colin, there was a shot. It woke me. I thought that I imagined it.'

'Why would anyone shoot Paul?'

—57—

Shuggie snorted. 'I can think of a few million reasons.'

Ingleby frowned. 'A few million? What are you on about. He was a bit of a shit at times but not enough for someone to shoot him.'

Shuggie lent back and stretched out to the breakfast bar. He was able to flick the letter on the counter until it nestled on his fingertips. He gathered it between finger and thumb, swung back to face Colin and Sandra, dropped it on the coffee table.

'A few million reasons. This is from Chicago and the man upstairs who shot Paul Leroy McNeil is an American. Said it was people in Chicago needed Paul dead. I don't think this letter is a coincidence. Especially as he wants me to make sure the body is found and is identified. Usually when you murder some one you want to keep it quiet. You hide the body. I wondered what all this was about and now… ' Shuggie prodded the letter. ' …I know.'

He was glad of the few moments of silence as Colin and Sandra digested this for his brain was racing. Hunter Dunbar would expect him back soon. He did not have much time but a way for him to have his revenge had been forming since he saw the letter and if it worked there was the bonus that he would be rich.

CHAPTER NINE

Sandra picked up the lawyer's letter from the coffee table. She knew it by heart but wondered if she had missed something. Shuggie broke into her thoughts.

'I need to get some things straight and I haven't much time, so nod or say yes if I have things right. When I am wrong, don't interrupt me; just shake your heads. Got that.'

Sandra's and Colin's 'Yes' was suitably subdued.

Colin adhered to the rules but Sandra could not restrain outbursts about McNeil being a selfish bastard at various points in his questioning. Despite her interruptions, he established in a few minutes that Sandra had been Paul McNeil's girl-friend and that she lived in the flat. Last night there had been a fight between Ingleby and McNeil. She had fallen out with Paul before the fire. They thought that McNeil died in the fire and Ingleby had come back with her as he believed that Shuggie would kill him if he knew he survived the fire; not wanting any evidence Ingleby could give, to be heard. They had spent the night together.

His final question was 'And Sandra, you knew about this Chicago great uncle and the inheritance.'

'Known for about six months. Didn't believe it at first. But Paul was cock-a-hoop. We'd been drifting apart but hell I stayed when that was in the offing. Was never sure how much but we joked that it must be a lot. And after Paul did some checking we knew it was a lot. God, a lot. We guessed about half-a-million.' Sandra had sat forward as she talked about the money but now she collapsed back against Colin. 'And now Paul's dead and the money's gone.'

'I have a way you can get the money.' He held up a hand to silence comment. 'Well. Not all the money. I'll have a cut. But I'm a fair man. I'll only take a third.'

The comment seemed to barely register on Ingleby but Sandra stiffened and stared at him in the moments of silence that followed.

Shuggie checked his watch. It was twenty minutes since he left the penthouse. He reckoned Dunbar would have no suspicions if he returned with confirmation of identity by 10.30, about forty-five minutes to find flat, search and return. He calculated that he had twenty minutes to pull together his ideas. He stood and began to pace up and down behind the settee. He had always found it easier to think if he was on the move. From time to time he stopped to ask a question about McNeil or the inheritance. When he asked how it was that McNeil was wearing Ingleby's ring, Sandra was unable to contain herself and started on a rant but fell silent as Shuggie glared. He took time over the most important point; cousins, Paul McNeil and Colin Ingleby were so alike in age, build and features that they had often been mistaken as brothers and even as twins. In the last few weeks Ingleby had lost weight from the worry about the restaurant going bust and also from his break-up with Geraldine. With the weight loss the similarity had been even more pronounced.

From way Sandra was animated during her explanations, Shuggie was certain that she would do anything for the money. Ingleby was sullen. He seemed to have become engulfed in gloom and stayed slumped beside Sandra. Shuggie assumed it was after the shock of the fire, but it did not matter. If the girl was on-side then he could cope with Ingleby. If necessary a threat of violence would bring him round. The girl might just have the savvy to pull off what he needed. Ingleby was the weak link but with her on side there was a chance that between them they could do it. They could carry him. Shuggie decided that it was worth a shot.

He returned to the settee to sit across from Colin and Sandra and lent forward, eyes deliberately wide and staring, like a weasel fixing its prey. Colin seemed to shrink into the cushions but Sandra flicking stray blonde hair from her face met his gaze. He noticed how she looked good despite the lack of sleep and no make up. The dressing gown slipped open a little to reveal the curve of her breasts. He was briefly distracted and she jumped in before he could speak.

'You said there was a way we can get the money?'

Shuggie half suppressed a laugh. He was right about this girl, for money she could do it. She was wasted on Ingleby.

'Yes. Do as I tell you and we'll all be rich.'

There was a flicker of interest from Ingleby as Sandra touched his shoulder and said

'Shoot.'

'Good opener, Sandra. It's because McNeil was shot that we have the opportunity.

'See, to put it bluntly, the mad bastard upstairs who came to kill him has blown half his face off. I've to dump the body so that it will be found and recognised. I will dump the body but it will have Colin's identity on it.' He saw disbelief on Ingleby's face. 'You see Ingleby, I thought the body was you. I saw that ring you always wore on the finger; until last night when you and McNeil fought over it and he took it. I saw a picture of the guy the American has been sent to kill and it looks like you.. You were often mistaken for each other. Well why not swap now. With your beat-up face no-one is going to doubt that you are Paul McNeil.'

Ingleby shook his head and muttered 'You're mad,' but Sandra was nodding and swung her legs back onto the settee so that she could curl into Ingleby, ran a comforting arm across his shoulders. 'Why not. Oh Colin. I'll be there with you. Whose going to challenge us.'

'Everyone who knows him.' Ingleby hesitated searching for reasons. 'What about his work?'

'I know all his friends and there are not many see him regularly. Paul had acquaintances not friends, not close kind of friends. We've his computer and diary we can sort out the work. How hard can it be to flog a few houses.'

Shuggie intervened. 'Forget work. You call in sick. Shock of the fire. Anything. Then you resign. No-one will suspect anything. Inherit millions and resign. Of course you would. As Sandra says, with her at your side it's a dawdle.'

'Colin.' Sandra laid her head on Ingleby's chest. 'Colin. Do it Colin. For me. For us,' she added quickly.

Ingleby stroked her hair, winding the ends round his fingers unconsciously and smiled. 'You really think we can?' She squeezed him tighter. 'Ok. If it's what you want. What have I got as me. A burnt out life?'

'You've got me, Colin.'

Ingleby perked up. 'Yes. You're right! I've got you.' He looked at Shuggie and there was strength back in his voice. 'Right, let's do it.'

Sandra kissed his cheek, before she unwound from him to address Shuggie. 'Mr Cameron, what have we to do now?'

'First thing I need is anything that would identify the body upstairs as McNeil.'

Shuggie saw the puzzlement on her face. 'It's why the American sent me down here. I have to take something back.'

'But we don't want Paul identified.'

'And we don't want Colin dead,' replied Shuggie. 'If I don't take the proof to the American. I am in shit. And you are in shit. He will come here for the proof of McNeil's identity. And what do you

—62—

think he will do when he sees Colin?'

'Shoot him.'

'You got it. So I need to keep him happy… For a time. Until my time.'

An edge in those last words sent a shiver down Sandra's back. She began to wonder what bargain they had agreed to but she wanted the money. She pointed to the door.

'We have his jacket hanging in the hall. Colin grabbed it when we left the restaurant. It has his wallet. His mobile. Probably other stuff in his pockets. He keeps,' she stopped, '*kept* notes on clients and houses in case they phoned when he was out of the office.'

'Ideal.'

Colin chipped in 'Don't forget that his business cards are in the inside ticket pocket. It's an expensive suit and Paul liked to flash the name as he gave out his cards.'

'I'll pick it up as I leave. Now I want you to have a couple of stiff drinks, then get down to the restaurant. You speak to the police. Tell them you're worried about Colin. That you were in the restaurant when it was fire bombed and managed to get away with him. Got that. With him. He got out with you, You went back to your flat and had some more drinks as were in shock. You fell asleep and have only just surfaced. Been trying to contact Colin without success. Last you saw him he was raging about some guy called McCluskey. Said he was going to sort it out and charged off.' He waited but there was no reply from either Sandra or Colin. He repeated the instruction. ' Did you get that?'

Sandra nodded.

'Can you do that. Play up being drunk. That'll cover any vagueness in your story and the time lag before you turned up. But keep to the basic story. The fire bomb bit is easy as you were there. Keep emphasising that Colin got out. Keep saying he was going to see McCluskey.'

Sandra was up from the sofa as he spoke. She poured two brandies. Looked at him.

'You want one.'

Shuggie shook his head. 'No. I can't go back smelling of booze.'

She pushed a glass into Colin's hand. 'You heard. Start drinking.'

She took a mouthful of her brandy, swallowed. 'Right first bit easy. Now when do you want us at the restaurant. Half an hour be OK.' Shuggie liked this girl. Spiky, fast on the uptake and great legs. He dragged himself away from lust. Headed for the door. 'Sure. Just as soon as you can. Show me this jacket.'

CHAPTER TEN

Hunter Dunbar threw open the penthouse door.

'What the fuck took you so long.'

Shuggie stepped inside. Avoided eye contact. Muttered, 'Sorry.' He needed to keep his image as subservient muscle. He risked a glance at Dunbar, 'Took a bit of time to find it and there was a girl in the flat.'

'Shit,' Dunbar exclaimed.

'Got away with it. She was in the shower. I heard her as soon as I opened the door. I slipped back out and hung about on the landing hoping she was on her way out. Then I remembered how long it takes women to get dressed. So I went back in quietly and had a poke around in the hall.' He held up the jacket. 'Bingo. This was hanging in the hall. Wallet, phone. She never knew I was there. Won't know its gone till the body turns up.'

Dunbar smiled. 'Fine.' He slapped Shuggie on the shoulder, a little harder than necessary. 'But you could still have been faster.'

Stepping into the lounge Shuggie was surprised to see that Dunbar had not been idle.

The body was dressed. It would have been an effort to get that dead weight manhandled into clothes and Shuggie had not been looking forward to it with the two of them. The American had managed it on his own and without getting covered in blood. He might be a bit debauched but taking him down would not be without risk.

Dunbar moved McNeil's body into a sitting position. Shuggie made great show of the difficulty he had in getting the right arm into the sleeve. There was a bit of pantomime as he manoeuvred the jacket past Dunbar and round the body. As he worked the left arm home, Dunbar pushed him aside, 'Goddam it', grabbed the arm and roughly forced it down, splitting the material. 'Cheap, Bastard.' Dunbar grinned at Shuggie. 'Always buy good clothes. Die with style. Don't end in rags like him.'

It occurred to Shuggie that he should have put on his best suit. If it was him with a body to be found this would be the place to leave it. An anonymous call to the police and that would be it. Bonus would be it was in McCluskey's penthouse. If he was Dunbar, this was the moment to kill Shuggie and then to track down Browne and kill him. When he left for London there would be no-one to say he had ever been here. He needed to get Dunbar thinking, throw him a plan that did not have Shuggie dead now.

'I know where to dump the body and it will be found immediately.'

Dunbar grunted, 'Yea.'

Shuggie cast his line, a place to get him and Browne at the same time. 'When done why don't I collect McCluskey and we take you to quiet station. You can catch the London train away from witnesses. Nothing to say you were here.'

Dunbar slapped him again. This time more playfully. 'Yea, that sounds good. A quiet place. Sure. Make it the night train.'

Shuggie nodded. Darkness suited him too. The American wanted no witnesses and he wanted a dead American and he had the ideal place for that. Getting Browne there to see how bad a move he had made when he crossed Shuggie would be an added bonus. He took out his phone. 'OK if I make a call. Get a good mate round with a vehicle. We need that to get this where we want.'

Dunbar's face tightened. 'We don't want no other fuckers involved.'

'He's good. Frightened of me. I turn up down stairs with a stiff and he'll ask no questions. Will say nothing. Knows what would happen if he did.' Dunbar shook his head.

'And I know of a murder he committed. He cannot cross me. Trust me on this. You don't want to be seen outside and we need two people to safely handle this.'

He could see the last point swung it.

'Yea. Do it,' said Dunbar.

Razor stopped the black Animal Pick-up at the entrance to the flats. Behind the glass doors he could see Shuggie supporting some drunk, slumped under a rain coat, Shuggie waved for him to come and help them. As he approached it struck him that the drunk was very, very not moving and as he opened the glass doors that the corpse was lacking a face.

'Fuck it, Big Man. You might have said. That could make you puke.'

'Doubt if there's anything would make you spew, wee man. Shut the fuck up and get an arm. When we're at the pick-up open the hard-top and I will jump in the back with this.'

Razor frowned. 'In the load bed? What? You in with him?'

'Christ. Let's not hang around asking fuckin' stupid questions. Do it. Once we're on board you drive to the in-shot by the railway bridge at Gallowhill. Got it.'

Shuggie did not wait for an answer before taking the weight of McNeil's body and dragging it and Razor out onto the pavement. It was barely five metres to the pick-up and with the body shrouded in the coat between the two of them it was seconds before Shuggie and McNeil were safely out of sight in the back and Razor drove off.

It took ten minutes to get to Gallowhill. They parked on the wedge of waste ground. Shuggie emerged from the rear and had Razor swing round so that the tail-gate of the pick-up rested against the red-sandstone parapet of the railway bridge. He climbed back inside and took a Stanley knife from his sock. The interior was too cramped for finesse and he wanted the jacket off quickly. Shuggie kept the knife handy, always useful to have a blade, but this was the first time he had to cut up a suit. When the jacket was clear he pulled the body onto the tail-gate

This was a quiet road and the vehicle screened what he was doing from view but he waited until the sound of a passing car had faded before he manhandled it on to the parapet. He edged it closer to the edge and climbed up. From here he could see the drop to the tracks and the short straight before the line curved toward Glasgow. Shuggie looked at his watch. They had been here about four minutes. He didn't fancy hanging around for long with a corpse but he wanted a train and at most it would be a couple of minutes before there'd be one. As he watched the bend the track begin to sing, the front coach appearing He yanked McNeil's body into a sitting position, threw it out into the void. The timing was perfect, body striking track, train ploughing over, throwing bits aside. Shuggie dropped back into the load bay and banged the roof. The clatter of stones from spinning wheels was drowned by the screech of the train stopping.

The pick-up swung right to cross the bridge then left heading back into town. Here the railway cutting flattened out and they could see the stationary train through the chain-link fence. Razor pulled over to let Shuggie out from the load-bed and the two stood for a few moments watching the activity below. The driver clambered out slowly and walked beyond the train shaking his head. He turned back as the guard, appearing from the far side shouted and pointed back under the bridge. The more curious passengers were standing at the windows trying to see what was causing the delay.

'Shit hit the fan, Big Man,' said Razor.

'Yes, job done. Let's get away before anyone clocks us. Drop me at the Cross. I want to see how the police are getting on finding Ingleby.'

'Was that no his body? I thought it was him ye were gettin' rid of.'

'Not Ingleby. And the who is something you should forget. Forget everything.'

'Sure, Big Man. Sure. As you say.'

Shuggie pulled up the number for Hunter Dunbar on his mobile, texted a cryptic. *Body found. Off to get McCluskey.*

CHAPTER ELEVEN

Detective Inspector Hamilton Scruffy McVey inhaled deeply. This was getting boring. The structural engineers could not enter the building until the Fire Brigade said it was safe. The Fire Brigade were concerned that there might be gas cylinders under the rubble and were continuing to hose down the hot spots. It would be another half-hour at least before the engineers went in and God knows when they would clear it for his officers. At least he knew that no human remains had been found, so far, but there was still Colin Ingleby to trace. As time went on it was more and more likely he had died last night. The Fire Officer was certain this was a deliberate fire, with an accelerant used. It was likely that this would be a murder investigation and he was standing twiddling his thumbs in the cold.

Ash from McVey's cigarette drifted in the breeze as he scratched his head. Some joined previous deposits to cling to his straggling brown hair as if he had a bad case of dandruff. Scruffy had never been one for sartorial elegance and the joke of the Station was that he combed his hair once a week on a Monday morning. As it lifted in the wind this Wednesday it could well be true. At least he had changed from the suede waistcoat his mother had bought months ago for his birthday and which had developed a peculiar pattern of egg and sauce stains, not that the state of it had caused its demise but his spreading waist had rendered it unwearable. It was replaced by an Argyll slip-over of a cream and purple found in one of the High Street charity shops which clashed with the dark blue suit. He kicked a loose stone into the gutter before wandering over to the barriers where a few spectators watched progress and Helen Green from the

Gazette was waving.

'Hi, Scruffy.'

'Come on Helen. A bit of respect. Mr. McVey when I'm working.'

'Detective Inspector McVey.' Helen smiled in what she hoped was a seductive manner and, as Scruffy had fancied her for years, was. 'What's the info? When will you get in there? Is Colin Ingleby missing? I've heard he's cremated?'

'You know better than that, Helen. I'm saying nothing.'

'But this was deliberate? I hear that Hugh Cameron has been seen recently. Here visiting.'

'Shuggie. Where did you hear that?'

'Ingleby's ex. Geraldine Kowalski. Gerry. The girlfriend the restaurant was named for. I'll introduce you. She's in the café waiting. Says she left because Colin Ingleby was a wimp. Folded to threats of violence. Wouldn't tell the police.'

'Well. Well. I shouldn't be surprised but not Shuggie's style. Fire. Not him, since his sister died in a fire. The one at the Cricketers, remember.'

'Mel McCluskey was Cameron's sister. I didn't know that. You sure?'

'I was brought up on these streets. Went to the same school as the McCluskeys, and as Shuggie for that matter. Few years earlier but I know the families. The Camerons and the McCluskeys go back a long way. Shuggie's sister, Melanie, was Graham McCluskey's wife.'

Helen Green shook her head. 'Before my time, The Cricketers. But that gap site with the sign painted on the gable wall overlooking it reminds you. It's still talked about in the office. Didn't realise she was Cameron's sister. A real looker according to the gossip.'

'She was indeed.' McVey seemed to become lost for a moment in the memory. 'And really close to her brother. So I can't see Shuggie fire-bombing anywhere. Now Graham McCluskey. I'd put him in the frame. Always a bastard and he was a suspect in the Cricketers' fire. But as usual we couldn't make it stick. Witnesses to give him an alibi. Mel had left him. You probable heard the story. She had taken up with the landlord. So there was motive and it was his MO. If you're talking protection for Ingleby my money would be on McCluskey.'

Helen Green took a notebook from her handbag. 'We should talk to Gerry.'

McVey put a hand on the barrier and contemplated swinging a leg up and over but even for him it was a stretch. He went back to the gap in the metal fencing where it was guarded by a constable. 'Make sure that the press are kept away' he said in passing,.

As he headed for the café, Helen fell into step beside him. 'You can't stop me coming to the café. I'll introduce you to Gerry.'

'And then you will disappear.'

Helen nodded agreement. She knew that Gerry was sitting at a booth. She would disappear to the next table from where she could hear everything.

'Wow,' thought McVey as Helen led him to a booth at the far end of the café and a slim red-head unwound from the bench. Gerry reminded him of a Pre-Raphaelite painting with legs forever and six inch heels so that she was taller than him.' As Helen introduced him, and they shook hands, her eyes swept him and from the expression which followed she was not impressed.

'Gerry. This is Detective Inspector McVey. He would like to get some information. Tell him what you've told me.'

Helen lingered as McVey slid onto the bench opposite, showed his warrant card.

'I would like a word, if that is OK.'

A young waitress appeared at the table.

'Are you ready to order

'I'll have a large Americano, milk.'

The girl looked up from the pad on which she was scribbling. 'Hot.'

'Cold.' McVey smiled at Gerry. 'Would you like another coffee.'

Gerry smiled back which he took as a yes.. 'And same again for the lady… Please.'

He did not look directly at Helen Green as she lingered beside the table and dismissed her with 'Thanks, Helen. Bye.'

Admiring Geraldine Kowalski's smooth pale skin, carved cheek bones, and long eyelashes framing pale grey eyes he failed to notice that Helen Green did not leave the café but slipped quietly into the next booth, her back separated from his by the width of the lattice partition.

'Gerry. I may call you Gerry? Great. Gerry I understand from Helen Green that you have information pertinent to the fire.'

'Too right. Colin is,' she hesitated, 'or is it was? Gerry watched for McVey's reaction. He lifted his hands in a who-knows gesture. 'Colin is a wimp. It's why I left. I mean you can't live your life with a man with no guts.'

'But you've come back?'

Gerry nodded. 'Yeah. When I saw the fire on the early news. I had stuff upstairs. Some sentimental stuff from my mum. Photos. Things like that.'

'There may be some things recovered but you see what I see. I doubt much will be saved. If that's what's keeping you I wouldn't hold much hope.' McVey leant closer. 'But are you saying Colin Ingleby means nothing to you? Perhaps you still love him?' He let the question hang in the air then added, 'Or do you hate him?'

Gerry shuffled a little on the bench. Her grey eyes bore into him.

'I gave him three years of my life. Still love him?' She blinked hard. 'Yes… and No. We had something. I thought we had a future. But I can't love him.' She turned away to look out into the street. 'He folded when I needed him to be strong. How can you commit to a man who has no guts. I saw bits of him that should never be seen. A weak child.' She sighed. 'Do I love him. Yes. But it's too late. Isn't it?'

There was such hope in the question that McVey wished he could be positive. The best he could offer was, 'We've not managed to get into the building yet. All you can do is wait. And he may have got out.'

'And if the bastard has got out and is hiding. I'll bloody kill him.'

The silence which fell over the café, as Gerry's raised voice turned heads, was relieved by the arrival of the waitress who tried, unsuccessfully, to stifle a laugh.

'One Americano, cold milk. One large Cappuccino. Enjoy.'

There was a brief pause as McVey opened three sachets of brown sugar, added milk and stirred.

'So you might kill him but don't want him dead. Seems reasonable.' He took a sip. 'About this wimp business. Who was he afraid of.?'

'Started with yon thin bastard.' Gerry rubbed fingers across her top lip wiping away froth from the cappuccino. 'Razor. That's the only name I ever heard. But it must be a nick-name.' She laughed bitterly, became lost in thought..

McVey tapped the table impatiently. 'What started with Razor?'

'It was about six, nine months ago that he came to the restaurant. Colin met him one lunchtime. Wanted a hundred to keep the restaurant safe. Colin, the daft bugger paid him. When I heard that night, I told Colin it was madness. But Colin was anything for a quiet life. Said it would be worth it. It would be OK. Well that was fine until the next time. The next time it was two hundred.'

'For a month?' asked McVey.

'Oh, nothing as formal, Inspector. Until the next time he came. And how he started to come. More and more frequently. More and more money and the place quiet. Colin became a nervous wreck. All moans and excuses. Whole thing was a bloody nightmare.' She threw herself back on the bench, eyes to the ceiling. 'Bloody nightmare. You can't live like that. I couldn't live like that. Told Colin. Said either he came to you and told them to bugger off or… Shit, he almost made it. He said that he'd spoken to Razor, told him it was finished. We might have made it but the big man turned up. Shuggie Cameron warned Colin not to do anything silly.'

'Colin told you it was Cameron?' asked McVey.

'Not told. actually. Cameron, I know from somewhere. He's not a man you forget. Was his picture in the papers? Anyway it was him I saw talking to Colin and it was after that that Colin said he was going to keep paying. Said that, now there were two of them, he had no choice.'

McVey smiled. 'You'll give me this in a statement? The protection money. Threats of violence.'

Gerry interrupted, 'Not just threats. One night last week Colin came home with a black eye.'

'So, you can give a statement about Cameron speaking to Colin, and hitting him.'

Gerry thought for a moment. 'I can say what I've told you but it was all from Colin. I heard none of it and saw nothing first hand. And the black eye he said was him being careless in the kitchen. Walked into a cabinet door.' She smiled thinly. 'Not very original, walking into doors. He didn't want to admit to me that he couldn't stand up to them.'

'But you saw Cameron and Razor threaten Colin?'

—75—

Gerry thought for a moment. 'Never saw them do anything. And never saw them, Cameron and Razor, together with Colin. Just Colin and Cameron that one time.' She paused. 'Not going to be much help is it. Not real evidence.' Gerry stopped to drink her coffee, cradled the cup with both hands, before she continued. 'And they destroyed us. It was too much. We didn't speak for days. Colin paid them again and I was off. We're going bust and he's crumbling. I'm better than that.' She half sobbed, then, almost an echo, 'I'm better than that.'

McVey rummaged in the depths of a trouser pocket and offered her a greyish handkerchief, which she waved aside. He shoved it back. Let her sit silent for a moment. Slurped his coffee.

'Thanks. The information is useful. But if this… if the protection money was being paid they had no reason to do this.'

'I told Colin I wouldn't be back. But while it was unsaid he knew that if he stopped paying, showed me he valued me, stood up to them, I would come back.' She sniffed. 'What if he did stop? What if this is down to me?'

McVey moved to place his hand over hers, thought better of it and changed the action to one of brushing away crumbs. 'If he did stop there would be retribution for sure. Things like this never end well, but they wouldn't want him dead. To torch the restaurant seems a bit heavy handed. You don't get money from a dead man or a ruined business. So don't blame yourself. You could not foresee this.'

Gerry's grey eyes bore into him. 'Maybe. But I can't get it out of my head. If it was them, you will get them. Won't you?'

He felt as if she was scanning his soul, waiting for the lie and if he said they would find who was guilty that would be a lie. He was not certain that they would. 'Rest assured, Miss Kowalski, we will do everything in our power.'

CHAPTER TWELVE

There was little activity in the road outside Gerry's Restaurant. One Fire tender remained but most of the sightseers had left and only a handful lingered in the cold breeze blowing across from the Abbey and the river beyond. Sandra steered Colin towards a gap in the barriers where a policeman kept watch. Whispered to him, 'Keep your nerve. This is the easy bit.' She smiled at the young cop.

'Hello, officer. We were wondering if you have any news of Colin Ingleby, the owner? We were here last night and when we parted we expected him to be in touch.' She stopped for effect. 'Since last night we've heard nothing.'

'You had a meal here last night. Miss?'

'Sandra Smith.' She took Colin's arm. 'And this is Colin Ingleby's cousin, Paul.' The constable's gaze moved from Sandra to Colin, who extended his hand saying, 'Paul McNeil. We both ate here last night.'

Constable Perry ignored the proffered hand and brought out his notebook. 'And you are worried about Mr Ingleby, Sir?'

'We are. We were with him, here, when the restaurant was fire-bombed. We all managed to get out but Colin stormed off. We haven't seen him since and we're very worried. Heard on the news that he was missing.'

'Have you and the lady been drinking, Sir?

'I'm afraid we were a bit drunk last night.'

'And this morning, Sir?' The constable sniffed. 'If you don't mind me asking?'

'Quick one to steady the nerves. We're upset about Colin.'

Constable Perry eyed them closely. 'Wait here' He stepped

–77–

behind the barriers, spoke into his radio. Waited a few moments and returned. 'Inspector McVey wants to talk you. He is in The Bell's Café. Will be with you in a moment.'

Colin watched the street outside the café for the Inspector. He shuddered when the large shambling man who emerged was followed by Gerry Kowalski. He lent close to Sandra, whispered.

'Shit, Sandra. Look who's with him. What do we do?'

Gerry had started to run. They could hear her shouting. 'Colin. Colin.'

Sandra reacted first. She ran to meet the advancing figure shouting in reply.

'I know Gerry. It's terrible. Paul and I are so worried.'

She grabbed Gerry's arm and moved her away from the following Inspector, waving to Colin to hurry up.

'We were with him last night. Here in the restaurant when it was fire-bombed.'

As McVey came nearer Sandra embraced Gerry. 'We got out when the fire started but we don't understand. Where's Colin now? We're so worried.'

At last, McVey caught up with them, breathing heavily, heard the last comment.

'Miss Sandra Smith?' Sandra nodded. 'and you were here last night?' She nodded again. 'Can I have a word?'

As McVey took Sandra aside, behind his back, Colin reached Gerry, put a finger to his lips and shook his head. He took her elbow and moved her away from the Inspector's hearing.

McVey's smile was meant to be reassuring and despite the bulk looming over her Sandra did feel at ease. A feeling that evaporated when she saw Colin and Gerry walking away, deep in conversation. At least Colin was not going to blow it with the Inspector, but could he persuade Gerry that he was Paul?

'Did I catch you right, Miss Smith; you were in the restaurant at the time of the fire?'

'Yes, Inspector. With Paul.' She pointed over to where Colin and Gerry were talking. 'We had a meal and then we stayed late with Colin. Paul's his cousin. We often stayed on after Colin locked up. Had a few drinks.' She shrugged. 'You know.'

'And last night. Was it just the three of you here, late?' Sandra nodded and he continued. 'The Constable tells me that you said there was a fire-bomb? Is that right?'

It did not take long for Sandra to tell of the night's events but, throughout the ten minutes that she answered McVey's questions, she was distracted by the scene unfolding between Colin and Gerry. They started close together but gradually the space between them increased and the body language suggested Gerry was becoming angry. She feared Colin was about to be exposed as a fraud and her answers became more disjointed. It was as well that McVey put her hesitation down to the drink he could smell on her and the shock of the night's events; someone who had escaped from a burning building was entitled to a drink and to be a little vague..

'And you are certain that Colin Ingleby said he was going to have it out with a man called McCluskey? Sandra agreed. 'And that was the last time you saw Mr. Ingleby?'

Before Sandra could reply they heard Gerry shout, 'No! No!' She stormed angrily past the few remaining spectators before turning to stare at Colin saying, 'You are a bloody idiot.'

Sandra was relieved to see Gerry depart. Whatever had happened, at least Gerry had not come to speak to the police. As Colin stood irresolute Sandra sought to explain Gerry's actions.

'Gerry Kowalski is a fiery woman. Her relationship with Colin was never smooth and she… I mean we're worried so she must be distraught.' She looked at McVey. 'Sorry you asked a question?'

'He definitely said McCluskey the last time you saw him.'

'Yes. Definitely McCluskey.' Sandra moved towards Colin and running over in her mind was her previous comment about Gerry. She saw that it could be interpreted by McVey as saying that it was Colin who was talking with Gerry. She had to reinforce that Colin was Paul.

'Paul heard it too. But look I better go to him. Gerry's antics have upset him. It's his cousin after all. He's feeling it. But would she see that!'

As Sandra came closer to Colin she could see that he was ashen faced and shaking. To her horror she heard McVey clumping behind her; realised she should have anticipated that he would want to confirm what she had just said. Wondered if Colin would be able to keep to the story. Dreaded the first question from McVey to him.

To her surprise the footsteps ceased to follow her. She glanced behind. McVey had broken away and was heading towards the small crowd. Shuggie Cameron was standing at the back. McVey was asking the question which came into her head.

'Cameron, how long have you been here?'

Shuggie shouldered through to the barrier. 'What's that? Couldn't catch it'

McVey faced him, hands resting on the metal rail. Sandra noticed what a contrast they presented. McVey was a similar height but unhealthily heavier and unkempt. If she had not known the relationship she would have said that Shuggie was the professional and McVey the thug.

McVey pulled himself up to his full height and stared into Shuggie's face. 'I asked you how long you had been here?' He scratched his neck and spoke over Shuggie's reply of 'not long' with, 'back to see your handiwork?'

Shuggie gave a false laugh, 'You know me better than that. Not me is it. Fire.'

The breeze whipped into a sudden squall. Thin rain stabbed McVey's face as he pulled up his raincoat collar. 'People change. Don't play the innocent with me, Cameron. I've known you too long.'

Shuggie seemed unmoved by the wind and rain. 'Aye, and you know why I don't like fires.' He lent towards McVey, and in a loud voice so that all could hear said, 'Aye, you'd like to hang this on me, wouldn't you. At least that would be one arson you could solve.'

The two men stood eye-ball to eye-ball, each determined to out-stare the other. The moment was broken by the arrival of the Fire Officer to say that the building was no longer a danger and that the engineers could start their survey. As McVey left with the Fireman he turned to Shuggie.

'I'll see you later.'

Catching sight of Sandra and Colin standing a little way off, bodies huddled together against the wind and drizzle, he swung away from the Fireman and came over to them.

'I'm tied up with this... ' he pointed to the building. ' ...at the moment. Come to the Station tomorrow, ask for me and I'll get a formal statement?'

Drizzle had turned to rain and the remaining spectators, seeing the Fire Brigade packing up hurried to shelter. Sandra and Colin broke into a run so that they over took Shuggie. Sandra appeared to stumble into Colin at that moment so they had to stop and momentarily were side by side. Sandra whispered, 'We've done what you said. But we need to talk. There's a problem come up.'

'Your place later this afternoon. Be in,' Shuggie muttered in reply.

CHAPTER THIRTEEN

By the afternoon the morning's squally showers had settled to steady rain as Shuggie Cameron strode along the footpath by the river. The pavement vibrated to the roar of the falls by the old mill. Spray hung in a think mist above the frothing river. The clouds parted briefly letting through a burst of sunshine. A rainbow flashed and died over the waterfall. Shuggie wondered if that was a good or a bad omen. Shrugged. Carried on walking. He should go and see Hunter Dunbar to make sure the American stayed in the penthouse but the less Shuggie saw of him the better. Hopefully with Browne sending a text confirming that tickets for the London sleeper train had been bought, the American would not want to be seen and would lie low until they picked him up at 11.00 pm. After that the threat Hunter Dunbar posed would be gone forever. That part of the plan seemed to be on track. Shuggie smiled at his pun, then became pensive as he wondered what problem he was about to find when he met with Sandra and Colin. He brushed rain from his face and quickened his pace. He would soon know.

As Sandra ushered him through to the lounge, he felt the tension. Gone was the spark between her and Colin of this morning. Colin was sitting huddled miserably in the corner of the far sofa. She ignored his pat on the cushion beside him and sat in the sofa opposite, grim faced and glaring at him across the coffee table. Neither said anything at first then Colin spoke.

'Well you asked him here. Tell him.'

She bristled, 'It's your bloody mess, you tell him. You and bloody Gerry.'

Colin looked more miserable, withdrew further into the cushions. 'It won't work,' he said. 'Gerry was at the restaurant this morning. We managed to keep her away from the police but she knows it's me. Recognised me right off. She'll have told them by now. So that's it. All over. No millions.'

Shuggie waited. There was more to this. Only an hour ago, Helen Green, from the *Gazette,* had quizzed him on whether there was any truth in rumours of Ingleby paying protection and that Shuggie was involved. Had he anything to say? Had McVey questioned him? The word on the street was that Ingleby had got out of the building. Did he know where Ingleby was? Helen was persistent when she got going and they had spoken for several minutes. If Gerry knew, this morning, it seemed that she had kept silent. Perhaps it was not all over

'She has not told the police.'

Colin looked puzzled. 'You sure? How do you know that?'

'You don't really believe I'll answer that,' said Shuggie. 'But I know that as of an hour ago she'd said nothing. You saw her at... what? About eleven o'clock and it's now after four. Plenty of time for her to have spoken to Inspector McVey and if she had, by now, you would be having a visit.'

Shuggie thought for a moment. 'Phone her. Get her round here.'

Sandra glowered at him. 'Over my dead body. My bloody home and I say who gets in here. And it's not her. Interfering, holier than thou, bitch.'

Shuggie ignored the rant. 'You're certain she recognised you? '

'Ran shouting my name. When I tried to say I was Paul, she totally flipped. So I said about the money thing... '

'You bastard. You didn't tell me that bit. You told her everything. Christ, how soft are you?'

For a moment it seemed that the torrent of words from Sandra would be followed by physical violence as she rose from her seat and thumped the table. Colin shrank back before the onslaught, stuttering.

'What. What could I do? I was trying to shut her up. Stop her shouting my name or going to the police.' He held out his arms pleading. 'It did work. She left at the time.'

'Knowing everything, you wimp.'

Shuggie stepped in, 'So she knows everything but it would appear she hasn't said to anyone. Now let's get her here and find out what she intends.'

He placed a hand on Sandra's shoulder and pressed her back onto the couch, sat beside her.

'Have you thought she could be bought?' Sandra spluttered as he continued, 'four way split is better than nothing. Phone her.'

Sandra hesitated, nodded. Colin stayed motionless.

'Well, wimp. Bloody phone. At least we'll know where we are.' She turned to Shuggie. 'But what she gets comes out of his share, right.'

God she was good-looking when she was angry, he thought. This was his kind of woman.

'Don't get ahead of yourself. Fix the cost when she agrees to stay silent.'

Shuggie placed a consoling arm round her and was pleased when she did not offer any resistance to the gesture. 'Actually this could work well. If she is in. There's no worry about identification of the body.' He smiled, remembered the splatter on the railway tracks, decided not to add, what's left of it.

That Gerry buzzed the intercom barely thirty minutes later said to Shuggie she had been expecting a call, perhaps hoping for one. Colin was despatched to greet her as Shuggie watched Sandra position herself on the sofa, back to the door, knees pulled up in posed nonchalance. She picked up a magazine and flicked the pages. Saw him watching and smiled conspiratorially.

'No need for her to think we are anxious,' she said.

Shuggie smiled back. 'I think she was waiting for Colin to get in touch.'

'You'll see. He lights her fire.' Sandra shrugged. 'Good on her. If she can stand hours with him…' Whatever she would have added was cut off by Colin coming into the room with Gerry close behind.

In her high heels she was slightly taller than Colin. She slipped off her coat, shook off the rain. Glared at Shuggie.

'You didn't say he would be here.'

Sandra half-turned. 'My flat. Get used to it.'

It was as if the temperature in the room dropped a few degrees. 'Hello, Sandra. Good to see you too.'

Gerry handed Colin her coat. 'Hang it up.' Warmed him with a slight purse of her lips. 'Please.' She moved like a dancer, lithely covering the ground to the far sofa. Folded gracefully to sit facing Sandra. Shook her long red hair, ran her fingers through it and let it fall, looked up at Shuggie. An attractive woman and she knew it.

Sandra tossed her magazine back onto the table as Colin came back in. Stretched, curved her back, raised her eyebrows in a question and smiled as she watched him go to sit beside Gerry. It seemed to Shuggie that Sandra was not disappointed and realised that he too was happy with this. Partly that it would be easier to strike a deal with Gerry if she felt that she had won her man but also because he did not like to think of Sandra and Colin as a couple.

While red hair, those grey eyes and that body should be an exciting package he was more taken by this little blonde. She reminded him of Mel which surprised him for she was petite and fair whereas Mel had been tall and dark. There was nothing similar but there was spirit here and a spiky mind, so like his sister's. He sat beside Sandra.

Gerry scanned the three, 'You don't think I am going to go along with this. Colin pretending to be Paul. And for some measly inheritance. You're pathetic.'

Sandra frowned, looked at Colin. 'Measly! I thought you'd told her. Could you not even get that right.?'

He shifted uneasily. 'There wasn't long to explain. I did say it was a bit of money.' 'It's a bloody fortune.' Sandra puffed. 'Listen, Gerry. His bit of money is millions of quid. Get it. Millions. So we are going to pull this off. He's stuffed at the moment. No house. No job. No prospects. No brains.'

Shuggie watched red rage spread over Gerry's cheeks and jumped in before she could reply. The last thing they wanted was both girls in a cat fight. 'Let's not lose our tempers. There's a bit of a misunderstanding.' He saw Sandra about to speak, continued, 'bound to be in the circumstances. Nobody's fault.'

'Gerry gave a brittle laugh. 'And I should listen to you. The bastard who is the reason Colin has no house and no Restaurant.'

'Not his fault he has no brains though,' Sandra chipped in.

Fortunately Sandra was quick to pull away and hindered by the table between them Gerry's slap missed.

Colin uttered 'seconds out, round two,' before he thought of the consequences, and it could have been disastrous. But Gerry froze, saw the humour and burst out laughing. Also she had registered the earlier conversation and was intrigued. 'This money's millions. No joke.'

'No Joke,' said Shuggie. 'Guarantee of about twelve million pounds if we can pass Colin off as Paul.'

'Won't Paul rather screw up that?'

'Aye. That's the problem,' said Sandra, 'a dead Paul does screw it.'

Understanding flicked across Gerry's face. 'Oh… eh, sorry.' She struggled for words. 'Condolences and all that. He died in the fire, then?'

'He's certainly dead. But not in the fire. A large American came to kill him… and has.'

In the silence, which followed, Shuggie added. 'Let's all calm down. Take time over a drink to explaining a few things to Gerry. Sandra, you have drinks, I assume?'

'Beers in the fridge.' She headed for the kitchen, remembered her hostess duties, 'Gerry, glass of red for you? I'm opening a bottle. Shiraz.'

'Make it a large one,' replied Gerry. She posed a conciliatory smile. 'Look, Sandra. About earlier, didn't like you insulting Colin. But I am sorry about Paul. Really sorry.'

Sandra replied in kind. 'Thanks. He was a bit of a bastard. But he was mine.'

It took a second bottle of Shiraz and a bit of argument but in the end a few million pounds swung it. It helped that there was a drunken promise from Colin to Gerry that they would be together for ever, would move far away from Paisley and these low-lives.

Shuggie stayed out of it as much as possible preferring to watch as greed undermined revulsion and respectability. It amused him to listen as they rationalised temptation. He also enjoyed watching Sandra. The way she manipulated the conversation so that Gerry became a mix of contrition at having left and jealousy that Colin might find another lover even if he was poor. How life with him could be of they were rich; painting pictures of world cruises and diamond rings. Why should they be poor when this money was theirs for the taking? And who was going to suffer? Some American gangsters who had killed Paul. It was just. It was only what they deserved.

All was settled until it struck Gerry that, for a time Colin would have to to stay in the flat with Sandra. Shuggie, to douse the jealousy, spoke up.

'There's two bedrooms. If he goes anywhere near her I'll beat his head in. He knows if he endangers this he's going to suffer.'

Gerry had seen how Colin wilted at the threat of violence. And in drink it made total sense to her that this solved her difficulty. Even if she could not trust his fidelity she could believe in his fear.

CHAPTER FOURTEEN

Inspector Hamilton McVey listened to rain patter on his office windows, raised his head to watch it gusting down the street. He picked up the half-eaten Mars Bar from his desk, took another bite. If he went outside he would be at the burnt-out restaurant in a few minutes. Not that he was going tonight in this rain and what would he achieve. The engineers had signed off and an initial search found no body. Colin Ingleby had not turned up, so more and more it seemed there was a death, but… He had two witnesses who said he got out. Two who heard him say he was going to see McCluskey. How good would it be to nail that little runt, Graham McCluskey.

McVey shuffled papers needlessly as he stuffed more chocolate into his mouth. Perhaps the sugar would help him think. Stop him craving a cigarette. He rubbed his eyebrows. But there was Hugh Cameron as well. Why had he been there today? And the girlfriend's testimony said Cameron had hit Ingleby and was involved in extortion, along with Razor Nelson. If this fire was about protection, it could be any of them.

He sat watching the rain. Thank Christ he was no longer on the Beat. Hell of a night to be out. His eyes caught the computer screen. It had finished the search for his typed request and the answer to his question about unidentified persons in Renfrewshire began to appear. The first leapt out.

Death on railway at Arkleston, probable suicide.

He read the initial report. The autopsy was to be carried out in the morning. It could be his man. Colin Ingleby could be a suicide. From what he had gathered today it would be understandable. But there was the niggle about McCluskey. Perhaps he didn't jump? First thing was to identify the body. He emailed for a copy of the report to be forwarded to him.

McVey checked his watch and saw that it was nearly six o'clock. He sighed and picked up the phone.

'Hi, Mum. Sorry it's been a busy day. Ah! you saw me on the news.' He listened pacing back and forth, saying 'yes' from time to time. 'Mum. Sorry I really must go. Yes. I'll get a hair cut. Promise.' He paced again, looking at his watch. 'Mum. I want to catch up with Helen Green. Yes, you do know her. The reporter at the *Gazette*. She'll leave her office soon.' He sat on his desk. 'No Mum. Not a date. Look, I have to go. Love you. Bye.' He put the phone down muttering, 'Spanish Inquisition.'

The *Gazette* office was at the corner of the High Street and normally he would have made the ten minute walk and left his car in the Police Station car-park. The rain driving against the doors as he descended sent him on down to his car. In contrast to Scruffy, the maroon 1976 Rover P6 V8 was pristine., paintwork and chrome shining, the cream leather seats spotless. He placed his hat carefully on the rear bench and slipped behind the wheel. As ever he sat for a moment and savoured the interior before heading for the Gazette.

The town centre was deserted. High Street misery afflicted Paisley more than many old industrial conurbations, Victorian buildings with ornate cornices and carved mottos lay empty and crumbling. McVey pulled up beneath the former glory of the private club where businessmen used to gather and look down on streams of mill workers filling their shops, buying their goods. Now it was abandoned and the chandeliers, visible behind the dust drab curtains of its first floor windows, did not blaze opulently. He counted five For Lease or For Sale notices in the shops which bordered the entrance to the

Gazette. Before he could become too maudlin he saw Helen leaving the building and waved her across.

'Want a lift.'

With the wind driving up the High Street, she did not hesitate to nip round to the passenger door and get in.

'Don't tell me. You just happened to be passing.'

McVey grinned. 'I could lie. You'd know I was lying. Wondered if you fancied an Italian.'

Helen Green laughed. 'Is he tall, dark and handsome?' McVey's puppy eyes pretended to be hurt. 'If you're paying, I'll not say no. What are you after?'

It was McVey's turn to laugh. 'There are a couple of answers to that… but I'll stick to the clean one. Want some info. What you've heard about McCluskey recently? Anything on Shuggie? But let's eat first. Mario's, overlooking the loch OK?'

'Bit expensive isn't it. And a bit of a run. Not want to grab the new place by the Abbey?'

He was already heading out of town. 'I fancied getting away from here tonight. Into the country. Unless you mind.'

Helen snuggled down in her seat. Listened to the thrum of the V8. 'You go for it. I like being pampered.'

Mario's was quiet, the heavy rain having deterred mid-week diners. They had a table by the window with views down the valley to the loch and beyond to the hills of the Muirshiel. When they arrived they could barely see those hills and indeed the view of the loch was distorted by streams of rainwater running down the large windows. Now, as McVey laid knife and fork together on his plate and pushed it away, the clouds parted and a red sunset sky glistened on the water.

Their young waitress was with them in seconds, clearing the table, then back with the desert menu. Helen shook her head.

'Not for me. Just coffee. Cappuccino.'

McVey took the menu and was tempted by the Tiramisu, swithered over the cheese board. 'Not having a sweet?' he asked.

'If had plenty. A coffee to finish is fine, Scruffy.' replied Helen.

Normally the nickname annoyed him but not when she said it. In her teasing voice it seemed to hold intimacy. He took in her slim figure, those deep brown eyes, her face crinkling as she smiled at him. He should make an effort, tidy himself up, get back into shape. It was hours since he had succumbed to a cigarette. He had checked and Helen was three years older than him but she looked younger. She was divorced from a husband who was a bit of a sportsman and they used to go hill walking together. He should make an effort. He patted his stomach.

'Good idea. I'll skip a pudding,' he said, handing the menu back, 'cappuccino for me.' As the girl was moving away he saw that Helen's wine glass was empty, called after her, 'and a red wine for the lady.'

'A small one,' added Helen. 'Scruffy, are you trying to get me drunk?'

'Faint hope,' he said. 'I've tried that before… not a chance and I couldn't afford the bill.'

Helen slapped his hand playfully

'Cheeky.' She paused, 'I've had a lovely meal, we've had a good chat and a laugh.' Her eyes flicked wider and a smile flashed briefly. 'You're good at making me laugh you know.' Scruffy glowed. 'But now I guess it will be payback time. What was it you wanted to ask?'

McVey sat silent. If he was honest he would tell her now that he didn't want to know anything. Since that morning he couldn't stop her slipping back into his thoughts and it had been spur of the moment to come here. It beat the hell out of his tiny cluttered flat and let him off the hook of visiting his mother. He struggled to think of questions about McCluskey or Cameron, the excuse he had used when he picked Helen up.

'Yes, McCluskey and Cameron.' He stalled. Was delighted when the arrival of the cappuccinos delay him having to speak for a couple of minutes as he put in four sugars. They might stop the desire to slip out for a smoke.

'It'll kill you,' she said as he stirred. 'You need to watch that weight, Scruffy.'

As he drank, from deep in his memory a rumour floated. 'Yes McCluskey. Heard anything about that mad wee brother of his. The one who's same age as Cameron. Is he back?'

Helen looked at him strangely.

'You hadn't thought about that before you asked,' she said.

'Yes. I recall something and wondered. If McCluskey's involved perhaps his wee brother is?'

She sat staring into space for a few moments.

'God! It was when you were off sick. After that nutcase broke your ribs, you went away to the coast didn't you? For three months?' McVey nodded. 'That's when his funeral...'

McVey cut in. 'Funeral?'

'Funeral. You're right in that he did come back. Came back in a coffin. Bad end. Violent; though that was no surprise. In some ways the surprise was it took so long for someone to cut his throat.'

'He's dead. Murdered?'

'Literally throat cut. One night in Salford.' Helen broke off. 'Good title for a book Eh! 'One Night in Salford'. Well for him it was a tragedy. They found him in a back lane. Broken jaw. Throat cut.' She motioned a knife slashing from ear to ear. 'Nearly took his head off'

'They make an arrest?'

'Not that I heard. As far as I know its never been solved. Mind you, would they try too hard. And there'd be a queue of suspects.'

'So it couldn't have been Billy McCluskey who threw a firebomb last night.'

'Billy McCluskey back from the dead,' she gave a pretend shiver, 'doesn't bear thinking.'

CHAPTER FIFTEEN

Sam Browne studied the pile of clothes and pair of scuffed Oxford brogues with disgust. Shuggie was already half stripped and putting on a pair of black trousers which were a size too big.

'I'm not getting into those,' he said.

'Suit yourself,' replied Shuggie, his voice muffled beneath the black sweat shirt being pulled over his head. 'If they trace the car back to you, I'll kill you.'

This was said with quiet menace so that Browne did not doubt he meant it and began to take off his clothes. Dressed in wine coloured jeans and a bamboo pattern yellow shirt he was an incongruous figure for a cold night. At least the long blue coat covered most of it but hard as he tried it would not fasten.

Shuggie, all in black, scanned him from head to toe.

'Aye, Razor really got you.'

'I look like a ponce at a poof's wedding,' said Browne.

'Now. No homophobic language. You could get arrested.'

At that moment being arrested for anything seemed preferable to a night drive with Shuggie to meet the American.

'Why do I have to come,' he said, for the umpteenth time that night.

'I told you. He wants you there.' Shuggie went to the door. 'Come on.' and as Browne followed said, 'I think he wants to kiss you goodbye.'

They stopped beside the car to pull on gloves. Razor had done well. Shuggie had specified a three door and preferably one where you sat upright. The five year old Toyota Rav4 met the bill and being black almost disappeared in the shadows. The number plates were mud splattered. Not enough to have the police stop them but difficult to read. Shuggie climbed into the back, behind the passenger seat.

Browne sat behind the wheel and twisted round so that he could see Shuggie.

'Won't you drive. This Hunter Dunbar scares me. What if I crash?'

'Don't' said Shuggie. He lent between the seats and grabbed Sam Browne's throat. 'Now shut up. Stop moaning and fuckin' drive. We pick him up and go to Westerton Station. The car park. Far end. Got that. No fuckin' parking by the entrance or under lights. Far end in the dark. He doesn't want to be seen with us.' He paused. 'Nor we with him.'

As they moved off Shuggie smiled as he saw Browne's hand shaking on the wheel. Pure chance that Razor had stolen an automatic but it would save crunched gears.

It was about fifteen minutes from Browne's house to the Old Mill flats so, by the time they drew up at the entrance, Browne had his shake under control. They phoned on route to say they would be there in ten minutes and the American had said he would be ready and waiting at the foyer. Shuggie didn't need to prompt Sam to leap out as soon as they stopped. Browne feared the American even more than Shuggie. Boot door thrown open as he raced round to meet Hunter Dunbar, grab his bag, passenger door held and closed like an over-efficient hotel doorman, case in the boot and Browne had the car speeding off, without a word spoken.

Normally Browne would have headed down the motorway and over the Erskine Bridge or at a push used the Clyde Tunnel but he had instructions to take a longer route by M8 into Glasgow, take Maryhill Road to Canniesburn and from there cut down to Westerton. It would be more difficult for the police if they tried to trace the journey on surveillance cameras.

Hunter Dunbar shuffled in the passenger seat, appeared to have some difficulty as he put away the train tickets passed to him by Shuggie and then, in adjusting his seat belt, he muttered about bloody English cars with no room. When he settled the pistol which had been in the holster, for his right hand to reach, was in his left hand, hidden from Browne by his jacket and from Shuggie by the seat. The two door car forcing him into the front seat had annoyed him at first but now he had altered his plans and was relaxed. In fact he was happy. If he had been in the rear of a four door it was relatively easy to plug driver and passenger from behind but there was a risk that a bullet hit nothing vital and one of them being able to get out. Once out the car it could take time to finish them off. This way he could shoot the driver, McCluskey, and be out before the clutz in the back knew what had happened. Easy job to shot him as he struggled to escape. As soon as McCluskey reached for the parking brake he was dead.

As they swung right off Maxwell Avenue, Shuggie slid his right hand inside his left sleeve, felt for elastic strap on the sheath of his grandfather's commando knife. He released the handle and let it nestle in his palm.

Cloud had cleared and the wet car park glistened in moonlight. There was a sole car near the station building but they carried on to where trees at the far end cast deep shadows. Hunter Dunbar's smile was never completed as Shuggie's left hand grabbed curly hair, pulled back Dunbar's head and with right hand, in one smooth curve of the blade, severed artery and tissue.

Blood sprayed the windscreen as Sam Browne slowed to park. The shock made him lose control, skid the Toyota so that it slid on and only came to a stop when they hit the verge. Shuggie held Dunbar's head tight to the seat-back as his body twitched violently for a few seconds before it slumped in death.

In the driver's seat Browne also slumped forward, head resting on the blood stained wheel and breath coming in gasps. He sat back wide-eyed, forcing down a need to be sick.

Shuggie wiped the knife on Dunbar's sleeve. He checked to the right and behind. Nothing moved. He let Browne sit and cry. There was no hurry. He would wait until the other car had gone. A train stopped and a lone passenger was met by the car's driver. Their headlights did not reach to the Toyota as they left.

One advantage of Browne being in shock and in the front was that Shuggie had time to compose himself before he had to speak or be seen. He swallowed twice to make sure his voice would be steady.

'Pull yourself together. If I hadn't killed him, it would be us dead.'

'Fuck you,' replied Browne. 'He was leaving. Christ another half-hour and we'd never see him again.'

Shuggie flicked Dunbar's jacket open with the knife. Pointed to the pistol resting in Dunbar's lap. As soon as we stopped, you were dead. You owe me your life.'

'For fuck's sake. You forced me to come. Bastard.' Browne started to shake and sob. 'You fuckin' played with my life.'

Shuggie sat in silence. It was too early for him to get out. A car dropped a traveller and left. The London train arrived and departed.

'Get a grip or you will be dead.' He tapped the knife on Browne's cheek. 'Now open the bloody door and let me out. We have things to do.'

Going to the boot he brought out two plastic packages and handed one of them to Browne.

'Get your outer clothes off, put on what is in there, then throw the ones you've taken off into the car. '

Browne stood looking at him in disbelief. 'It's bloody freezing.'

Shuggie ignored him and returned to the boot for the American's case. Taking his knife he ripped it open and began to empty Hunter Dunbar's clothes onto the back seat.

Still shivering with shock as Shuggie tossed the case on top of the clothes and began to undress, Browne was stirred to action by a growled command .

'I'm getting pissed off with you. Get stripped. Do it.'

Shuggie was already half undressed.

Like an automaton Browne followed suit. In the plastic bag he found a grey, one- piece, nylon overall, even the feet were included. He stood disconsolate. How far would they have to travel dressed like this?

'Get the bloody clothes in there.' The angry voice again forced him to move.

He threw his discarded clothes onto the front seat as Shuggie appeared from the back of the car with a petrol can and began to pour petrol over the car interior. Browne watched him methodically make certain that the body and all the loose clothing was saturated before leaving the can in the driver's foot-well. Next Shuggie took out his mobile phone and sent a text. In two minutes car headlights cut the gloom. Razor drew up beside them. With relief Browne crawled into the back of the car. From there he dared to watch as Shuggie searched through the American's pockets and made a pile of the contents on the passenger seat. He tore out the pages from the passport and rolled them into two tapers. As Shuggie moved at his task, at one point, his back was towards Razor's car. While the view of the body was obscured, it seemed to Browne, something was slipped by him into the nylon overall, before he used the remaining petrol in the can to saturate the pile then flicked a red disposable lighter to the tapers. One was held to the debris of Hunter Dunbar's life until they caught fire and the other was tossed onto the clothes on rear seat.

Briefly Browne saw the grotesque corpse of the American, head almost severed from the body. Flames carved patterns in the trees as they sped off.

Shuggie spilled a little of the drink as he placed a brandy for Sam Browne on the coffee table, listened to the gagging noises from the bathroom and took a mouthful of his own. It was only thirty minutes since they had returned and this was the second time Brown had been sick. All those swash-buckling scenes in his acting career had not prepared him for the reality of violence. However it was a blessing that he kept having to leave the room as it gave Shuggie time to recover and not have to maintain his pretence that killing a man was easy for him. It was only the third time he had killed with a knife. Both of the others had been when his own life was on the line but this was a first, for him, to have planned ahead. The moment he saw Hunter Dunbar in the penthouse, he had known that one of them was going to die. From then on it had been a case of making sure it was the American who did.

Shuggie took a deep breath and lowered himself slowly into the white leather. He placed his drink carefully by his side and flexed his fingers, focused on the framed posters of Browne's career highlights, to block out the memory of resistance of flesh and sinew, the gush of blood. The adrenalin of the night was wearing off and he did not want Browne to see him shaking.

When Browne returned and dropped into the armchair, Shuggie

saw his eyes flick to the feet on the couch, the slight grimace, but nothing was said. He guessed that whether his shoes scratched the leather, after tonight's events, was no longer important. A side effect of the killing was that Browne was even more in awe of him. Browne had not bothered to dress after removing the nylon overall and was in a pale grey dressing gown. Wiping the corners of his mouth, he picked up the brandy left for him. His face was strangely bloodless and with the white leather and grey dressing gown was like the ghost he played in the horror movie celebrated on the wall behind him. .

'You bastard. Why did you do that.' The brandy revived a conversation started on their journey from Westerton. 'You could have killed him without putting me in danger.'

Browne rose and poured himself more brandy. 'Fuck, you could have killed him in McCluskey's place. All this pantomime with old clothes and overalls and fuckin' Razor.' He drank long and hard. 'Bastard.'

'Time you learned some truths about the world you joined when you took up with McCluskey.'

'McCluskey! McCluskey! Shit, he hasn't taken me out at night to watch a man's throat slit.'

'But he got you into this.' Shuggie let the thought simmer. 'Believe me it was the only way. You were my bait. Kill the American in the flat. Big bastard. A pro. A pro with a gun. I had to get him off guard and you were my bait. My first priority was keeping me alive.'

'Fuck you. You could have let him leave. Christ we were at the station. He was going. A few minutes and it was over.'

Shuggie chuckled. 'Aye. Over for you and probable me if I hadn't got there first. You saw the gun. Think about it. The only witnesses to Hunter Dunbar being in Glasgow are you and I. You think he was going to let that be. I said he was a pro. These guys don't leave loose ends.' He pointed at Sam Browne. 'You were a loose end. I was a loose end. I offered him a way to get us both, on a dark night, in a lonely spot. Knew he would check it all out. Knew he would bite.' Shuggie gave a quiet grunt. 'I sold him a slow fool, a bit of muscle and he bought it.' He finished the brandy. 'Aye, he bought it.'

CHAPTER SIXTEEN

Inspector Hamilton McVey was late but he still took a detour on the way to his office. He wanted to visit the burnt-out restaurant. Constable Perry was surprised to see a rather neat-looking Inspector approaching, hair combed, shirt tucked into trousers, and not a stain in sight. Rather than the usual cigarette the Inspector was chewing gum.

McVey stood for a few moments surveying the lack of activity. 'Is the search finished Constable?'

Constable Perry nodded. 'Yes, Sir. Nothing found. Certainly no sign of a body.'

McVey wandered towards the Police Station. If there was not a body at the site of the fire it did suggest Ingleby had got out. If that was true why had he not turned up? If it was true that Ingleby had gone to see McCluskey, as the cousin and Sandra Smith had told him, anything could have happened, but nothing had come from searches of local hospitals.

There were several surprised looks as he passed down the corridor to his own office. A cry of 'new suit' followed him to the door. He stroked the lapel as he entered, thought how you got good bargain in the Stroke Charity shops. He would see Graham McCluskey this afternoon and hopefully that would give him a reason to talk to Helen. This was his wedding's suit. Time it came out of the wardrobe.

On his desk was a preliminary report about the death on the railway. There was an attached note from Robbie Fleming the pathologist. 'You asked for this. You were getting it anyway.' He flicked through the file then rotated the chair so that he sat side-on to the desk. Resting his feet on the radiator by the window, with one elbow on the chair arm and the other on the desk he began to read more carefully. This was an interesting corpse.

Interesting that a man killed sometime late Tuesday and early Monday had managed to end up on the railway lines at Arkleston and be hit by the 12.03 train to Ayr. A man whose body matched the information on Colin Ingleby's height and build, who had been shot in the head and whose face was missing. A body without any identification. Someone did not want him traced? Yet had chosen a very public way of dumping a body?

McVey looked a the sparse list of belongings. Trousers and shirt label from 'George' at Asda. Belt, brown, fake leather. A silver Luckenbooth ring. McVey's eyes glinted as he whispered 'Yes'. Emptied out the photographs and picked the enlargement of the ring with the engraved 'G to C' clearly visible. He had no doubt that this was Gerry Kowalski to Colin Ingleby and that the ring was Colin Ingleby's.

He dropped his feet and swung back to the desk. So the major line for enquiry must be that Ingleby had gone to find McCluskey. If he had it was likely that the meeting had not gone well. First get the body identified. He rang the mortuary and spoke to Robbie, asked for the ring to be brought up. He sat quietly then telephone again to ask if Sandra Smith and Paul McNeil had come in to make their statements. They had arrived and were with Sergeant Jenkins in Interview Room 4.

Sergeant Jenkins was small fat, fifty and bored. It had taken this pair an hour to agree statements that could have been done in twenty minutes. He had a mugging and three house break-ins sitting on his desk and with the sun shining should have been in the scheme beneath the Braes and breathing fresh air. Not in this windowless dump with the overwhelming smell of body odour which dousing with Lynx deodorant had not concealed, merely added another irritant. Sandra Smith made and signed hers relatively quickly but this idiot, Paul McNeil, had taken ages to make his with any semblance of clarity and now was reading it for the fourth time. It was as if he thought it should be a literary master-piece and not a single page document, waiting to be signed.

It was a relief when the silence was broken by 'Scruffy' McVey knocking and coming in. Sergeant Jenkins took a few seconds to recognise that it was the Inspector, for the neatly combed hair and the suit, without permanent creases and shiny elbows, was not the usual appearance. It disconcerted him for a moment as the Inspector entered.

'Statements done?' asked McVey.

Sergeant Jenkins held up Sandra's so that the signature was visible. 'One done.' He pointed to Ingleby. 'Just a final read through and that's it.'

'I'll take over, Sergeant. I want a word with Miss Smith and Mr McNeil.' He smiled at both, 'if you can spare me a few minutes?'

The Sergeant tidied his papers said, 'Yes, Sir' and was out the door before they had replied.

The Inspector arranged three photographs of the ring in a line along the desk.

'I wondered if you recognised this ring?'

Sergeant Jenkins popped his head back round the door and held out a small plastic bag. 'Sir. This was brought for you. They said it was urgent.'

'Thank you, Sergeant.'

McVey shook the ring from the bag onto the table and Colin immediately picked it up As he twisted it in his fingers, he made to slip it on but was stopped by Sandra taking it from him. He caught her frown and realised his mistake.

'Oh. it's Colin's' said Sandra. 'But how do you have it? He never takes it off,' she glowered up at Colin, 'does he?' She emphasised the 'Paul.'

Ingleby raised the ring to peer inside. 'Look inside,' said Colin. 'It's a gift from Gerry. Almost an engagement ring really. It's engraved G to C. That's Gerry to… '

Sandra jumped in sensing another faux pas coming. 'Yes. Look here it is, G to C, Gerry to Colin. It's his. Oh you've… ' her voice trailed away, 'you've found him.'

There was a brief silence before McVey held out his hand for the ring.

'There's no doubt that this is Colin Ingleby's ring?'

Both nodded.

'I'm afraid it was found on a body which has yet to be formally identified but does fit the description of Mr Ingleby. And with your identification of the ring I have to tell you that it is likely that it is Mr Ingleby who died sometime last night.' McVey let the news sink in. 'I am also sorry to tell you that I have reason to believe that his death was in suspicious circumstances.'

Sandra Smith had been around actors for long enough to know that the way to portray grief and shock was to underplay it, so she sat stiffly, and hidden by the table stabbed long finger-nails into the palm of her hand until her eyes watered. Colin on the other hand went into so many 'Oh, my Gods,' that Sandra had to kick him to bring it to an end. Fortunately McVey, who had seen every possible reaction to bad news, thought his sudden yelp was just the effect of grief.

CHAPTER SEVENTEEN

There was a soft breeze blowing from the loch as Graham McCluskey padded across the decking to lean on the rail. His short spiky hair showed signs of going grey and there were stress lines round mouth and eyes. The cord on his cream dressing gown strained to contain his expanding waist. The wood was pale at this point, where the stain had been worn through, a testament that standing here was a regular occurrence. McCluskey liked to survey how far he had come from the council schemes of Paisley.

On this beautiful morning the air had that quality which came from being close to water. From the loch came the putter of a small outboard and on the far shore wisps of morning mist trailed up the shoulders of Ben Lomond.

Graham McCluskey breathed deeply. From below the faint shouts of his boys made him smile. He remembered his own childhood and playing in the street or on the old railway embankment behind the cricket ground. Perhaps this morning he would join them in the swimming pool beneath the deck. It would be good to lie and gaze through the expanse of windows at how the clouds patterned Ben Lomond; but he knew the boys would not let him float in peace. He wondered if he was in the mood for their boisterous play. He should grab the opportunity before they returned next week to boarding school. Footsteps had him turn to see the housekeeper placing a tray on the table overlooking the loch.

'Your rolls and coffee, Sir.'

'Thank you, Mrs Lightfoot. Brown sauce on the sausage?'

Mrs Lightfoot raised an eyebrow. 'Of course, Sir. Would I forget.'

There were times when his housekeeper spoke, with a hint of annoyance in her voice, that she reminded him of his mother so he was suitably contrite as he replied, 'Thank you.'

As McCluskey sat drinking coffee and eating his rolls he watched a pair of bullfinches in the trees between the house and the water. From this raised viewpoint the tops of the trees were level with his gaze. He envied them their morning together and thought about texting Jennifer. It was after nine o'clock and her day would be well underway at Ross Hall Hospital. The boy's laughter made him wish he could shut out the future as easily as they did, but then they did not know his fears. He texted 'Morning. love you.'

He had barely put the phone down when it bleeped and he grabbed it in anticipation; but it was not from his wife. He threw the phone down when he saw it was from Sam Browne. Messages from that wanker could wait. He returned to watching the finches and behind them the trailing wake of the small boat cutting the water as it journeyed north. He tossed the end of his second roll to the grey squirrel which appeared from the edge of the trees, to run across the slope leading to the swimming pool windows. He wondered if his two sons were equally amused with the almost human way it spun the titbit in its paws and nibbled. His reverie was disturbed by another bleep of his phone.

This time, it was his wife and he lay back in the lounger and chatted. Happy, for she was happy. A good night and a suggestion she could be home in forty-eight hours had lifted her spirits and his rose with hers.

He returned to watching the bullfinches and was almost dozing when the phone interrupted the peace. He stretched for the phone, angry thoughts driving sky, loch and nature into darkness, when he saw that it was Sam Browne; what did the tosser want now? No doubt to check in and say that Hunter Dunbar was safely away on the evening train. Bugger. He better get on to 'The Team' about clearing the flat of any traces of the shooting. Bloody Americans owed him big time. Browne's bleating voice broke into his musings.

'Didn't you get my text. It was urgent.'

'Yes. Sure. And I haven't a hundred urgent things to deal with!' Something in Browne's voice made Graham McCluskey hesitate. 'What's happened?'

'Its Shuggie. He's gone mental. Gone ape shit mental. Only killed the American last night.' Browne gulped, struggled to get the words out. 'Christ, he slit his throat ear to ear. Right beside me.'

'What!' The voice had been rising and for the latter part was shaking badly so that McCluskey was not certain he had heard properly. 'Get a grip, man. What do you mean killed the American? You were taking him to the train. Why the fuck was Shuggie there? And why would he kill him?'

Any chance of peace was gone and McCluskey paced the deck as Sam Browne answered his questions, explaining how Hunter Dunbar had died. However, while he listened, six words kept niggling at McCluskey, 'slit his throat ear to ear.' Billy had died like that. And Shuggie hated Billy. And Billy's murderer had not been caught.

As soon as the call was over McCluskey phoned Chicago. He was nervous as to how Dunbar's death would reflect on him so, no matter it was the early hours of the morning over there, he had to get this done. He relaxed when a sleepy Liebermann answered and after the initial anger at being disturbed, Liebermann laughed. The lawyer did not have a problem with Dunbar being dead. The hit had been done so the mad Scot had in a way done them a favour. Now they did not have to pay Dunbar. In fact Liebermann said, they would send a little bonus to McCluskey for his help in getting it done so quickly.

With the difficult international call having gone well, McCluskey turned his attention to local matters. He arranged for 'The Team', The Wilson brothers, to start on his penthouse; lounge and mezzanine to be stripped back to bare concrete, everything that could be burned, would be burnt, and what couldn't would be tipped. If it wasn't a bare shell in twenty-four hours, 'hell would descend on them.' As he went into the house for a whisky he wondered why he had added that warning. They had known him long enough to realise how he would react if they failed.

His two boys ran in from the pool, dripping onto the polished wooden floor. He snapped at them and they swerved away sensing his anger was real. He cursed his reaction as their play screams echoed on the stair down to the basement playroom. Shit. He didn't need these problems now. Jennifer recovering from the operation and the chemo to come. He wanted time with his wife and children, not this. At least he was still in favour with the guys from Chicago and the South American cocaine was secure.

CHAPTER EIGHTEEN

After lunch Graham McCluskey settled in his office to checking through emails, but his mind kept wandering. He had to face it, Shuggie Cameron was now a liability. He poured a whisky, opened the desk drawer, and took out the old album. The photographs of him and Mel brought back the fun when they first married. It was the cocaine that split them but she could not see what he saw. This house, the security, the way he was respected. Her bloody sense of what was right and the constant nagging had broken the happiness. She said it was dirty money and went to work in the Cricketer's pub. She would have seen sense if it hadn't been for the bloody landlord. If only she had not met and fallen for Robbie Stanton. He shut the album with a bang. Well, he owed Mel nothing now. He had given her brother a job these last years and look where that had got him. And was it coincidence, the way Billy died? He poured another whisky, knocked it back in one. Time to tidy up loose ends; flat cleared and Cameron removed, and if Shuggie Cameron had been responsible for Billy's death then it would be sweet revenge.

He was about to go down to make it up with the boys for his morning anger and abrupt dismissal of them when he heard the buzzer from the driveway gate. Mrs Lightfoot came in.

'An Inspector McVey would like to speak to you, Sir. Are you in?'

McCluskey felt his stomach tighten. Scruffy was not what he needed this afternoon. He had told Jennifer he would visit the ward at 3.00pm and he wanted away by 2.00pm to be certain to get there in time, but there was nothing to be gained by refusing to speak. Thank God he had the flat being worked on for it was too much of a coincidence Scruffy being here today. Now he would stall for time.

'Of course, Mrs Lightfoot. Always happy to speak to Scruffy. Open the gate.'

He went to the door, adopted a cheerfulness and was waiting with a broad smile as Scruffy's maroon Rover pulled up. 'Hi, Scruffy, long time no see.'

'Morning, Graham. How's your mother?'

'She's fine. Yours?

McVey gave him a baleful look. Graham McCluskey winked back.

'Same as ever, eh! Come on in. Coffee? Mrs Lightfoot does a brilliant cheese scone.' McCluskey paused by a phone. He punched two keys for an internal number. 'Jackson. Bring the car round in forty-five minutes.' He placed a hand on the Inspector's shoulder. 'Sorry, Scruffy, I have to leave by 2.00pm. Hospital visit. Jennifer.'

They briefly discussed his wife's illness as they walked down the corridor to the study where the sounds from the play room increased in volume.

McCluskey grinned. 'The boys are full of energy after lunch. Perhaps the high sugar drinks were a mistake.'

In the tiled space below, the cries echoed loudly, became more strident, mixed with sounds of running and thumps as Scruffy replied. 'Sounds like a fight.'

McCluskey gestured out to the deck. 'Outside might be quieter and it's a lovely day.'

McVey followed him out to the loungers. Not the easiest place for an interview but it would be a pleasant change from the stuffiness of his office. They disturbed a squirrel which having ventured up to search for any crumbs jumped onto the rail and sped away. Mrs Lightfoot appeared in moments with coffee and scones.

'Have a word with the Boys,' said McCluskey as she withdrew.

'Scruffy,' he saw McVey grimace, 'Sorry, The Inspector and I need a bit of peace.'

It was an easy half-hour chat for both. Scruffy asked his questions and McCluskey answered. The scones were a delight. The sun shone. All was right with the world, certainly from McCluskey's point of view, for it all hinged on Colin Ingleby and the restaurant fire and he knew there was nothing to tie him to that. If anyone was going down it was Sam Browne, Shuggie Cameron and Razor Nelson who were well up the line before him and he had cast-iron alibi for all the recent events.

To his relief, McVey said nothing about America, drugs and an American hit-man with his throat cut. He kept an eye on the wrought-iron clock set into the rockery below and when he felt he had been sufficiently diplomatic drew the visit to a close.

'Right, Scruffy. Policing over as I have to go. I promised Jennifer I would be at the hospital in an hour or so and I want to pick up something for her on the way.' Mrs Lightfoot's warning to the boys seemed to be wearing off and, as if choreographed, a fresh bout of shouting echoed out from below. 'And a couple of hyper kids to deal with before Jackson brings the car.'

McVey sat in his car for a few minutes before driving off. Through the trees Loch Lomond sparkled and, above the mountain, puff-ball clouds moved slowly across a pale blue sky. His gaze changed to the wing mirror where behind him the white painted house shone in the sunlight. He shrugged and surged off spinning tyres on the gravel of the drive muttering, 'Crime doesn't pay.'

He had to stop for the security gate, cursing its slow upwards arc. As he had driven out from Paisley he had thought this journey was pointless, but now something in Graham McCluskey's reactions bothered him. There had been tension beneath the bonhomie and not just Jennifer being ill. McVey had known McCluskey for years and was certain the easy banter was hiding something. But he could not see how it was to do with the death of Colin Ingleby. The man had died sometime during the night and had been seen leaving the fire on foot, there was no way he could have got out here unless brought by someone. No-one would bother to bring Ingeby all the way out here to kill him and then take him back to Paisley? Christ there were woods where you could bury a man and a loch in which to sink a hundred bodies. Why throw one from a railway bridge? Unless you wanted it to be found?

McVey pulled off at the sign for The Duck Bay Marina and parked at the rear of a row of cars. He sat, looking out over the water, sunlight flickering on the rippled surface. Could he trust the statements made by Paul McNeil and Sandra Smith? McCluskey could account for his whereabouts for the whole of last night; at the hospital visiting his wife, home by ten and Mrs Lightfoot had brought him supper. McVey was certain she would swear to his return and that he had not left the house again. She was a long served and loyal servant and would lie if told to. But even if she would lie there were the security cameras recording everyone who entered and left. It was mounted on the gate and triggered by the buzzer. McCluskey had volunteered the tapes. Was there a way to by-pass that? Were the witnesses reliable? McVey was beginning to doubt them.

The loch shimmered and laughter from children in the park contrasted with the problems he was mulling over. Aroma from the hotel kitchen drifted on the breeze and he was hungry, despite the recent scones. Why not take advantage of the good weather… and he deserved a break. There was no need to rush back? He could investigate those bothersome statements tomorrow. This hotel did a rather tasty roast which he could eat on the veranda and enjoy the sunshine. If it was as good as he remembered this would be a place to invite Helen; a pleasant evening drive in the country and a meal. The thought drove away his worries about Ingleby.

CHAPTER NINETEEN

Colin Ingleby shredded the last of the sheets of signatures with relish. Sandra had kept him signing 'Paul McNeil' for most of yesterday afternoon until it was second nature. By the time it was evening, he had become bored with the her nagging and resisted demands that he keep practising. He was confident he could carry it off and told her so. Much to his annoyance, she had him back at it this morning but now she had left the flat he was free. When he told her that Gerry was coming round she had found a reason to go out. He could switch off for a while.

In a way he was enjoying this deception. It certainly beat the worries of the last few weeks when he had been unable to see any future. He checked his watch. Gerry was due shortly. Life was looking up. Gerry was back and this time he would hang on to her no matter what he had to do. There was a prospect of money and they could do what they liked. He was attracted by her suggestion of moving to France. It made sense for, if he was to live from now on as Paul, it would be easier to do so in a place where Paul was unknown. It also appealed that Shuggie Cameron would be out of their lives. He fingered the bruises on his face, fading but still visible. If he never saw that psychopath again it would suit him.

He put on the kettle and searched for biscuits, ready to greet Gerry. As he waited he scribbled a couple of signature and admired his handiwork. Nodded to himself. These would fool anyone. He was tearing them up when the buzzer from the entry system sounded.

'Hi. Come on up. You forget your key?'

Colin Ingleby jerked back to stress when the answer was not

Gerry's voice.

'This is Inspector McVey, Mr McNeil. I have a couple more questions if you can spare a few moments?'

Ingleby scanned the apartment for anything incriminating. Saw the bin full of scrapped paper and stuck it into a cupboard. Thanked God that, in his happiness to be free from Sandra, he had removed all evidence of his forgeries from the room. Hopefully Gerry would be there soon as moral support.

The policeman did not sit and refused the offer of coffee, said that it was to be 'a brief visit, to confirm a few points'. Their initial conversation went over, once more, what had been said about McCluskey in the aftermath of the fire. When out of the blue came the question, 'Do you happen to know who was Colin Ingleby's dentist?' It seemed such a strange request it was all Ingleby could do not to laugh.

It amused Colin to answer this question about himself while pretending, as Paul to have to think about it, but he managed to maintain his composure.

'Don't know why I'm puzzling about this, Inspector. Colin did not have a dentist. In fact Colin and I shared a phobia of dentists, were terrified by the thought. As far as I know, Colin had no truck with a dentist since he was a child and was forced to go'.

It was only as they talked further that Ingleby realised how fortunate this was; no adult dental records removed the teeth as a major factor in identification. It was a natural step from there to McVey discussing Mitochondrial DNA and ancestry. Colin struggled to follow this but it seemed that as cousins, on their mother's side, he should be a match and that would assist in identifying the body; if the body was that of Ingleby. Colin readily agreed to the mouth swab and McVey said that he would get it organised.

When Gerry came in, shortly afterwards, she found Colin grinning from ear to ear.

'You look pleased,' she said.

'I had a visit from Inspector McVey.'

Gerry looked at him quizzically. Run-ins with authority were not usually Colin's strength. 'And it went well?'

'Oh Better than well. Do you realise that Paul had no dental work done? I had forgotten that until the Inspector brought it up. It's brilliant. Isn't it.' Colin was almost jumping up and down. 'Couldn't be better.'

'Colin. You're making no sense.'

Colin jigged to the kettle. 'Kettle's boiled. Sit down and we'll have coffee. I'll explain.'

As they drank he went over the method of identifying a body and Gerry too started to smile. 'To think of the times I nagged you about your teeth.' She put her cup down rather forcibly. 'When we have the money, phobia or not, first thing, you get them fixed… mind you it's lucky you didn't do it earlier.'

Sandra found them, still buzzing with excitement, sitting on the couch arm in arm, computer on the coffee table, scrolling through properties in France. Colin was quick to boast of how he had handled the Inspector, explained their good luck with dental records. In his exuberance he had forgotten that it was her boyfriend whose broken body he was discussing with such glee. Sandra cut him off.

'Thanks for that, Colin. You're a heartless bastard. Paul's body so smashed up that the only method of identification is DNA.'

Her outburst stopped the smiles and in the silence that followed Colin and Gerry returned to the computer screen, became engrossed, once more, in vineyards and chateaux. Soon they forgot Sandra was there and their giggles annoyed her. That, and the stroking and cuddling; did they have to do that?

'You've decided on France, then. Fixed on an area.' She could not resist a dig. 'Massif Central sounds like a place for you, Colin. Remote and backward. Sort of place you'd both fit in.'

Colin shrugged. Gerry did feel a little guilty about how they had discussed Paul's body and, with the prospect of France, her mood was good. She did no more than nibble at the bait.

'You should think of moving. Nothing for you here, is there?'

Sandra taking the hint, said, 'No, there isn't' and mooched off to the bedroom.

It was true, what did she have; no job, no boyfriend. She should make plans and with a few million she could do anything she wanted. She threw herself onto the bed and began to daydream of world trips, a private yacht, the Aegean and a hunky skipper. Somehow, when she envisaged the skipper, he morphed into Shuggie. Two could travel as cheaply as one and there would be double the share to spend. She wondered how Shuggie Cameron would fancy a private yacht… and her. A burst of laughter from the next room seemed far away and no longer caused her to be jealous.

She texted Shuggie. *Fancy a drink tonight.*

A few moments later her phone pinged and her mood darkened as she read. *Don't want us seen together.* She tossed it away when it pinged again.

Sorry, sent too soon. Go to the Old bill buildings. I can pick you up there without being seen. 7.00. Meal in Ardrossan OK.

She wanted to text *Yes Yes Yes.* But sent *See you 7.00.*

CHAPTER TWENTY

Normally Shuggie would have blasted his horn at the skip lorry which forced him to pull sharply to the left, but he did not want to draw attention to his car. Ahead he could see Sandra, waiting as arranged, a short white skirt and long black boots certainly showed off her legs. Despite her attractions his eyes strayed to the full skip lying at the rear of the flats. The figure tossing a further load into it was familiar, the older Wilson boy. He had only had a quick view of the cab of the lorry before he had to swerve but it could have been the younger Wilson brother sitting beside the driver. Shuggie had no doubts they were working for McCluskey and it was the penthouse getting a major refit.

Sandra slipped into the passenger seat. Flashed a smile. 'Hello. Right on time. I like that in a man.'

'You're looking good.' Shuggie returned the smile. 'I like that in a woman.' He was pleased when she laughed. Sometimes his attempts at humour misfired but it seemed they were on the same wave-length. The night had started well.

The roads were quiet and Shuggie relaxed into the drive to the coast. Sandra took the opportunity to bring him up to date on McVey's visit and the way he hoped to identify the body. He sympathised when she moaned about the heartlessness of Colin and Gerry, but as the miles trundled by a thought niggled. Nothing that Sandra said about McVey related to the penthouse.

As they slowed for Beith he asked, 'Have the police been anywhere in the building other than your flat?'

'Not that I've seen.'

'Or heard?'

Sandra grunted.

Shuggie continued, 'Has McVey asked about the penthouse?'

'I haven't spoken to him since yesterday, but not that I know of. There's work going on somewhere up there. We had hammering and thumps into early morning. Was going to complain if I saw the men.'

'No need. I know who it is and they'd ignore you. But why has McVey not stopped them? They're in the penthouse clearing up after the American.' Shuggie swore, fingers tightening on the wheel. 'He doesn't know about McCluskey owning the penthouse.'

'Paul was trying to sell it. He spoke about McCluskey. Surely the police would know?'

'They wouldn't be letting the Wilson boys strip the place. Damn.' He pulled off the road.

'Sandra. Phone this number. Helen Green at the *Gazette*. Tell her you're upset by work going on into the middle of the night. Spin a sob story. Paul gone missing and probably dead. You need peace. Mention McCluskey being the owner. You know the idea.'

'A reporter? Will she do anything about noise?'

'It's not the noise I hope gets her going. It's the ownership by McCluskey. Hopefully that feeds back to McVey.'

Helen Green had not expected to be out again with Scruffy McVey so soon, but the invitation was welcome. A trip out to Loch Lomond and a good meal was an attractive prospect but there was the added bonus of possible information. The fire and disappearance of Colin Ingleby had gone National and her bosses wanted more. It had been good to sink into the Rover's leather seats and be chauffeured to this view from the restaurant.

As she watched him sit opposite she realised he was not a bad looking man. He had made an effort with suit trousers pressed and hair tidy. Well she could do with a bit of attention and besides, this fire and the death of Paul McNeil had mileage. Scruffy was worth keeping in with, at least until the story was exhausted.

The Ride of the Valkyries sounded from her handbag, caller unidentified. The female voice introduced herself, 'Sandra Smith,' had her immediate attention. She shrouded the phone and whispered to Scruffy. 'It's Paul McNeil's girlfriend.'

McVey fidgeted as the call progressed. He could make out little of the conversation from the one side he could hear. Talk of building work and disturbance, lost sleep, disgrace. Skips blocking up the place. He ordered red wine for Helen, ginger beer for himself. Pretended to read the menu. His attention came back to the call when he heard 'Oh it's owned by Graham McCluskey.'

As soon as the phone was put away he lent over. 'What was that about owned by McCluskey?'

'A penthouse in those mill flats is owned by Graham McCluskey.'

'What… ' exclaimed McVey, 'and disturbance?'

'Just that there's major work going on and it lasted into the early hours. Totally ruined her sleep.'

McVey went a strange reddish colour. Helen saw a vein pulsing in his neck and worried he was about to have a stroke or heart attack.

'Scruffy. Are you alright? What is it?'

He pressed the palms of his hands together and held fingers to his lips as of in prayer. It seemed to relax him and he breathed out in a long sigh.

'Sorry. Just a bit of a shock that we missed McCluskey having that penthouse.'

Helen looked puzzled. 'And?'

Before he knew it he told her about Ingleby and McCluskey, how he had been following a line of enquiry. How he had been dismissing it today when he saw how far McCluskey lived out here. Too far for it to be realistic that Ingleby came there in fact. A flat in the town made sense and he should have found it sooner. He knew he should keep this to himself and stopped his rant.

'Just for your ears this. For now.' He raised his eyebrows in supplication. 'Please.'

She nodded and laid her hand on his. 'You want to get back. I'll understand.'

'Too late. And anyway I don't have enough for a search warrant. I'll see what I can salvage in the morning.' He waved a waiter over to the table. 'We're ready to order. Helen what are you having?'

As Shuggie drew up, out of sight of the flats, Sandra snuggled close and kissed him lightly on the cheek.

'Thanks. I needed to get away.'

He shifted awkwardly in the driver's seat. 'I'm worried we're seen.'

She laughed. 'Ok but… '

He did not struggle as she pulled his head round and they kissed properly, until he pulled away.

'I'll make an excuse tomorrow night and we'll get away. If you want?' she said.

'I do want that. But you must realise we don't want them to suspect we're together. No idea how Colin… '

'We must call him Paul' she cut in.

' …Paul will react and I don't trust Gerry.'

Sandra nodded, slipped out of the car and ran off. At the corner of the old gatehouse she turned and blew a kiss.

Shuggie drove off wondering why he had not booked a room in Ardrossan, but it had seemed a bit quick on a first night out. It was the return journey had cemented what had grown during the evening. 'God, she is a looker,' he said out loud. 'And spiky to boot. Or to… '

He smiled at the prospect.

CHAPTER TWENTY-ONE

Razor Nelson was on edge. The Saturday collection had gone well. As he had said to Shuggie, on the morning after the fire, everyone was afraid of retribution. The easy collection should have meant Razor could concentrate on the task ahead, but Shuggie was in a strange mood.

Razor wondered if he was reading something into the quietness and the affability expressed to the shaking punters. It stirred questions as to whether Shuggie had got wind of what Razor had planned. All evening he had expected a challenge from Shuggie, but none had come. Now they had the last of the money and it was time for action.

Razor fingered his switch-blade knife. They always took the shortcut from the courthouse. The lights on the lane had failed weeks ago but, as ever, the Council had yet to repair them. No-one else used this route in the dark. Shuggie was ahead and Razor took the opportunity to wipe his hand on his trousers. He did not want the knife to slip.

Shuggie stopped at the foot of the lane and waited for Razor to arrive. He tossed the leather satchel which he carried on their night rounds.

'Catch. There's three thousand in there. Be sure that is what McCluskey gets.'

Razor plucked the bag easily from the air. 'McCluskey? But you take it to Sam Browne.'

'Not tonight. Tonight you go back to that slug McCluskey, the real boss.'

Razor gripped his knife. Christ, why this tonight? He had it all planned. Did Shuggie know?

'Browne. We work for Sam Browne.'

Shuggie laughed. 'Yeah. Keep up the pretence. Anyway I'm out. That's the last time I do the dirty work. Tell who you want.'

He headed into the dark of the lane and Razor hurried after. This was his time.

'Have a pint, Big Man. We're a team. It's easy money.'

Shuggie was walking quickly and had reached the junction with the road up from the station. Here steps rose to Church Hill and Shuggie hesitated to let Razor catch up. Now they were close, the click of the blade locking sounded so loud that Razor expected Shuggie to spin round but there was no reaction as they carried on to the first step. As Shuggie placed his right hand on the metal rail, Razor stepped tight behind. He stabbed hard under the left shoulder blade throwing all his weight into the blow. The force of assault lifted the big man off his feet. Shuggie's gasp echoed from the stone walls of the lane as his back arched, before he slumped to the ground, hand sliding from the rail.

The weight of the falling body ripped the knife from Razor's hand.

He kicked violently at the slumped Shuggie. 'You or me, Big Man. It was always goin' t' be wan o' us… '

He jumped back, turned onto the road to the town centre, and raced off clutching the satchel. Perhaps he should go straight to McCluskey. There might be a bonus for tonight's work.

There was no-one around as Razor slowed to a quick walk. A running man would draw attention at this time of night. Alert for any sound of the discovery of Shuggie's body or worse that the Big Man was not lying, dying, but was in pursuit, he sighed with relief when he reached the pick-up. He wondered about driving out to Loch Lomond but realised it would be after midnight before he arrived. He began to dial then stopped. McCluskey would not take kindly to being disturbed. He expected Shuggie dead and would see no reason to be told. The money would go to Sam Browne as usual. The body would be found by the morning and that would be the time to speak to McCluskey.

Shuggie Cameron listen to the retreating feet before hauling himself up using the railing. Razor's knife fell from his back and clattered on the cobbled steps. He winced as he breathed. 'Christ,' he grunted. 'Thank fuck for the stab vest.' He looked down at the knife blade which was twisted by the impact. 'Wee bugger has some bloody strength.' He winced again as he set off up the steps. The vest had saved his life but, by the mix of pain and numbness spreading across his back, Shuggie reckoned the blow and the kicking had broken at least one rib.

He turned right at the top of the steps, grateful that his flat was a short walk passed the Observatory and then downhill. He stopped frequently and took shallow breaths to avoid expanding his ribs. The street was deserted so that his slow progress went unnoticed. At the close door he steeled himself for the climb to his flat.

Checking that no-one was on the stairs, and having to stop frequently, meant that it was some minutes before he was home. In the living room he undressed with difficulty. The stab vest was placed over the back of a chair by the window. Fingering where it was ripped and dented Shuggie undid his belt and let his trousers fall to the floor.

In his underpants, he moved gingerly back into the room, taking a bottle from the top of a small cabinet as he passed. Sat in the armchair by the fireplace, he poured a generous brandy and found a semi-comfortable position half lying on his right side. Despite the discomfort he grinned. He was alive and tomorrow Razor would realise that no body had been discovered. How would Razor explain that to McCluskey, for there was no doubt in his mind who had ordered this? Razor did nothing without being told. He imagined a conversation between McCluskey and Razor as they wondered how badly he was injured. Revenge would be sweet. But he would need to lie low for a while until recovered. Shuggie toasted towards the stab vest, 'To planning ahead. Aye, and letting the bastards worry.'

As Razor turned off the motorway he could see that only the occasional flat in the old Co-op building was lit, despite it being Saturday. He wondered if any were managing to sleep for, as he left the pick-up, music blared from three wide-open windows. Two girls in the street were laughing loudly as they smoked. He guessed that they were exiles from one of the parties; smiled at the incongruity of parties he had attended where those who still favoured tobacco were banished to the pavement while he passed round a spliff. He could see Browne's window wide to the world but it took three long buzzes before Browne released the security door to the building.

Browne was hammered. Slurring his words and weaving down the hall to the lounge.

He waved a hand in Razor's direction.

'Where's your bastard mate. Killing someone?' He laughed coldly.

'Naw.' Razor had an image of Shuggie slumped on the steps in that Paisley lane. 'He couldnae make it. Sent me.'

'Drink? Whisky?' The bottle was already in Browne's hand and he poured without waiting for an answer. He passed Razor the drink and took the satchel. 'Fair exchange.'

'Three grand in there. Nae bodies holdin' out after what happened to Ingleby. Telt Shuggie that would do the trick.'

—128—

Browne slurped his whisky. 'Death. Alas poor Yorik.'

Razor was puzzled at first then dredged from past schooldays that this was in a play.

'Aye. Him an' all.'

'Jester to the court. That's what I am here. Court jester to my Lord McCluskey. When will he decide I should be dead… or you?'

'How much have you had to drink?' Razor noticed the light flickering on the answerphone. There were 23 waiting messages. He pointed at the phone. 'You not taking your calls.'

'No need, I know what they are.' Browne poured more whisky.

'Does the spirit tell you?' Razor laughed at his own joke.

'It's the director doing his nut about me being off sick. 'Fuck me. Sick. Of course I'm sick but can't tell him I'm sick of life. Of you bastards. Of bloody people getting killed.

'Shit, I've seen a man's head nearly severed with a blade and he wants me to prance around with a bloody sword spouting romantic shit as Cyrano de fuckin'g Bergerac.' Browne downed his drink in one. 'Fuck it, I should go to the police. Get protection. Get out of this whole shithouse.' He began to sob. 'Don't worry. I won't , of course. Who'd believe this old has-been. So I drink and am off sick.'

The idea of Browne going to the police unsettled Razor. He was not sure this was drink talking. The man was cracking up. Razor had seen this before and when they cracked they did stupid things. McCluskey would have to be warned and no time like the present, but not with Browne listening in on the call. He poured Browne more whisky. 'Get that down you. I'll phone for a carry-oot. You need food.' He Made a show of staring at his phone before saying. 'No signal I'll go pick one up along the road. Fish an Chips? Curry?'

'As if I care,' muttered Browne.

'I'll not be long. Give me a key. You're in no fit state to let me back in.'

Outside he texted to McCluskey. Late as it was this need to be dealt with urgently. *Sorry Boss. With SB. He's lost it. Drinking. Says can't work. Hates us all. Talking of going to Police.*

Along the road he saw the sign for an Indian takeaway. He headed to pick up a curry.

As he waited in the queue his phone rang.

McCluskey barked as soon as Razor answered. 'What about Shuggie.'

'Done. Can't talk I'm in a queue.'

'Queue.?'

'I had to leave Browne so I could contact you. Said getting food. I'm in a curry house.'

'How bad is he?'

'Bad. Very drunk… and dangerous I think.'

'And serious about the police?'

'Possibly. he's in such a mess I don't trust him.'

'Get rid of him. We don't need him now. Make it look like an accident. Shuggie and him gone suits me fine.'

'Tonight?'

'Do it.'

The few minutes it took for Razor to collect the chicken curry gave him time to figure out a plan. On the way back to the flat he stopped at the pick-up, reached up behind the tow-hitch and pulled down a packet wrapped in oilcloth.

Browne was surprised when Razor walked in.

'How the hell!'

Razor held up the key. 'Key, remember. And I've got Chicken Madras. Rice. Bombay Potatoes. And these.' He held out three tablets, green, blue and white.

'What?'

'They'll give you a lift. What you need.'

Browne reached out and took the three tablets in his palm. Shook his head, slurred a question.

'You sure?'

'Aye. You've had them before. These are on the house.'

He spread the takeaway on the table. Opened each and explained the contents to a befuddled Browne. 'Fried rice, Chicken madras, Bombay potatoes. He unwrapped four popadoms. 'Get stuck in, man.'

Browne sat staring vacantly at the three containers, lying open on the table before him. He began to spoon rice onto his plate, spilling nearly as much as he successfully dished out. He stretched for the chicken curry, actions laboured with booze and the tablets.

'You not having any?'

'No hungry. I'll skip it. You get that down ye.' Razor placed an open can of Lightning cider beside the food. 'Have a cider. Wash down these.' He gave Browne three more pills. 'Have ye back on yer feet.' Picked up the satchel of cash while Browne sat bemused staring at the pills cradled in his palm.

'Didn't I just take these?'

'We talked about it. You've still to take them.'

Browne shook his head slowly, 'Was sure…' but he swallowed them. Drank half the can of cider in one long gulp.

Razor slipped away into the night.

CHAPTER TWENTY-TWO

A disembodied voice stirred Shuggie from a disturbed sleep. The radio alarm in the bedroom sounding far away from the armchair in which he had spent the night. 'This is the seven o'clock news.' Shuggie groaned as he tried to move, nearly knocking over the remains of last night's brandy. It had helped him sleep but lying, semi-naked, in a chair had not been a good idea. He had to roll from the chair onto his knees and use the chair as a leaver to get to his feet. The left side of his back, which had been throbbing when he awoke, now went into spasm. Shuggie cursed, clinging to the arms of the chair, until it passed. 'Shit, shit, shit,' he said as he hirpled crab-like to the small kitchen. He slurped water from the tap then filled a kettle. It was an effort to lift it onto the electric base, requiring concentration to overcome the pain. He shook his head. 'Bugger this. Can't even manage to boil a kettle.' He abandoned the idea of tea.

The few steps to the bedroom were achieved with difficulty and he lowered, carefully onto the mattress, with a sigh. The voice of Radio Scotland newsreader, Gary Robertson, distracted him from the pains stabbing below his left shoulder.

'And now a breaking news story. Sam Browne, the well know Glasgow actor has been found dead in his flat at Morrison Street, Glasgow. Neighbours discovered his body early this morning when they went to his door to complain about noise. Being unable to get a reply the police were sent for and Mr Browne's body was discovered. Our reporter Fiona Walker is outside the property. Fiona, what is latest from the scene?'

'Yes, Gary. News of Sam Browne's death has shocked neighbours and friends. Despite the early hour, already flowers have been left at the entrance to the flats. His many fans have been posting on the internet. He was found dead in the living room of his flat in the early hours of this morning. I spoke to the upstairs neighbour, Mr Josh Turner, who raised the alarm. He said that it was about three o'clock this morning when he went down to remonstrate with the actor about, what he called, mournful music keeping him awake. A Leonard Cohen CD had been playing for some hours and Josh has an early start to get to his work. Being unable to get a reply, Mr Turner called the police. On entry to the flat the body of Sam Browne was found.'

'And have the police made any statement about cause of death. Are there suspicious circumstances, Fiona?'

'It is early days, Gary. As a sudden death there will of course be an investigation but for the moment it seems that this is a tragic accident. Sam Browne has long been the go-to leading man for home-based dramas. Tall, dark and handsome, he fitted the clichéd description. Probably best known as the dashing Doctor Mclean in Victorian Doctors. He has had trouble in the past with drugs and did spend time in rehab at the Priory Clinic. But it seemed he had put those troubles behind him and was currently back home in Glasgow to shoot scenes for his latest film. He was playing the lead in Cyrano De Bergerac, a remake of the classic swash-buckler. There will be many fans mourning the loss of a star of the large and small screen.'

Shuggie turned off the radio. Slumped back on the bed. Suspicious circumstances. Too bloody right. Razor had been busy last night. There was no way this was an accident. It had McCluskey written all over it. Loose ends being sorted. Razor better watch his back. McCluskey might just get rid of him as well. Shuggie started to chuckle, grabbed his chest and winced. Said aloud. 'Jesus, Razor, that's me and McCluskey goin' t' kill you. Hope I get you first.'

Razor Nelson was puzzled and worried. There was no talk of any stabbing in Paisley. He had risked going back to the lane and had found his knife with the blade bent. There were no Police, no tape, no search going on. Worse there was no sign of blood in the lane or on his knife. And what or who had damaged it. Christ he had heard Shuggie cry out, seen him fall, had given him a kicking. There should be a bloody body.

His nephew was duty Sergeant over-night and said no report was filed at the Police Station. He phoned a mate who portered in the Royal Alexandra Hospital. No-one fitting Shuggie's description had been brought in with a stab wound. How the fuck was he to explain this to McCluskey?

He rolled a cigarette. For two hours he had hung about here at the foot of West Brae and there was still no signs of life in Shuggie's flat. The living room window was open a crack but, apart from the curtain moving in the draught, nothing had happened. Razor racked his brains to think of where the Big Man could be if he wasn't up there. Nothing made sense and soon McCluskey would have to be told. At least Sam Browne had croaked it as planned. That would get him some leeway if Shuggie had escaped. But shit, how? Razor could feel the satisfaction of the blow. Never mind McCluskey if Shuggie was on the loose… Razor backed tight against the tenement., glanced anxiously around, then set off for the Pend across the road. From here he could watch the house and the approach to the Brae. Standing in the street he was too exposed. If he needed to avoid anyone it would be easy to slip out of sight through the Pend; now the buildings at the back were derelict no-one went down it.

As he lent against the white tiled walls, Razor ran through the stabbing. Shuggie must be dead or holed up somewhere badly injured. There was no friend he could think of who would give Shuggie shelter. For sure, not voluntarily. And would the Big man be in a fit state to force co-operation. Razor doubted it. He looked at his watch. Bugger if he would phone McCluskey and get a bollocking. He texted. *As far as I know Shuggie's stabbing not reported. Not traced in Hospital. I am watching his flat. No sign of him.*

He waited for an irate call but none came. It was half-an-hour before his phone pinged. *Your problem. Sort it.*

Razor grunted. Typical McCluskey. He should have expected it would be for him to deal with. At least he had been spared the lecture. But, aye, it might be his problem but in the end if Shuggie wasn't dead or dying it wasn't just him that should be afraid. McCluskey must know that.

As he began to roll another cigarette he wondered about disappearing himself. If Shuggie was still around it might be best to be somewhere far away. He had a little money stashed for a rainy day. And there was last night's protection takings, if he dared to steal from McCluskey. Christ if Shuggie was on the loose McCluskey would be well worth the risk. For the moment he would keep watch and see what developed.

Razor settled in for a long day.

CHAPTER TWENTY-THREE

Inspector McVey had the Sunday morning blues. Yesterday, his mother had been unusually difficult when he took her for a drive. Probing away at who he had been picking up from the Express offices in the High Street on Friday night. Was it that Helen Green he'd said he was meeting on Wednesday? A second date? Her army of informants would have made MI5 jealous but this time they had failed her badly, for all they could tell her was that it was a woman. She kept niggling about him being fit to drive. Ask if he had a good night's sleep with chuckled innuendo in her voice.

Scruffy rubbed his eyebrows. Last night's sleep had been disturbed by the stress of fending off those persistent questions from his mother as to when he would find a good woman and settle down. Friday night, on the other hand, he had a good sleep, unfortunately. Scruffy drifted into a reverie, wondered how Helen Green would react if he asked her back to the Duck Bay Hotel and this time booked a room. His flat was not a place to impressing a lady, not conducive to seduction. The thought of Helen, in their hotel room, at a window looking out onto Loch Lomond, brightened his morning. He would do that. He would ask her. At least with Helen there would either be a crude laugh of rejection or… Forgetting his coffee was fresh made and boiling hot Scruffy burnt his mouth.

He put the cup beside a pile of files waiting to be reviewed. That was his Sunday morning sorted and this afternoon he had a court appearance to prepare. Ingleby's death would have to wait. Soon he must have a look at McCluskey's flat. Perhaps someone had seen Ingleby on his way to it? It was a faint hope anyone sober enough to remember had been around in the middle of the night but cases could turn on luck.

It was early afternoon before the inspector pushed the other cases aside and picked up the file on the restaurant fire and the body which he was certain was Ingleby. He flicked through the pages. Something niggled at the back of his mind. Why was Ingleby going to see McCluskey about the fire. Police information was that McCluskey had stepped back from protection and was concentrating on drugs. He stood to pull another file from the cabinet behind his desk but stopped with hand extended. Turned back to his desk and dialled out.

'Hello, Helen. It's your favourite inspector here.'

'Scruffy.' Helen laughed. 'And what makes you think your my favourite? That there's not a long line of inspectors beating at my door?'

'OK. One of your favourites.' Scruffy hesitated. Hoping for a better reply. In the silence which followed he felt a slight shiver of disappointment. 'Hopefully.'

'Yes. One of my favourites. What do you want?'

He relaxed. 'We'll come to that later.' Was glad when she laughed with him.

'Thought you'd be working today. No rest for the wicked.'

'Or from them, eh Scruffy?'

'Too true. Hence the call. You did an article, a month or two back, I think, about the protection racked in Paisley. No names but you must have had background info to write it.'

'Yes.' Now Helen sounded hesitant. 'I can't reveal sources, Scruffy. You know that.'

'Not wanting you too. Wouldn't ask. I have more respect for you than that. But who did you hear was running it?'

'Come on. Are you telling me I have more information on the racket than the police?

If you are there's a story in that.' She paused for effect. 'And a big one. I could get a national by-line for that.'

This was not going how Scruffy wanted. 'No. No. Don't dare. I wanted to know what the word on the street was. Who did the guys paying protection money think they were paying off?'

'You said the other night.' Helen chuckled. 'In one of your moments of indiscretion. Shuggie Cameron and Razor Nelson were the muscle. Why are you asking, when you know?'

'But who were they collecting for? I have another name in my head. Nothing confirmed. Bit out of left field.'

'Scruffy, I won't say on the phone.'

'Drink. After work. There's a nice pub in Lochwinnoch. Good beer garden and it looks as if it will be a warm night.'

Pick me up from the office. You can buy me food too.'

'It's a deal'

McVey hung up highly pleased with his ruse.

The rest of his afternoon was taken up with reviewing papers for his appearance in court in the morning. Domestic violence was an area he wished he could avoid. He said, she said, and then when you got to court someone, often the wife, no longer did keep to their script; usually fear of retribution from the man, or his mates, or a perverted believe he still loved her. But he had to be prepared. At times like this he wished for the old days, as told to him by his dad, when these cases did not make it to the courts but were sorted by a good beating of the perpetrator. He recalled a story of his dad walking with his sergeant down Paisley High Street and seeing a couple of guys walking towards them. The sergeant was a big Highlander and punched one of them in the face as he passed, knocking him out. As the man lay in the gutter the Highlander said to the shocked mate, 'Tell him, next time his team loses don't hit the wife.' As he stepped away he stopped and expanded a little. 'If he touches her again I'll find him.' Nothing more said, the two policemen walked on.

As he re-read his notes, here was a man Scruffy would like to take up a back alley.

With the streets quiet, Scruffy parked the Rover outside the Express office, got out and stood waiting. If his mother's spies were around he wanted them to get a clear view. The tongues would be going overtime with this third time in as many nights. He could hear the telephone call in the morning and his mother's excited enquiry as to whether this time there was a future. If he could not shake her off he might as well wind her up and you never knew perhaps this time it would last. He smiled as Helen appeared, thought how striking she was. It was certainly better fun than sitting at home alone. Held the car door open as she slid into the leather seat of the Rover.

Helen smiled up at him. 'Why thank you. I'm not used to this chivalry.'

'You deserve it.' Scruffy gently closed the door wanting to add a compliment but could not think of anything that would not sound crass. When he sat in the driver's side he said, 'A beautiful evening, a beautiful lady what more could a man want.' In the corner of his eye he saw Helen Green cut him a quizzical look.

'What I want is a cool drink and food. So less cackle and lets get going.'

Weekend traffic was light as they left the town and it was a pleasant drive along the A737 towards Lochwinnoch. The loch, catching the low sun, gleamed silver.

'You had a good day?' asked McVey

'I'm not sure any day is a good day any more. Not since they cut back on staff. There are so few of us now it's a constant chase your tail.' Helen pointed out to the valley. 'Look. Hen harrier.'

McVey flicked eyes right. Saw the tell-tail flight of a raptor. 'Hen harrier is rare. Is it not a buzzard.'

'I know my birds, Inspector McVey. Unlike you.'

The inflection in the voice made Scruffy turn towards her.

She was laughing, at him or with him? 'Keep your eyes on the road,' she said, placing her hand over his and pretending to help him steer. Scruffy felt the warmth of her flood through him.

'Stop distracting me.' He negotiated the roundabout, looked over at her again. 'Actually don't.'

'Don't what?'

'Don't stop distracting me.'

She raised an eyebrow. 'No?'

'No. I like the way you do it.'

In the village Scruffy drew up outside the Italian fish and chip shop. 'Let's eat first.

Fancy taking them down to the loch side? Seems a shame to sit in on an evening like this.'

They bought fish suppers and drove the short distance to the loch. Sat on a bench at the water's edge surrounded by gulls, swans and geese, hanging on every move of fingers to mouth, waiting for thrown tit-bits They ate in silence. Helen licked her fingers. Crushed the tray and papers into a rough ball. 'Brilliant. Scruffy, that is what I call a treat.'

Scruffy crushed his remnants and took hers. 'Was good. Wasn't it.' He took the rubbish to the bin. Returned to Helen who, eyes half closed, drank in the sun. 'Good company makes everything better.' Before she could answer, he added, 'So the beer should be a cold elixir.' He held out his hand. 'Brown Bull.'

She took his hand, replied, 'Brown Bull, ' linked her arm with his and headed for the car. 'But mine's a glass of red. A large one. Cheapskate.'

'For you, I'll stretch to a bottle.' He replied pressing her arm tighter to him.

As they reached the car she spun him to face her. 'For an Inspector you're pretty dim. How many clues do I have to give?' Sighed. 'Kiss me you idiot.'

There were many who were taking advantage of the balmy evening to sit out in beer garden of the Brown Bull but they found a seat at the far end. Scruffy swatted away a wasp as they settled on the bench. They sat in silence for a time but there was no awkwardness. It seemed right that they should be together on a night like this. It was Helen who spoke first.

'Wasn't there information you wanted? Or was that just an excuse?'

For Scruffy, it was a shock to the system to be pulled back from this to the reality. He thought of lying and decided Helen was too shrewd for that to work. Anyway he did not want to lie to her. To buy time he took a drink from his half pint.

'Good stuff, this Kelburn beer.'

Helen playfully kicked his ankle. 'And, was it an excuse?'

He pretended remorse. 'Excuse. You've got me to rights.'

She sipped the Shiraz, large glass as requested. 'I may have to impose a long sentence.'

'As long as there are visiting rights,' he replied. 'Look,' he said, 'there's your bird of prey.'

She looked up scanned the sky. It was empty. 'Where?'

'There.' Scruffy pointed to a carved eagle on a post in the garden.

This time the playful kick was little more forceful. He pulled his leg back spilling beer.

'Careful. I break you know.'

Helen recalled the reports on the beating, the broken ribs, his three months away from the town, the haunted look that only recently had left his face. 'Yes. I know.' She put a hand on his arm. 'You are OK now though. Aren't you?'

'Oh! Yes, that. Well over that.' He looked at his watch for no reason. 'Wee bastards will be out in about a year. Time moves on.'

It was becoming colder as the sun moved lower and the garden dropped into deeper shade. Tables began to empty.

'I confess, I had a reason other than to see you,' said Scruffy.

'Always the detective! Even tonight.' Helen drained her glass. 'What was it?'

'Who is behind the Protection Racket, hiding behind Shuggie Cameron and Razor Nelson? I know that it used to be McCluskey, but he had stepped back from that to concentrate on the drugs. More money less hassle.'

Helen nodded. 'That's what I heard. Couldn't put names in my story, of course. The lawyers would have spiked it.'

'Did the name, Sam Browne, the actor bloke, come up?'

Helen nodded. 'But you can forget about him.'

Scruffy was puzzled. 'Forget? How. Has he moved on? I thought he was up here filming for a while?'

'Did you not hear the news today. He's dead. Died last night. It's the main story on local TV and radio. Film and television star found dead by neighbours in the middle of the night. Rumours of suicide. All the usual suspects pulled out to say what a wonderful man he was. What a great loss to the Scottish stage. My colleagues on the entertainment pages say his latest role is not going well. He was not liked by some of the crew or fellow cast. So the suicide thing might be true. The *Gazette*'s information is that the Glasgow Police suspect a drug overdose.'

Scruffy wondered. Was it a coincidence that it came so soon after the fire. If only he had made the connection sooner. Bloody inconvenient of Sam Browne to die just when enquiries were implicating him in the death of Colin Ingleby. But Scruffy had other, more pressing, problems on his mind. He should ask Helen back to his flat and it was in no state to be seen; decided it was best to face the fact head on.

'Helen.' he stopped, how to word this.

'Yes.'

'There's no point me trying to put this well. I want you to come back to my place but it's such a mess, I can't have that. Your place is out, as my car would stand out like a sore thumb.' He sensed she wanted to cut in and hurried on worried that she would misinterpret his comments. 'Look, if I'm out of order I'm sorry, but how about I book a room at Duck Bay for the weekend.'

'You ashamed to be seen with me?'

He was glad to see her eyes twinkle as she said it.

'No. No. It's nothing like that. But gossip. Especially as you're reporting the case. A little circumspection.'

'Indeed, Scruffy! Now there's something I didn't associate with you. And yes. This weekend would be lovely.'

'Let's get back. Can I see you tomorrow?'

'Is that circumspect?' She was laughing again.

'More than me being seen leaving your place in the morning.' God, he wished he had more practice at this. 'Well can I see you?'

'There will be hell from me if you don't.'

CHAPTER TWENTY-FOUR

Sandra checked the message on her mobile phone. West Brae, first close. That had to be it. She looked into the two carrier bags for the fourth or fifth time, running through the list of purchases for Shuggie. She had not forgotten anything. She hoped he would like the whisky she had added to the list. Celebration of him inviting her to his flat, even if the invitation had been the cryptic message. *Can't go out. Need some things brought round. Do it tonight when no-one around. Do not be seen or tell anyone about this. NOT ONE Must be our secret.* Followed by a list of essentials to bring.

She nearly knew it by heart, having read it umpteen times during the day. Although it was getting dark there was no signs of life in the upstairs flat. Curtains open, no lights, not a sound. Shuggie had said go straight up but she could see the key-pad for the secure entry system on the door frame and he had not sent any code or flat number.

The streets were deserted so now was the time to go for it. Sandra stepped from the shadow at the entrance to Walker Street. A flicker from a lighter in the shadow further up Broomlands, caught her eye. There was a man and, in the brief moment as he lit his cigarette, Sandra saw a sharp hatchet face. That was Shuggie's side-kick, surely. Colin, Paul… she must stop thinking of him as Colin, had spoken of the threats, described Razor Nelson and this man fitted it to a T. She could not cross to Shuggie's without being seen. Perhaps Shuggie had asked Razor to come too. She should go talk to him. As her eyes became accustomed to half-light where Razor lingered, she noted that everything about him indicated he was watching the flat. It was clear he did not want to be seen by anyone. Sandra ran over in her mind that Shuggie had emphasised she was to tell no-one. Also the tales of Razor's nastiness made her flesh creep as she got closer. It was an easy decision to walk on past the pend where he stood, being careful not to be seen examining him. She walked briskly away. She would have to figure out a way to Shuggie's without him seeing.

It took half an hour for her to walk the circle of roads back to the High Street and up to the top of West Brae. She slowed as the Brae curved back to Wellmeadow. She was right. The close door was a few metres up the Brae and from where Nelson had chosen, she could reach it without being seen. She glanced anxiously around, worried that Nelson might have moved but there was no sign of him. Nobody to see her as she tried the door. The handle turned and the door swung inwards. As she pushed it shut behind her, she saw the Yale was snibbed to prevent it locking.

The corridor was lit by a single bare bulb. She noted, with relief, there were no doors. Hardly daring to breath, in case someone heard her in the close, Sandra tip-toed to the end. Stairs to the right rose to a half landing and then turned back, leading to a rear balcony. Last of the evening light filtering down from the sky behind the rooftops of the adjacent properties, assisted by a grime covered bulkhead lamp, showed three doors opening onto it.

For the first time since she had started on the stairs Sandra drew breath, muttered to herself. 'Shit. He didn't say which door.' To remain unseen ruled out taking pot luck, knock and see who answered. She remembered Shuggie saying he could watch the comings and goings on the main road. The one at the far end would be for the flat looking in that direction.

She almost dropped the bags when a toilet flushed in the middle flat, then took advantage of the noise to head for the end door.

As she approached she saw it was slightly ajar and stepped silently inside. It seemed right to whisper.

'Shuggie. Are you here?'

The reply came from the room to her right. 'In here.'

She began to search the wall for a light switch. Shuggie's voice became curt. 'Don't turn on a light. Shut the door quietly. When your eyes get accustomed, there's enough light from the street to let you see.'

Door shut, the hall was dark but Sandra began to make out features. The room door was open and she saw it was a bedroom, a little brighter; lit by the street lamps. Shuggie was lying on the bed wearing underpants beneath a dressing gown, thrown open across the bed.

'I'm supposed to be dead,' he said. 'The flat was being watched earlier. Probably still is.'

Sandra went over to the bed reached down and kissed him. He groaned and she pulled away. 'Thought you wanted me to come. You send a message for help and groan when I kiss you.'

'Christ, Sandra. I have the pain of hell in my back. That's why I groaned.' He sat up and let the dressing gown fall from his shoulders. Sandra saw the dark bruising spread across his back, gasped. 'What happened?'

'That bastard, Razor. He tried to kill me last night. If it hadn't been for me wearing protection, he bloody well would have.' He pointed at the bag. 'Have you brought the paracetamol'.

She opened the carrier. A bit annoyed that he had to ask the question.

'Of course. I have everything you asked… and more.'

He took the offered packet, tore open and pressed out two tablets. Swallowed dry.

—146—

'I'm not sure you ought to do that', she said.

'Aye. But I've needed these.. You're sure no-one saw you.'

'No-one saw. But you are being watched. Razor Nelson. At least I'm sure it was him. Recognised Colin's description. he's standing in that Pend up the road. I would have been seen coming to the flat but he's so sinister, he caught my eye. Went round over the top by the church.'

Shuggie pressed her hand. 'Sorry I was short. Bloody pain gets to you and I've been lying here for the whole day.' He pulled her towards him. 'Thanks. Thanks for coming, and for the kiss.' They kissed again.

'You mind if I get in,' said Sandra. She slipped off her jacket and unbuttoned her blouse as Shuggie grinned, shuffled carefully over the bed and patted the space beside him.

As her skirt fell she watched him eye the curves of her figure, the black silk, the smooth glow of her skin. Pleased with his attention.

She, in the crook of his arm, lay tight against him, right breast pressed against his chest. Felt the warmth of him, the beat of his heart increase as she traced fingernails through the hair on his chest.

Shuggie moved his right hand to stroke her hair. 'Christ, it's good to be alive.

Razor stomped in the pend, his feet becoming numb. Looked at his watch. Whole bloody day and not a sign of Shuggie. He had spent hours out here without seeing a flicker of life inside the flat and asking around had brought no joy. Last anyone had seen Shuggie was on Saturday night when he was with Razor doing the collections.

A heavy shower drove him deeper into the shelter of the building. A late night bus rumbled towards Johnstone, a handful of passengers staring out dolefully. Razor felt the chill spreading up his legs. Bugger, he didn't have a coat. He would get soaked going home if the rain kept on. Razor pulled his jacket tighter, flicked up his collar. Alright for McCluskey to say 'sort it' but how if he couldn't find the bastard. He scratched his head. Tomorrow he would widen the search and ask around the usual haunts again, probable check the flat a couple of times, but if Shuggie was not found maybe it was time to disappear. Fuck McCluskey. It was both their problems. In Paisley he was a sitting duck if Shuggie was alive and healthy… shit.

He rolled a cigarette. Watched two girls run down Well Street, feet splashing in the rain. Dam it, rain or not he had had enough. He was going home. If he had no joy in the morning it would be time to leave. At least if he disappeared Shuggie would have to find him. Razor lit a final cigarette, trudged off towards his basement bedsit.

CHAPTER TWENTY-FIVE

Colin and Gerry stirred as morning light stole across the bedroom.

'Sleep well?' he asked.

'For once. Thank God those builders are finished. You?'

'Yea. Keep wondering if I can carry this off. You know, being Paul.'

'You'll be fine. You're his cousin and you've always been close. You know more about him than anyone. '

He shook his head slowly.

'Sandra will fill in any blanks,' said Gerry, trying to sound confident.

'Maybe.'

Gerry sat up and leaned over so that she looked straight into Colin's eyes.

'No maybe about it. We're in this and it will work. There a twelve million reasons you can do this.' She stroked his cheek. 'And think of us, on a beach in the south of France, or on our yacht in the Med.' She slid her hand under the blankets down his chest . 'If you're not up for it, I can leave now.'

His mood changed as she swung her head to dragged her hair over his face, leant in and kissed him. 'You can do this.'

He laughed, grabbed her shoulders and rolled her onto her back. 'This... or a burnt out future. Got to be this. No more talk of failure. We're going to be rich.' He heard a key in the flat door. Grimaced. 'Bugger it, Grumpy's back. We'd better keep the noise down.'

'Stuff her. She's jealous. But I wonder where she's been all night. New lover, you think? Or keeping out of our way/'

Who'd have her greetin' face? Anyway, who cares? Come here

you.'

Sandra heard their giggles. Shouted, 'Jesus, do you two never stop.' She clumped around in the hall, doing nothing but making noise. If she had to leave Shuggie why should they lie on? The thought of his fingers teasing down her spine as she rose to leave the Broomlands flat, his smile when she promised to return when it was dark, mellowed the moments anger. 'Col… Paul, Gerry want tea, toast? I'm putting the kettle on.'

Gerry shouted back. 'Yes. Thanks. We'll be through in a minute.' She whispered to Colin, 'It's definitely a lover to make her like this. Wonder who?' Pulling on a robe she prodded Colin out of bed. 'Come on let's get her while she's in a good mood. See what we can wheedle out of her.' Colin was slower to follow rather liking the warmth of the bed and Gerry had to throw off the covers before, reluctantly, he got up.

Sandra was sitting at the computer as they came through from the bedroom. Toast in hand nibbling, scrolling down emails.

'You sound bright,' said Gerry. 'We were worried when you weren't home.' She nudged Colin. Scowled as he stood open- mouthed. 'We were worried, weren't we.'

'Oh! Yea, Worried.'

'No need to worry about me. I'm a big girl now.' Sandra stopped on an email, pressed to open.

'Old friend was it?' But Sandra ignored Gerry, peering at the email. 'Anyone we know?'

'What? Eh.' Sandra scrolled back to the top. 'I was fine. No need to worry.' The toaster popped. 'Tea's in the pot.' She looked round. 'This email to Paul is from those Chicago lawyers, Geland Shuster and Leibermann. Asking him if he can fly out. Meet this Tony Simpster, his great uncle.'

'Shit.' Colin's hand shook as he poured tea into a mug. 'Christ, I can't go to America as Paul. Send a reply. Say I can't possibly get away.' He pulled a chair beside Sandra. Scanned the email. 'Come on think of an excuse. Get typing.'

Sandra shook her head. 'No way. We do not reply. This is a trap. Got to be. I mean last we heard Simpster was barely conscious. Didn't know where he was.'

'But it's the lawyers. If we don't reply how will we get the money when Simpster dies.'

'Listen, fat head.' Gerry grumphed at the insult. Sandra ignored her. 'Paul was killed for the money. They think he's dead. Do you want to tell America that he's alive? What do you think happens then.' Sandra paused, waited. Colin shrugged. 'They come over here and kill him. Fuck do you want to be shot.'

Colin stood in silence staring at her. Gerry went to his side.

'OK, smart ass. If we don't speak to the lawyers how does it work? Eh? How do we get the inheritance?'

Sandra returned their stares. 'I'm phoning Shuggie. I'm sure he'll agree.'

'We don't have to do what he says,' replied Gerry.

'You think. Have a look at Colin's face, the bent nose. Ask him if he thinks that.'

Shuggie lay back in the bath, felt the warm water ease the tension in his back. The radio played so quietly that it was barely audible but he was concerned that no sound should escape from the flat, though that might be a lost cause after last night. He sank deeper into the bath, let the water run down his chest. At least he knew that his ribs were not broken. Even with Sandra being cautious there was no way he could have made love if they were. There had been pain but it was worth every spasm. God, was he into masochism. He wished she was here now, in the bath with him.

The bath water was beginning to cool and he was wondering about getting out when the close door banging shut had him reach for the radio and switch it off. He was certain that Sandra would have made sure it was securely shut. She had made great play about saying she would, so much had he emphasised the importance. That bugger Henderson was always forgetting to pull it hard and leaving it unlatched. Shuggie looked at the display on the radio.

Henderson would be well away to work and Old Ewan never stirred before mid-day.

Shuggie lay still, head cocked to the side, listening. There were muffled scuffs from the stairwell and then on the balcony the unmistakeable sound of someone trying to tiptoe noiselessly to his door. Shuggie heard rasped breaths, fingers feeling round door frame, lifting the mat to see if there was a hidden key. It could be his imagination but he thought he could smell the sour whiff of Razor.

As the chill from the bath spread deeper into his bones he did not dare to move fearing the sound of the water would carry into the hall. He could see the shadow of a figure on the wall. Someone was pressed against the frosted glass trying to peer in.

'Shuggie, are you in there? Razor's voice was high pitched, edgy.

Hell, the man was a fool. Did he think any one you had tried to kill would shout out a cheery hello? Part of Shuggie wanted to leap from the bath, throw open the door and strangle the little rat. But not today. Not with his back locking up as the water chilled.

The shadow muttered 'Fuck' Moved off and shortly after the close door banged again.

Shuggie realised he had not needed to resist the idea of leaping anywhere for his strength drained with the bath water. Muscles spasms had him gasp and he could not get purchase on the plastic, slipped back, grew colder. Finally he managed to twist onto his knees, get his shoulders over the lip and half roll, half fall, onto the floor. Lay groaning. It was twenty minutes before he was able to rise, wrap his dressing gown round and sit with a coffee. As he cradled the mug it occurred to him that Razor must be desperate. It was an idiotic move to come to the flat. He nearly spilled the coffee when his phone vibrated on the table. Picking it up he saw it was Sandra. She had not long gone why the call.

'Sandra? What is it?'

He listened as Sandra read out the email. 'I've told Colin not to reply. It's a trap, isn't it. But they think we'll want to keep in touch, make sure that Paul gets the money…'

'Christ.' Shuggie cut in. 'Put this on speaker. Are they nuts.' He waited a second or two. 'Is it on speaker?'

'Yes. We can all hear you.'

'You daft bastards want to die. I've just killed one fuckin' American to keep you alive.'

'Wouldn't surprise me if it was the fuckin' lawyers who set it up. He talked about Liebermann. This is bad shit were dealing with and you want to tell them Paul isn't dead. Jesus. Give me strength.'

'Ah but… ' He cut Gerry off.

'There's no fuckin' buts. Do not reply. Fuck it, reply and I'll contact them. Get paid to fuckin' come round and kill you.'

Gerry persisted. 'But how will we get the money. If they don't believe Paul's alive they won't pay out.'

Shuggie took two deep breaths, calmed, spoke quietly. I've that in hand. Don't you worry. As soon as I know Simpster is dead we speak to a lawyer here. Prove Colin is Paul. Get the money. Leave the thinking to me. And Christ, don't reply to any fuckin' emails, letters, anything without getting my say so. Agreed.' There was silence. Shuggie shouted 'Agreed.'

'Agreed, Shuggie. They both nodded.'

'Say it you bastards. No misunderstandings. This is fuckin' important.'

He relaxed as both spoke at once. 'Bye Sandra. You keep them right.' Hung up.

Sandra looked at Gerry and Colin. 'We don't contact the Americans. Right.' Ok. Ok. We've got the message.' Gerry began buttering a slice of toast. 'Marmalade, Colin?'

Colin moved to join her, both turning their backs on Sandra who took the hint and left for her bedroom.

'Smug cow,' said Gerry.

'She'll hear you.'

'Good. Telling tales to that thug. We should cut both of them out. You and I can make the claim. Email the lawyers. How would they know?'

'But they would sometime. No. We can't. If we move without them they could blow the whole thing. Remember Sandra was Paul's girl friend. If she said I wasn't him we would lose it all. We have to go with it.'

Gerry nibbled toast. Stood silently thinking.

'How come she had a number for Cameron? Don't remember him giving a number'

Colin shook his head.

'She had a number and he knew it was her straight away. So it's not the first time she's called.' Gerry slumped into the settee. 'That's it, That's where she was last night. Shuggie Cameron is her bastard boyfriend.'

'You think.' Colin dropped beside her. 'Them. An item.'

'Makes sense to me. We need to keep an eye on them. They've kept that quiet.'

'Wonder when it started? How are we to know there ever was an American? Perhaps it's all made up and Cameron killed Paul to get Sandra and the money?'

Colin mulled this over. 'Can't see it. Sandra could have died in the fire. And me. If he wanted to get the money he needed me if Paul was dead. And he could have had Sandra and the inheritance anyway. Paul would have folded if threatened with violence. He valued his looks too much.' He shook his head. 'No., there was an American. Sure of it. But them we'll watch.'

CHAPTER TWENTY-SIX

'Damn an buggery.'

An old woman, coming out of West-end Deli, gave Razor a smile and he realised he had said this with more vehemence than intended.

'Aye, son. Take it from me. It don't get ony better.'

What had possessed him to try the door? Did he expect Shuggie to pop out with a big grin and give him a hug? Jesus. Had he heard something inside? He could have tried breaking in but he'd seen Shuggie's door and it was set up to withstand a police battering ram. Him kicking it would have got nowhere. 'Damn an buggery.' This time he meant the old lady to hear. Gave her a wave as he swung away towards home. Bloody McCluskey could go hang, time for hitting the road. Disappear for a while and let McCluskey take the heat.

Back at his flat it took minutes to pack what he needed. He always kept a bag ready for quick get-a-ways, so all that was needed was a final check of contents and adding toothpaste and toothbrush. He swithered about the protection money. Realised he couldn't leave it in the flat and no way was he going to see McCluskey. Bugger it, he needed the cash. Replacing it? He would face that problem when he came back. If he came back.

McGill's coast bus headed out through Renfrewshire. Usually Razor had no time for countryside but today he enjoyed the passing fields, for the first time since Saturday he felt safe. Clyde coast was where you had days out and summer holidays. He began to hum 'I do like to be beside the seaside'. Grinned at the old man who nodded in appreciation. At Largs he boarded the Ardrossan bus, pleased that it was busy enough for him to go unnoticed. Good thing about his journey was the breaks in the trail. Not that he thought he was being followed but he checked anyway when he left the bus at Main Street in Ardrossan. A light shower was falling but, if anything, this increased his feeling of freedom as he walked briskly to the ferry terminal.

On the ferry, Razor settled himself in a corner of the rear deck. Sheltered from any wind he was free from worrying about Shuggie suddenly appearing at his back and could watch Ardrossan harbour shrink as they crossed the Firth. He should have done this as soon as he found out that no body had been found. The further he travelled the less he liked the idea of coming back. He texted his nephew. *Heads up if you hear anything. Will be at usual place.*

As a child Razor had spent many summers with Great Granny on Arran and that feeling of stepping back in time came as soon as he stood on Brodick pier. A feeling that grew as he left the coastal bus at Corrie and took the curving dirt road up to the cottages of High Corrie. The key for Great Gran's house were under the rock at the side door. The door that led into the old cowshed which formed a separate room. He wondered about using this as his bedroom. Many years back he had taken refuge there. His mother had hidden him in that cowshed; being windowless it was perfect for no-one to know the room was occupied. Razor looked out across the Firth to Ayrshire. Decided it was unnecessary. Last time was winter, any light would have been seen for miles. It would not be much use in any case as, with no no-one to look after him, he would have to use the main house during the day. Most of other cottages were occupied and it would look strange for him to spend the night in the byre.

The cottage was damp and he lit a fire in the front room, sat in the rocking chair by the hearth, took a lager from the shopping and popped the ring-pull. He checked his mobile.

As expected there was no signal.

As he rocked he ran over the events which had brought him to his hide-a-way. Hard to believe that it was only a week since Colin Ingleby had taken the hump and told him and Shuggie to 'Fuck Off'. If only Ingleby had just paid up... and now life was shit. For the moment he was safe here but that could not go on for ever. He had seen a new hardness in Shuggie that frightened him. Never known him kill before and the America's death was cold-blooded. Christ, and he had tried to kill Shuggie and failed. Well there was no doubt about it Shuggie had to die before he could resurface. When he left for Arran it had to be with a plan to disappear permanently, or to achieve Shuggie's death. Unless, with any luck, McCluskey had lost patience and done it himself.

Razor drained the last of the can and tossed it in a lazy arc into the basket by the fire.

Took the coal scuttle and went out to the back of the cottage. Time to stock up with coal and fire wood. It would be some time before he could work out what to do. In the meantime he might as well be comfortable.

As he rummaged the shovel in the bunker, a call 'Hello' made him start.

Looking up he saw a woman crossing towards him, two ewes reluctantly moving out her way.

'Mrs Ford. Yer nae lookin a day older,' he replied.

'Freddie. You've not been for awhile. Robin well? Good to see the place in use.'

'Oh, Robin's fine. I'm over for, not sure how long, break between jobs, few days onyway. You well?'

'Can't complain. Come over any time. Will be good to chat over the old days. Catch up. Tell Robin we're asking for him. He's missed.'

'Will do. Polis keeps him busy. But he'll be down this summer as ever. Kids wouldn't miss it.'

It occurred to Razor that this encounter was a bit of luck. He would have spoken to Mrs Ford at some point but this early meant he could sort out delivery of food and drink.

'Does the van still bring you an order? Could I drop over a list and you added it on to yours.'

'Aye. But why don't I get him to come over and you give it to him direct.'

'Dinnae want onyone tae know I'm here. Last job, the customer was… well you know. Fittin a kitchen an…' Razor shrugged. 'Shall we jist say the Mrs liked my work; her man didnae.'

He knew Mrs Ford well. She stepped closer, pretended to skelp his ear.

'You. Still Jack the lad. Aye we'll keep it quiet. You give me a list. Not too much drink now. Don't want to ruin my reputation.'

The scuttle was full, 'I'll pop over the night.' He smiled, 'couple of drams, eh!' and made his escape.

CHAPTER TWENTY-SEVEN

'And this is the open plan living room/kitchen, double height with mezzanine floor, third bedroom.' Scruffy refrained from pointing out that it was unnecessary to explain what was clearly visible. Estate agents' desire to speak jargon put him off viewing property but pretending to be a buyer did let him see McCluskey's flat without trying to get a warrant.

Helen agreeing to come with him was a double bonus. He got to see her and it added credibility to his subterfuge.

The estate agent led to the kitchen area. 'This has just been refurbished to the highest standards.' That Scruffy could agree. But rather than seeing the quality he saw marble flooring, white tiled walls, a fortune to rip out if he ordered a full forensic search. And for what? A hunch that a man had been shot here. But where here? The blasted place had been gutted and rebuilt. Damn McCluskey, the bastard knew the score. No search in here until he was certain of a result. Bloody budget for the year to rip this place apart. The girl was extolling the range stove, induction, of course. The American style fridge.

'Big enough to store a body.' Scruffy could not resist the interjection.

She cut him a strange look but ignored as she pointed out the state of the art combined oven-microwave, the instant boiling water from the mixer tap. Thin, dark haired, bright red lipstick, regulation dark suit, he couldn't help being distracted as she climbed the curving staircase to the mezzanine. Helen followed his gaze, gave a small cough which drew the girl's attention.

'And I am sure Mrs McVey will love the art deco mirror, a feature of this guest accommodation.'

Helen dug Scruffy in the ribs, whispered. 'I didn't even hear you propose.'

Scruffy's bad day in court receded. Bloody Social Work reports. Waste of a whole day hanging around for a cut and shut case of wife abuse. At least the husband had been found guilty but lock the guy up, let the poor woman get some respite. Now there was a bloody fortnight waiting for Social Work reports, at least the husband was on bail with conditions to stay away from his wife.

It was a last minute thing, phoning Helen, and a risk, but she had responded as he hoped. Playing as a husband and wife wanting to view the penthouse had appealed to her. Propose? She was a good looking woman. Three years older than him but didn't look it. Scruffy eyed the estate agent three steps ahead, the narrow waist, curve of her bottom. She looked over her shoulder as she arrived at the mezzanine, smiled seductively. Wondered how often she got the men to buy because of her long legs. She must be twenty years younger than Helen but her beauty was plastic, face a masque, those thin eyebrows, the lips overdone. A magazine look, not life. He let Helen go before him. That was what he called a woman. Propose? What would be the chance of a yes?

Helen lent close. Another whisper interrupted his thoughts. 'You're supposed to be admiring the house.' She said aloud. 'Lovely property. Beautifully presented.'

Her hand lingering on his arm encouraged him. As the girl pointed out the striking mirror over the bed which reflected the view out to the Abbey, he put his arm round Helen's waist, slid his hand down. She placed her hand over his and he waited for her to pull his upwards but she linked fingers let it stay where it was. Desire flooded

Scruffy. Damn it why wait till the weekend.

He took out his phone began to text.

'Scruffy.' Helen sounded exasperated.

He glanced up. 'Sorry. Couple of things I have to check.'

It took longer than he hoped but after few moments he was done. He was aware that the estate agent had stopped talking and that both women were staring at him.

'Ah!' He thought quickly. 'I was just looking at the listing on your website. I see it is shown at offers over three hundred and sixty-five thousand. But it was advertised initially at three hundred and fifty thousand. Seems odd?'

'It was on at three hundred and fifty but the owner felt it was not being seen to its full potential. You've seen the quality of the finish, Mr McVey. Most of this is brand new. Updated to the latest spec and highest standard. The new price reflects the work done. Indeed I am sure you can appreciate that more than fifteen thousand pounds has been spent.'

'I'm sure the work was worth every penny,' replied McVey, thinking it was a small sum to cover up a murder. At least it was probable that was the reason, but there was no way he could afford a forensic search unless he was cast-iron certain.

'It's beautiful.' Helen sought to smooth any awkwardness. 'Isn't it?'

Scruffy looked round the penthouse. It was a cracking flat. A place where he could see Helen as hostess. For the first time he considered it like a buyer. If he sold his place, if Helen moved in, they could afford something like this. They deserved something like this.

He slipped an arm through Helen's. 'Thanks for the viewing. It is certainly worth consideration. Now if you'll excuse us, we are expected down the coast.'

Descending in the lift he could sense Helen mulling over his parting comment. Refrained from satisfying her curiosity. It was only as they reached the car that he spoke.

'Hope you're free tonight as I intend to kidnap you.'

'Oh, Yes!'

'That comment about the price in the flat and my interest in the internet, was just to cover the real reason for using the phone. I've booked a room in The Waterside Hotel at Seamill for tonight. Get in. We're on our way.'

Helen laughed as she climbed in to the Rover. 'You seem rather certain I'll agree.'

Scruffy was in determined mood. For once he would take the lead 'You're in now. Put the seat belt on. We're off.'

'If I am going to a hotel, we need to stop off at my place. Pick up things for the night.'

'There's nothing we need.'

'Nightie, dressing gown, pyjamas?'

It was Scruffy's turn to laugh. 'Don't intend us to need any of those. For once I'm not being sensible. I'm not waiting till the weekend. Will you come?'

She gave him what his mother would have called an old fashioned look. Belted up.

'Seamill it is.'

His arm was becoming numb under her head, but he did not want to move the warm nakedness of her. They lay for some minutes, nothing said, letting breathing slow. He wanted to say something but nothing seemed right. Waited for Helen to speak. She rolled half away to pick up her watch from the bedside table. She checked the time and sat up.

'Nearly eight-thirty. We said we'd have dinner at nine. I'll have a quick shower.'

She lent over and kissed him. 'You should too.' He tried to pull her down back into the bed.

'Not now,' she said, 'we've all night.'

He watched her as she threw off the covers and stood. Wondered at his luck. Wondered about saying, bugger dinner get back in here. Didn't.

'Would you open the window?' he asked.

'You want me arrested.' She took a towel and draped it round her body before going to the full height glass door and sliding it open. 'Watch you don't catch a chill.'

'I'll think of you,' he said. 'that'll keep me warm.'

She blew him a kiss, letting the towel drop, and dragged it behind, like an actress playing the seductress in a nineteen twenties film, as she left for the en-suite.

Scruffy enjoyed the gentle sea breeze playing over his body. Had it been good for her? Surely. God it had been a long time since he felt like this. He shut his eyes, felt ready to nod off, jerked awake.

He threw his legs to the floor. His clothes were strewn on the carpet, scattered where they fell in his haste to get in beside Helen. He gathered them on the bed. Looked round for hers. Remembered they were draped neatly over the chair; how she had taken the lead when they came up from Reception, undressing as he stood like an idiot. He sighed, what did she see in him?

The remote for the TV was on the dresser. He took it and lay back on the bed. Better get his mind off Helen or he'd be in the shower with her and… he had a feeling it would be a bad move.

Scruffy did not usually watch the news. He saw enough violence and misery in his job to not want to hear about the misery in the world, but the television was tuned to a news channel when he switched on. Outside, on the dark blue water, the white of a yacht caught his eye. Beyond he could see specks of white on the side of Goatfell; the cottages at High Corrie, imagined exploring Arran with Helen, untrammelled by work. The words 'police ask for help' brought him back to the TV. Grainy CCTV footage was playing as the voice continued, 'do you recognise this man? He is thought to be the last person to see Sam Browne alive. Here he is on camera buying a curry at 'Pick an Spice' curry house, off Morrison Street, in Glasgow. Police believe that this is the last meal the actor ate. Did you see this man around midnight on Saturday?' Inspector Charles Hodgson asks you to assist in his enquires'

The image was hazy but McVey had no doubt, it was Razor Nelson. Would Charlie Hodgson still be in the office? Knowing Charlie it was likely. Scruffy reached for his phone. It was answered almost immediately.

'Scruffy, you old reprobate. How are you.'

'Well, Charlie. You.'

'Same as always. What can I do?'

'You're involved with the Sam Browne death? Just saw the appeal on the news.'

'You got it. It's one of mine.'

'I recognise the bloke buying the curry. It's Frederick Nelson. Known to all as Razor, Paisley muscle for Graham McCluskey.'

'Interesting. And… ?

'Plenty to chew on, Charlie. Recent info was that the protection money in Paisley was being paid to your Sam Browne. Seems he had extended his career from screen to the streets. But what got you onto this one? Not your usual beat.'

'We still think just an overdose but reason I'm investigating is that when the news broke about Browne's death they ran all those pictures of him, I thought I spotted a connection with a murder case I'm already working. Unidentified male body found at Westerton Railway Station in a burnt out car. Punter throat cut. No ID survived the fire. But car leaving the scene was on CCTV and there was an image of the rear passenger; brief, but when I saw the footage of Sam Browne, seemed to me there was a likeness. According to our boys there is a strong likeness. It was decided I should look into it, see if there was any connection. That would be easier if I could have talked to Browne… '

'And he's dead,' said Scruffy. 'Inconvenient of him.' He stopped momentarily. 'Or convenient for someone. Charlie, I think I may have a linked enquiry. Too many coincidences. I have a body, identified as Colin Ingleby, local restaurant owner. Ingleby was shot and body dumped on the railway line at Arkleston. Dropped from the bridge in front of the Largs train. His restaurant was burnt out last Tuesday night. Night he was shot. Possible paying protection to Razor Nelson and to another nasty piece of work, Hugh Cameron, known as Shuggie. My info is that Nelson and Cameron were collecting for Sam Browne. Not keen on coincidences, Charlie. Possibility we have a gang war here. Browne trying to cut in on McCluskey's patch. I've spoken to McCluskey in connection with the Ingleby case. Just wondering… He may be behind Browne's death.'

Wisps of steam from the bathroom caught his eye. Helen came through rubbing her hair with a cream bath towel, breasts swaying. She stopped in mid stride to look quizzically at him. Mouthed 'Who?'

'Sorry Charlie. Got to go. I'll talk tomorrow OK.' He smiled at Helen leapt up to give her a kiss. Whispered in her ear, 'You're beautiful.'

'Did anyone know we were here? Who was on the phone?'

'I called them. Sorry. Will explain over dinner. I better have a quick shower too.' Disappeared before she could ask more questions.

'Brandy? With the coffees?' asked Scruffy.

Clouds flared spectacularly over the Arran mountain ridge as the sun dipped the skyline. Scruffy breathed long, wistful. 'This is when I miss a cigar.'

Helen laid her napkin by her empty plate. 'Well I don't and I doubt the rest of the diners do. Glad to be able to enjoy a meal without the air filled with tobacco. And look at that view, Scruffy. This was genius.'

'What about brandy?'

'Do you need to ask!' She waved a waiter over as she spoke, ordered for them both returned to an earlier conversation. 'You were certain it was Razor Nelson.'

'Unmistakeable, even on those crappy CCTV images.'

'You think he's working for McCluskey. Taking back the racket from Browne? With him out the way I don't see any other competition in Paisley.'

'Possibility. It's what I said to Charlie Hodgson.' He studied Helen's face. The setting sun highlighted the cheek bones. He loved the wrinkles round her eyes. And she knew the world he inhabited. 'Makes sense to me. But then there's this dead man at Westerton Station. You heard anything.'

'Not my paper's area. Wouldn't pick up any gossip. Interviewed Sam Browne twice over the years. He did the Paisley lights once and some charity thing at the Abbey. Didn't strike me as a man capable of violence.'

Scruffy put his left hand over hers. 'But who does? Look, tonight

I want to forget all that… '

Helen slapped her left hand on top of his. 'Well you brought it up. Never heard of a post-coitus telephone call to a colleague before. Not very flattering.'

He slapped his right hand lightly on to the pile of hands. 'Do we start that childish slapping game here? Or shall we go up to the room? No telephone call this time. I promise '

CHAPTER TWENTY-EIGHT

The town hall chimed six o'clock. Gerry cursed the double glazing that failed to keep the sound at bay. Like some haunted wolf the bells had marked her inability to sleep. It did not help her mood that Colin snored steadily beside her.

It was lucky Sandra had been out at her boyfriend's or she would have overheard them as they argued into the small hours. Colin could not see that it made a difference if Sandra and Shuggie were an item. Not that Gerry trusted either of them; a thug and a stuck-up make-up girl. But if they were together that changed the dynamic. Colin was an innocent, when it came to deception, and refused to acknowledge the important people in this scheme to get Simpster's millions were him and her. OK they needed Sandra to back-up passing Colin off as Paul but why the hell give Cameron anything. Get the money and tell him to get stuffed. Cameron couldn't go to the police or anything without incriminating himself in a murder. And despite what Colin argued, how did they know there was an American hit-man. Cameron was a violent psychopath. Perhaps he killed Paul thinking it was Colin. Gerry slid from beneath the duvet, put on a dressing-gown, and tiptoed from the bedroom, closing the door quietly behind.

In the living room the whirr of the cooling fan seemed impossibly loud when she started up the computer. She sat unable to breath, waiting for a noise from the bedroom. Sighed with relief when none came. Shuggie Cameron did not rule her. If the American lawyers believed Paul was dead why would they ever pay out. Time that she took the initiative. Cameron could get stuffed for the money was hers and Colin's. They deserved it after what he had done to them. Sandra could get something to keep her mouth shut but they could sort that out once they had the inheritance.

Gerry began typing; pressing the keys as softly as possible, aware of every sound. Giggled quietly. And if Shuggie thought he should get money let Sandra pay it to her new boyfriend.

She read over her draft to Geland Shuster and Liebermann.

Pleased to hear that great uncle able to have visitors. Would love to come over to meet him. Difficulties with work and to be honest the cost. Will see if I can organise something but I doubt if can come in the near future. Keep me posted. Give my regards to great uncle Tony

Paul

As the door opened behind her she hit send and changed screen to the card game she had pulled up in readiness for being disturbed. Colin came to bend over her chair, gave her a peck on the cheek.

'Not sleep? How long you been up?'

'Not long. Thought a couple of games of Patience would help settle my mind.' Bleary-eyed, Colin watched as Gerry shut down the computer. Gerry slid a hand under his pyjamas, made certain that her dressing-gown fell open as she rose.

Let's get back to bed. If I can't sleep at least I can have a cuddle.'

In his flat at the foot of West Brae Shuggie snuggled comfortably into Sandra's back and pulled the blankets tighter round his right shoulder. The bruising to his back was fading and now there was little pain when he moved. He could not resist tracing the line of her neck with fingertips as Sandra half-stirred. He kissed her ear.

'What's the time,' she whispered.

'About five thirty,' he said. 'But lie on. No need to slip away before dawn now.'

She moved her head so that he could see her puzzled face. 'The back's pretty well good now. I don't care if Razor knows I'm here. He'll not dare try anything. Anyway we haven't seen a sign of him for days.'

Sandra lifted her eyebrows 'But... '

'No. Nothing to worry about. I can take Razor. And anyone McCluskey sends. I don't want you skulking around any more. Who cares who knows.'

'Think Colin and Gerry have guessed. They made catty remarks when I left to come here.' Sandra paused, thought a little. 'Should I come out with it?'

'Let them bring it up. She's a proper stirrer that Gerry. Let her stew.'

'What about Razor? You letting him away with it?'

Shuggie chuckled, pulled her tight against him. 'You think? That's what I'm going to do when I get out of this bed. Find the wee bastard and... but for now I'm in bed and have other things in mind' He had been sliding his hand up under her arm as he spoke, and conversation ceased for a time as he gently teased her nipple and they kissed.

It was Sandra who broke off. 'As long as you do. I want him out of our lives. I can't settle knowing he is out there wanting to kill you.'

Shuggie shook his head, said very deliberately. 'It will be sorted. Trust me.'

'Oh! I do,' she replied as she drew him close. 'Am I a fool? Are you a dangerous man to trust?'

She was laughing but at the back of Shuggie's mind was a voice that said, 'Perhaps?' From somewhere a quote, 'put not your trust in dangerous men'. It sounded Biblical but it could be a false memory. But should anyone dare to love him? Could he really love anyone? His embrace was hard, fiercer than he meant, but Sandra surrendered to him. Willingly.

The road from Loch Lomond into Paisley and on to Crookston was unusually crowded for a Tuesday afternoon. At least Graham McCluskey thought so. But he was on edge, annoyed that he had delayed by the pool. Annoyed that he wanted to get to the hospital and get the news, annoyed that he dreaded the news. Jennifer had sounded bright, optimistic but she had such a positive attitude to life. He wondered if he had seen too much bitterness and envy. Knew how life kicked most to death. Only the strong survived. He could do nothing to frighten cancer. This one Jen had to fight on her own. Well with him there, fucking useless but there. He would give his body if it would help. The doctors were good. He was sure of that. Wasn't he? Was he? Best money could buy, Only an hour till he knew the worst. He blasted a slow Nissan. Sunday bloody driver. He managed a rueful smile. And on a Tuesday.

The mobile rang and he checked the car screen. Sighed with relief that it was not Jen, or the hospital. He toyed with ignoring it then decided he would only worry what Liebermann wanted and pressed to accept the incoming call.

'Hi there. How y' doing.' Sol Liebermann sounded bright.

'Hi Sol. Fine and you.'

'Good. The family well?'

McCluskey flicked eyes to the sky. They would go through all this polite routine when all he wanted was to cut to the quick.

'On the way to the hospital. Jennifer's results are today.'

'Gee. Sure. Well God be with you both. The operation went well thought?'

'It was fine. Jennifer is recovering well. It's just the test results. You know.'

'We will pray for you.' There was a brief hiatus. 'Can you talk?'

'Yes.'

Suddenly the tone of Sol's voice became darker, angrier.

'What the fuck is it with the McNeil guy. You tell me he's dead?'

Dunbar is dead. Fuck it, I get an email midnight. Bastard McNeil is alive. Wants me to pay for him to come visit old man Simpster. Are you fuckin' real. Holy shit, do I have to come over there and kill the guy myself. You'd better believe I will and... fuckin' believe you'd be next.'

McCluskey swerved round a Beemer, cut up a Range Rover Evoque, accelerating with rage and confusion.

'McNeil is dead. What. I mean. What?'

'Yea. Sure, a dead guy sends emails. He emails this morning that he's ready to meet Simpster. You've fucked up, McCluskey. I don't like fuck ups.'

The silence in the car seemed minutes. Graham McCluskey trying to grasp reality.

Did he need this shit? Jennifer was waiting. Shit Liebermann could break the business. The Columbians would pull out with a wrong word from America. Shit, where did that fuckin' Vauxhall come from?

'I don't understand, Sol. What you have is my info and that is that Dunbar killed him.

Job done.'

'It fuckin' aint. Dead don't send emails. Sort it. It's too late for a second guy from here. You get it done. '

McCluskey was off the Motorway, straight through the traffic lights and slowed through Hillington. The hospital was minutes away and he had an urge to say 'yes, you're the bloody problem' and hang up.. But it wasn't just Liebermann's problem and McCluskey knew it. Now it was his bloody problem.

'You want McNeil dead, he's dead. Take my word on it.'

'Right answer,' said Liebermann. 'Good speaking to you. God be with you and Jennifer. Trust in the Lord.'

Ward visiting was open-all-hours and McCluskey was in no hurry to leave. In their private room he felt relief from having to think about Paul McNeil. He sat holding Jennifer's hand. Seeing for the first time that there was colour returning to her cheeks, he realised how much this had drained her and him. Her sense of humour had never left her but he could feel the tension easing in them since their meeting with her Oncologist. Cancer had not spread to the lymph nodes. The news was beginning to sink in. He realised how tense he had been and how much those words meant. Now he could really plan for her coming home, plan that holiday in the sun, Italy… or America.

Bugger, America brought him back to Liebermann. That was a different problem but it too had to be addressed. He would go to the flat instead of back to Loch Lomond. He could check out McNeil's place and see if there was any truth in him being alive. It would take five minutes to get to the old mill buildings and Heritage Tower.

There was no response to his ring but McCluskey had the impression of being checked on through the spy hole. He heard faint sounds and rang again this time holding until the door opened.

'Yes? Can I help you?'

This was not McNeil. There was a strong resemblance but the

man did not recognise him. McCluskey let the silence linger. Watched the growing uncertainty in this man's eyes. Whoever he was, this was a weak man.

'I'm looking for Paul McNeil?'

A brief hesitation. McCluskey watched as the man swallowed. The answer was dry throated, hoarse.

'I'm Paul McNeil.'

Weak and a liar. But why pretending to be McNeil?

'You're selling a flat for me. Upstairs. The penthouse.'

'Oh… '

Behind him a woman appeared. McCluskey smiled disarmingly. Indeed he was rather taken with this red haired, large eyed, beauty. Much too good for the man at the door although the way she placed a protective arm round his shoulder suggested that they were a couple.

'Hello.' She returned his smile, looked to the man 'What is it, Paul?'

The man glanced to her then back to McCluskey but his dry throat had stolen words.

McCluskey met her eyes, large, dark as they returned him. She did not flinch.

'Hello. I was just saying to… ' McCluskey deliberately hesitated switched his gaze, for an instant, back to the man. 'Paul? That he is selling a house for me. The penthouse in this building. I'm Graham McCluskey.'

She gave a flick of her hand. 'Gerry. Nice to meet you.' He saw her nudge the man who smiled tightly and nodded. 'But Paul has left the Estate Agents. He's not acting for anyone now.' She nudged the man again. 'Isn't that so.' Emphasised the name. 'Paul.'

This time there was a response to her prompt.

'Yes. Sorry. Of course, the penthouse. I should have realised. But as Gerry says, I've left Yellow Brick Road. You'd be best to go to their office.' He looked at his watch. This is their late night. You'd catch Diane. She's taken over my portfolio.'

McCluskey hit him with a full beamed smile.

'Actually. It is you I really need to talk to. Can I come in?'

Although phrased as a question he gave no time for an answer. His outstretched arm eased them aside and he was into the flat before they could stop him. They followed him down the hall, the woman angrily started to speak. 'What do you … ' but he turned, cut her off, stared at the man.

'I don't know who you are, but you're not Paul McNeil.'

He went on ahead of them through to the lounge and sat in the far settee. Indicated they should sit opposite.

She blustered in. 'You can't push your way in here and say that. Get out. Now.'

The man stood open mouthed. He had looked pale but now was ashen. Stammered.

'I am… '

The woman grabbed his arm and they moved behind the settee, as if it would protect any assault on them.

McCluskey sat in silence, waiting.

'Tell him, Paul. Tell him to get out.' She glowered at McCluskey, her voice cracking, part rage, part fear. 'I told you to get out.'

He settled back on the settee, stretched an arm along the back, indicated for them to sit. 'I'm going nowhere. I'm guessing you know my reputation.' They pulled closer together. 'Now, I met with Paul McNeil when he was selling the penthouse.' He let silence hang. 'I know you are not Paul.'

It was the woman who spoke. 'Please go.'

'I also know you are not Paul McNeil as Paul McNeil is dead. And you know he is dead' He pointed again at the settee opposite and this time they sat. 'And if you were Paul McNeil... I would kill you... So before I decide whether to kill you... why are you pretending to be a dead man?' They shifted uncomfortably, sat in silence. He lent forward as if to go. Put a hand on the man's knee and as he shrank away said 'Pity. Next time you see me... well actually next time you won't see me...' Spoke to her, 'You'll look good in black.'

The man was panicking, garbled his words. 'No. Listen. I'm Colin Ingleby. The cousin. It's a long story.'

McCluskey patted his knee. 'Now that's sensible. If it's a long story. How about coffee. eh. Maybe... ' he moved his hand to the woman's knee.

'Gerry,' she replied.

'Gerry, could get us all coffee... and a biscuit. A biscuit would be nice... civilised. We can have a nice civilised conversation.'

Sandra jerked awake. There were voices in the hall. She struggled to get her bearings. She must have dosed off. Her book lay open on the bed beside her. Someone was at the door talking to Colin and Gerry. She heard a commotion and realised that who ever it was had entered the flat and Gerry was angry, 'What do you... ' cut off by the stranger's reply. 'I don't know who you are, but you're not Paul McNeil.' Now Sandra was fully alert. Bugger what had the idiots done?

She lay hardly daring to breath. Listening, but now the voices were muffled and she realised that they were in the lounge. She tiptoed to the door and eased it open. Now she could catch the odd word but nothing clearly. She had to get nearer. She opened the door slowly and edged into the hall She would like to have been able to see them but if she could see them then they might see her and she could not risk it. She froze when she heard 'Selling the penthouse'. The stranger had to be Graham McCluskey. What the hell had brought him to the flat?

She listened as Colin and Gerry crumbled under McCluskey's questions. The whole story given away. How Paul McNeil was heir to a fortune. Shuggie's visit, the plan to replace McNeil with Colin. Gerry provided a little resistance but with Colin betraying every secret she soon fell in with full disclosure. Sandra shook her head as their plan was explained to McCluskey then in disbelief as Colin and Gerry fell in with an alternative route to wealth which involved cutting out her and Shuggie. How McCluskey could protect Colin and Gerry for a smaller cut than they would pay to Sandra and Shuggie. She slipped back to her bedroom realising how easily Colin and Gerry surrendered her and Shuggie to this thug. She had to speak to Shuggie.

She was about to phone when she heard McCluskey leaving. Quickly lay back on the bed, picked up the ear phones from the bedside table and turned on her radio, balanced the book back on her lap and lay waiting. She caught the whispered conversation at the bedroom door.

Colin asked, 'You think she heard.'

'If she had she'd have been out here. She couldn't keep her nose out'

'But if she did?'

Sandra smiled and under her breath said, 'yes, I did, Colin. You should be worried. Shuggie will go mental.' She saw the door handle turning and adjusted the ear phones so they were only partially inserted. She could still hear what was happening. Let her head fall as if she had dropped off while reading.

Gerry gloated. 'See. Told you. She's slept through it all. We're in the clear.'

After a few moments the door clicked shut.

Sandra lay on, hardly breathing, not daring to move in case they were lingering outside her door. When she was certain they had gone she reached for her phone then changed her mind. She needed to see Shuggie and what if Colin or Gerry overheard her call?

CHAPTER TWENTY-NINE

Blue light from the computer screen flickered over Shuggie's face giving him a ghostly look as the night darkened. Shuggie blinked and rose to put on a light.

He found it difficult to break the habit of keeping the flat looking as if it was unoccupied, although he was sure that Razor had given up on his vigil outside. There was no reason to sit in the dark. Soon he would be fit to start hunting the bastard. Not that it would be difficult for he knew exactly where Razor would hide. Daft bugger would go to Arran. Probably believed he was safe there. Shuggie recalled a drunken night's maudlin tale of Razor's mother, some cowshed in the hills and never being discovered..

He returned to the computer and the latest on an insurance case in Chicago. Resting at home had the advantage of giving him time to research the American lawyers who were involved in the killing of Paul McNeil. Geland Shuster and Liebermann had a rather colourful internet history with organised crime featuring in their profile. Yesterday he had discovered a current court case, a breaking story on the local TV Station, WTYP, with their star reporter, Caroline Probert, running daily updates

Rainwater Care Home, situated just outside the city, was involved in a court case where Liebermann was their defence attorney. Caroline Probert built up the gruesome details of the charge; the home kept resident bodies in cold store until insurance policies were arranged on their lives. Fraudulent claims totally upwards of a million dollars had been made on policies arranged after death. Joint accused were two doctors at the home who signed the death certificates.

Shuggie noted with interest Probert's assertion that the main stumbling block for the prosecution was that in all the cases the dead had been cremated. However the insurance company investigator had built up an impressive list of informants. There were also quantities of hacked email's and text messages. So they had paperwork and testimony but no physical evidence

What interested Shuggie was that this care home had come up through his search for Tony Simpster. This was where the old gangster was supposed to be clinging to life. Or was he in deep freeze waiting for the death of McNeil? After all, Simpster was notorious in Chicago and until recently there had been a number of reports of his curmudgeon hand on the local underworld. How, even from his sick bed, he continued to wield influence. About four weeks ago it had gone quiet. Shuggie traced a YouTube video of a blacked out ambulance going to Rainwater Care Home. Since then all had been quiet, apart form intermittent postings by his lawyer, Sol Liebermann, saying Simpster was weak but responding to treatment.

Shuggie began trawling the TV company site. If he could get through to Caroline Probert perhaps she could look for a frozen corpse, one waiting to be defrosted when there was news of McNeil's death. It was a long shot but if he was right Simpster was in cold store and with any luck they would not have had time to cremate the evidence. Wouldn't she jump at the possibility of a scoop? He checked the international time zones. In Chicago it would be around midday, a reasonable time to try phoning.

He went to the bottom drawer of his computer desk and pulled it out from the runners. Underneath were the phone and gun taken from Dunbar before he torched the car. He phoned WTYP, gave the receptionist the name Graham McCluskey, said he was phoning from Scotland with vital information relating to the Rainwater case, must speak to Caroline Probert urgently. He held for minutes, as jazz tracks played, before the receptionist came back on the line.

'Miss Probert can give you a few moments, sir. Please hold the line.'

After five minutes the jazz was beginning to grate when a velvet voice said 'Hi, Caroline Probert. I hear you have information on the Rainwater case,' and Shuggie thought what an asset her voice was for an investigator. This was a voice that you wanted to charm.

'I have indeed and thank you for taking my call.'

'You intrigued me. Calling from Scotland with information for an insurance fraud case in the States. How and why, are the immediate questions? I don't have long as I have to be back at the court by 2.00.'

'Ok. Short version. I live in Paisley near Glasgow. Let's say I am well known in the town. You need something fixed, I can fix it. Sol Liebermann contacted me. There's an heir to the Simpster millions in Paisley. He sent a hit man to kill him and it's caused me big trouble. A dead Chicago hitman. Guy called Hunter Dunbar. Killed at Westerland Station, in Glasgow. Look it up. There's another body dumped on a railway line in Paisley. You can look that up too. You'll see it checks out.'

'Yea. Sol Liebermann is a shit. Tell me something I don't know. How does this help my case?'

'All this is tied to Simpster. He needs to be alive until the Scottish heir is dead. If they can do that the money stays in Chicago. Simpster is in Rainwater Care Home. Nothing heard of him for weeks... except what Liebermann reports. I'm certain he's dead and that he's in a freezer. And this is one body not yet defrosted and burnt. They couldn't move till the Scots guy was dead. It's only just happened and the court case you're following will have held them up. You search their freezer and you'll get your proof of freezers used to store the dead. That's the Rainwater case blown wide open and a scoop for you.'

There was a brief pause when he finished.

'This heir. What's his name.'

'Paul McNeil. They think he's dead but the hitman got the wrong guy.'

'Gee. You sure about this?'

'Sure as I can be. Check it out. Simpster's not been heard from in weeks.'

'Weird, real weird. OK, I'll look at it. Get back to you if needed. On this line?'

'No. This is it. One call and you can't quote me on any of this. The police here are already interested in me without this. I want Sol Liebermann out of my life. I never phoned you. Will deny it if you say I did.'

Shuggie hung up. Hopefully the call would stir things State-side. He carefully wiped the phone of all prints and put it in a padded envelope addressed it to Caroline Probert.

There was a sparkle in Jennifer's eyes that Graham McCluskey had not seen for weeks. She squeezed his hand.

'And... go on.'

He had hurried back as soon as he left Ingleby and Gerry, the girlfriend. He had to talk with Jennifer. It would be a big step to side with Ingleby against Sol Liebermann but a share of millions was tempting. As he outlined the afternoon's events he could see life flowing through Jennifer. This was the woman he knew, skin glowing, animated. Questioning his account. Nodding as he spoke.

'So I left it that we could shut out that runt Shuggie Cameron and I would pretend to Liebermann that I had killed Paul McNeil.' He chuckled, 'Again. They would go into hiding and, when Simpster was dead, I would back them in their claim on the estate.' He felt her grip tighten nails digging into the back of his hand. 'What do you think? Am I mad?'

Jennifer lay back on her pillows. He watched the little creases round her eyes, the purse of her lips. Lusted for her. It had been weeks since they made love. Weeks when he did not know if she would survive. Now she was so alive. So Jennifer again.

'Not mad. I see the temptation. A few million dollars and we could leave all this in the past.' She lifted his hand to her lips kissed it. 'I know how you think.'

He nodded, 'We could disappear. Just us and the boys. Spain. South America even. No more watching for the police, the next rising tuppenny hard man, another Shuggie Cameron. You and I… '

Jennifer cut him short. 'You're wrong. This isn't the right opportunity.'

There was silence as he waited. How often had Jennifer kept him right? The last time he had ignored her was in taking on Sam Browne to run the properties so he could employ Cameron. His sop to a guilty conscience. And look where that got him. She said it was a mistake, would end in tears and…

'You said yourself that Ingleby is useless. He folds easily. He told you everything. You really think he can sustain this deception. He was putty for you. He was putty for Cameron. Will be putty when anyone threatens him. The man is the weak link. It sounds as if that Gerry woman is the strong one and it's not her you'd be relying on.' Jennifer stopped but he saw she was thinking, said nothing. 'And you'd need to kill McNeil's girlfriend. And if you had to kill her you'd probably have to kill Cameron.' She laughed. 'Not that that would be bad.'

'Aye,' he agreed.

'But it adds up to hassle and as Ingleby's useless, all pointless. Can you see him in a court? Can you see him face a smart lawyer? More to the point what if Liebermann sent over another thug. Ingleby, stand up to that pressure? Never.'

'So what should I do? Will I tell Liebermann to stop worrying? McNeil is dead and that Ingleby is trying to work a scam.'

McCluskey felt her nails again pull down the back of his hand. Saw the flush of excitement in her cheeks. 'You can if you want but you know what he'll say.'

'I do?'

'Kill him. He's in the way. They don't need more problems with claims and courts, with hit-men, with Scotland. Clean. Quick. Dead.'

'Of course. You're right.' God he loved this woman. Her brain. Her body. 'Ingleby signed his death with that email to America. I'll tell Liebermann it's a scam. But you're right. He'll want him dead.'

Jennifer pushed back the covers. 'That's the man I married. Now give us a kiss. I want you to hold me.'

He looked at the door, the window, thought of the hospital beyond. 'What here? Now?'

'Drop those blinds. And get in. They'll not be in to check on me till much later.'

He had seen the scars. Could he? Would he? He feared this moment. Lowered the blinds.

'What if I hurt you?'

'I trust you,' she said. 'But don't worry if you hurt me a little.' She slid lower in the bed, opened her arms. 'I want to feel alive.'

Although the flat was dark, the window was open and in the street Sandra could hear Leonard Cohen singing 'Closing Time'. It confirmed that Shuggie was on the mend. Not caring who knew he was alive and at home. In he few days they had been together she had discovered that playing Cohen was a sign Shuggie was at his happiest. It was just as well.

He was sitting, feet up, whisky in hand. He greeted her with a kiss. She leant back to look into his face. 'You look in a good mood.'

'I am. Excellent bit of stirring. McCluskey, hopefully, will feel the heat.'

'McCluskey. Well, you'll not be pleased when I tell you my news.'

He let her go. Took a drink.

'McCluskey has been to see Colin. The bastard just wilted.'

Shuggie sat and she started to walk back and forth, unable to settle as she recounted what she had been able to hear. From time to time, breaking away from what had happened to curse Colin Ingleby, Gerry, bloody fate that had had Ingleby answer the door, that McCluskey had actually met Paul. She was in a rant about that painted hussy Gerry, only there for the cash, 'I mean who could love a cretin like Colin,' when Shuggie spoke.

'Yes. Yes. I know she's a gold digger but… wait I have to get this clear. Graham McCluskey has the whole story. Me, the American, Dunbar, the body on the railway. The whole fuckin' shebang…'

'Yep.'

'…And he said that he would not kill Ingleby if they cut him in.'

'Yes.'

'And cut me out? Cause he could protect them from me?'

'Too right. Big headed bastard was gloating. I could hear it in his voice.'

'Christ, I told the bitch not to reply to that email. She's fucked up everything.'

Shuggie rubbed his eyebrows, sighed, dropped into thought.

Sandra poured more whisky, took one for herself. As he chinked his glass with hers it seemed to crystalize what he was mulling over.'

'They'd be idiots to trust McCluskey. But, if they have thrown in their lot with him, you can't go back.'

She frowned, gave a slight shake of the head. 'Why?'

'Don't you see. They told McCluskey you and I were working together. He wouldn't trust you to keep your mouth shut. You were Paul's live in lover. You blow the whole scheme if you decide to expose Colin. Working with me. McCluskey can't have that risk. If he doesn't kill Colin...' Shuggie indicated for Sandra to refill both glasses. '...he kills you.'

Sandra paused for a moment mid sip. Swallowed.

'Oh! I hadn't thought of that. Would he?' She saw the look on Shuggie's face. 'Don't answer. I know he would.' She smiled weakly. 'If it was on the other foot, would you?'

'Not you. Do you have to ask? And anyway I've never killed for money; self preservation, revenge, But not greed. I've seen greed. It eats you up.'

'I'd better go back. Pack a case. What do I tell them? They don't know I heard of course.'

'Say nothing. Wait till early morning. I'll come back with you. We slip in, get what you need and leave without being seen. Let them stew.'

'But McCluskey will guess I'll be here. And you can't be with me all the time.'

Shuggie pulled her down beside him. 'And why not. But we'll not be here I've an idea where to hide. We're going to Arran.'

'Arran? Why Arran?'

'It's as good as any. But I think Razor is there. And we have unfinished business.'

Sandra snuggled into his chest. 'Self preservation, revenge.'

'You told me to get him.'

She traced a finger through the hairs on Shuggie's chest. 'Will you do everything I ask.'

He kissed her. 'Depends.'

CHAPTER THIRTY

The first light of dawn crept from the east as Sandra and Shuggie parked at the old mill flats. They could see the workers in the nearby supermarket readying for the opening in a couple of hours and cars passed on the road, the other side of the river, but here all was quiet.

They had agreed to wait for dawn before collecting what Sandra would need as it avoided turning on lights in the flat. The lift sounded loud as they rose to the tenth floor but it couldn't be helped. In the hallway Shuggie held up a hand to stop Sandra. Pointed to the flat door. She saw splinters of wood round the lock and that the door was slightly ajar. Sandra would have spoken but for Shuggie's hand urgent on her lips. He shook his head, eased the door open and she followed him inside.

A light burned in Colin and Gerry's room. There was a strong smell, sickly sweet and yet acrid. Shuggie stepped inside and whispered, 'Fuck.' He tried to stop Sandra coming in, holding up his hand and saying in his normal tone. 'McCluskey came back. Don't come in. It's not ...'

But she was beside him before he could prevent it, gasped as she saw the bed. 'Christ.'

Colin and Gerry lay side by side. A black hole in their foreheads, blood soaked pillows supporting their heads. The duvet had been thrown off but whether by them or the killer was unclear. In each body there was another bullet hole through the heart.

Sandra stared, blinked rapidly, as if to make the image disappear. For reasons she did not understand, asked, 'Are they dead?'

Shuggie gave a low dry chuckle. 'Not that long ago by the look of it.' Shook his head. 'The stupid bitch. I told her.'

Sandra stood staring for a moment, swallowed hard, managed a reply. 'She wanted the money. I don't think she really loved him. She only came back, the day of the fire, to get some things. She admitted as much in one of our arguments. It slipped out.' Sandra took Shuggie's arm, pulled him out into the hall. 'That smell is turning my stomach. Let's get my stuff and get away. Christ, she was a selfish bitch and he just a weak fool, but they didn't deserve this.'

'Forget getting stuff. Don't you see there's no need. You're not at risk any more.' He pulled her closer. 'Listen, you must realise we can't go away now. If we do who do you think the police will believe is in the frame for this? My prints are all over the place in here. If we run we've thrown away our alibi.' He let her go, lent against the wall. 'Let me think.'

The sound of the lift broke the silence. Sandra grabbed Shuggie's hand. 'God. Oh God! He's coming back.'

Shuggie took their linked hands up to her lips. 'Shush. Not him. Shush.'

The whirr of the lift grew louder, stopped. From the floor below, they heard the doors open, close and then the descending lift growing fainter, the first of the morning commuters off to work. Both began to breath again.

'We phone the police and report this.' He rubbed his eyebrows. 'And… ' Drummed fingers on his forehead, spoke in bursts as he thought out loud. 'Bugger there is something… we can tell them what happened tonight… we can tell the whole story.'

Sandra interrupted, 'Why phone the police?' but his wince cut her short.

'We have to get our story right… stick to the truth… yes, of course… Listen Sandra. We tell them the whole thing. The American hit-man, Colin pretending to be Paul, McCluskey visit. The bit you leave out is me being in on it from the start. We met in Morrison's supermarket... after Paul's death, right. Nothing about me and the American...

Damn, that doesn't work... how would you know about the American?' Shuggie began to pace. 'How did you know Paul was dead? Yes. Yes. He didn't come home. You thought he died in the fire. Of course. Right. Got it, Sandra.' He took her by the shoulders. 'It's easy, any questions you tell the truth except about me telling you about the American. If you say anything about that say you heard it from the conversation between McCluskey and Colin and Gerry, this afternoon. Got that?' She nodded. 'Good. We met in the supermarket. Right. Don't give too many details. Just saw me got into conversation, etc, etc I asked you out. You wanted away from Colin, etc, etc. You can do that?' She nodded. 'Good. We have to do this, Sandra. You do see that?'

She hesitated, 'Why can't we just pretend we weren't here? Never saw them?'

He shook his head. 'Too risky. What if someone saw us this morning? We're probably on tape somewhere driving over. Trust me. This is best.'

She put her arms round his waist. 'Hold me.' He obeyed. 'Tighter. Really tight.'

She pressed her head against his chest. 'I trust you. You do love me don't you?' He kissed her hair. She bent her back so that she could see his face. 'It's just struck me. You will love me now I'm poor? I mean with Colin dead there's no money.'

He kissed her forehead. 'I love you. Forget the money. Just remember we met in the supermarket, everything else is as it happened. OK?'

She smiled, 'As long as you love me.'

The telephone was on Helen Green's side of the bed. She wriggled free from Hamilton McVey's arm and stretched for it. At the same time was aware of the buzzing of a mobile in Scruffy's jacket slung on a chair and of the musical ring of her own mobile on the dressing table.

When she answered her mobile also stopped ringing. 'About time. I've been ringing this and your mobile for five minutes.' She recognised the voice of her editor.

'Christ, Jimmy.' She checked her watch. 'It's just turned seven. I do sleep you know.'

'Forget that. Freddy the Fox phoned.' Helen shivered. 'God, you woke me for one of Freddy's leads. He's probably drunk and wanted to tap you for a few quid.' The commotion had stirred Scruffy and she saw he was retrieving his mobile. 'I have a private life, Jimmy.'

'This one's a goer. I've checked and there's police activity at the Heritage Mill flats. Freddy says there's been a double shooting. If we move fast we could get that in the late edition.'

Helen was about to dismiss this as another of Freddy's exaggerations when she noticed that Scruffy was trying to pull on clothes with one hand while speaking on his mobile.

'Helen, we need you out there. And you've that tame Inspector. McVey isn't it? See what you can get. Double shooting and in the luxury flats. It would be a great headline.'

As she agreed to go Scruffy was hopping on one foot trying to pull on his trousers. He was about to fall when she grabbed him and getting the trousers by the belt hauled them up. He smiled his thanks, rang off.

'I think you've had the same call as me,' she said. 'two shootings?'

'Come on Helen. You know I can't say.' He scrabbled by the bed. 'Can you see my socks?'

'On the chair where you left them. But it is a double shooting. Isn't it? According to Jimmy.'

McVey tried to look serious saw her face and grinned. 'Yes. You're bloody sources are better than ours. See you there. We better take two cars. Although I think we're rumbled, no sense flaunting it.

'You ashamed of me.'

He was glad to see that she was mocking him, not serious. 'Of course,' he replied planting a kiss on her cheek. 'Last one there buys lunch.'

As he went to pass her she shouldered him onto the bed. 'No, dinner, and a good one. None of your cheapskate,' and was first out the door.'

The rotund shape of Sergeant Jenkins waited in the foyer of the flats.

'Morning, H.'

'Morning Tommy. What have we got?'

'Two dead. A Paul McNeil.' Sergeant Tommy Jenkins hesitated. 'At least it appears so. That is the registered owner of the flat. And Geraldine Kowalski, his girlfriend. Looks like a professional job. Clean shots to the head and to the heart.'

Inspector McVey scratched the back of his neck. 'Bit of over kill. Two shots. That's not like a professional?'

Jenkins tilted his head a little in response. 'But good shooting. The head shots were between the eyes. Seems our intruder broke the flat door, into the bedroom and both shot before they had a chance to move. For me that's professional.'

'Who found them?'

'Aye, you'd never guess. Hugh 'Shuggie' Cameron and a girl. Sandra Smith. She shares the flat with McNeil.' 'They say they came in about five and found them.' he checked his notes. 'They phoned emergency at five sixteen. So that would fit.'

As they entered the lift McVey muttered, 'Strange'

'What's that, H.'

'You said Sandra Smith was Shuggie Cameron's girl and the girl in bed with McNeil was Geraldine Kowalski.'

'That's right,'

'But when I met them after that fire in Gerry's Restaurant. Smith was McNeil's and Gerry was the girlfriend of Colin Ingleby. The body on the railway line.'

Jenkins shrugged. 'Christ, young folk nowadays in and out of each other's beds.' Sergeant Jenkins tapped his notebook against the knuckles of his other hand. Coughed.

'Mind you? I said it appears that the man is Paul McNeil. But there is a question as to that?'

McVey waited. 'Spit it out Tommy. What question?'

'Well I said it was Paul McNeil as… according to Smith's statement that was who he was now… but she said that until a few nights ago he was Colin Ingleby. But I know we have Colin Ingleby's body in the morgue so…

'So we think it's Paul McNeil.'

'Yes?'

There was a niggle at the back of the Inspector's mind. It grew stronger as they left the lift and entered the crime scene.

'Speak to the pathologists. Have them check this body's right knee.'

Jenkins flicked his hands open, questioning, 'right knee?'

'You know there was something bothering me about that body on the railway line, the identification as Ingleby's;. I couldn't put a finger on it until now. There was no mention in the report of damage to his knee. Yet Ingleby walked with a slight limp, an old rugby injury. I'd have expected it to show on the pathologist's report. Maybe the one on the railway line isn't him. And if it's not Ingleby, could it be McNeil?' As they pulled on latex gloves and shoes, he lent against the wall. 'But why would Ingleby want to pretend to be McNeil?'

'He'd run up debts. That restaurant of his was struggling. Maybe that fire was an insurance job.'

'But you wouldn't do that and disappear, Tommy. You'd claim the insurance. Wouldn't you?'

McVey proceeded Jenkins into the flat, stopped to glance back at the Sergeant. 'Anyway didn't we establish that Ingleby had forgotten to renew?'

Sergeant Jenkins sighed, 'True. Forgot that.'

Examination of the bedroom confirmed for McVey his sergeant's opinion; the clinical precision of the shots were not the work of an amateur. These killings were the work of a hardened man. McVey stopped mid-thought, or woman. Could it be a woman? No reason to discount that. This was not a crime that required strength. A little, to force a way in, but in all honesty the builders had not gone overboard on security; a child could force that door. All the signs suggested it couldn't be more than a couple of hours since they were shot. McVey imagined the events. Early hours, deep asleep, the jerk awake, what was that, a figure in the room, lights come on, eyes dazzled, sit up, try to focus. By the time they saw the gun… He indicated to Jenkins to follow him and went through to the kitchen. Began to check the room. Poking out from under the computer keyboard he saw an edge of folded paper. Pulled free a letter. Read it. Passed it to the sergeant.

'Well, well, Tommy. What do you make of that?'

Jenkins scanned quickly. 'Bloody hell, H McNeil was to inherit from some American. Christ, wish someone would leave me an inheritance of millions. No wonder these lawyers talk of being able to advise on US investments and property. See the number of partners and associates. Doesn't sound like this is from any tuppence ha'penny firm.'

'Yes. Tommy. Was to inherit.' he stretched out a hand, took the letter back.

'Geland Shuster and Liebermann, From Sol Liebermann. I think we better talk to this lot.' He nibbled a thumb nail, absent mindedly, lost in thought. 'Or maybe he already has inherited? See the date. Wonder who benefits from McNeil's death?'

'It's only a week. And who would know?'

'Still time enough for a man to die. Perhaps that's what this is about. Wonder who inherits?' There was a lull in conversation as the two men searched on before McVey returned to the letter. 'And Shuggie Cameron has hitched up with McNeil's girl? There's something fishy there. Let's get him and Sandra Smith back to the station. We're doing nothing here. See what they have to say for themselves. For starters, why were they skulking about in the early hours?'

CHAPTER THIRTY-ONE

A ringing telephone greeted Hamilton McVey as he arrived at his office. He placed coffee and sandwiches on the desk and answered. Sergeant Thomas Jenkins dropped into the chair opposite, tore open a pack of Cheese and Onion crisps and began to crunch. McVey mouthed 'bastard' at him as his sergeant broke open a triple pack of All-Day Breakfast Sandwiches and, after struggling to free Sausage and Egg from the trio, bit off the corner and chewed extravagantly. Scruffy McVey pointed to his own pack of Prawn Mayonnaise, indicating for Jenkins to open them. Tommy Jenkins smiled and ignored, until a glower said he was pushing his boss too far and he obliged. McVey sank back in his chair and mumbled responses as he ate. Hung up with a sigh.

'Problems, H?'

'No. Just that bastard of a husband who I was up in court with on Monday, breached his bail last night, went round to see his wife.' McVey took a bite of sandwich. They chewed in silence.

'Hit her, did he?'

The Inspector nodded. 'Of course. Bloody social work reports. He's a fuckin' nutter who hits women.' He drank coffee, ripped opened a large packet of plain crisps, spread it on the desk. 'Help yourself.' Picked up a handful, stopped half way to his mouth. 'What he needs is a bloody public flogging. Let the women at him. Social Bloody Work.'

'She OK?'

'Yea, luckily. Neighbour heard it. Stepped in. That's the only good bit. As the husband was leaving he fell down the close stairs, is in a bit of a state.'

Jenkins smiled. 'We charging the neighbour?'

'Fortunately three other neighbours say they saw him trip. Anyway enough of that. Down to serious business. You got those statements from Smith and Cameron?'

Jenkins passed a folder across the desk. McVey took out four sheets, kept two, passed the others back to the Sergeant. They sat in silence reading until the Inspector sat back, stretched out his hand and they swapped pages.

Carefully brushing crumbs from his jacket into his hand and depositing them in the bin, McVey tapped the desk and pointed at the trail of crisps left by Tommy Jenkins.

Jenkins mumbled, mouth full, 'Getting awfully house proud.'

'Fed up with you leaving my room like a pig sty.' He held out the basket and Jenkins gathered up the remains and threw them in. He missed popping out for a cigarette, taking a break from the office, took out a packet of gum, and unwrapped a piece. He pushed the packet across his desk offering them to the Sergeant. Jenkins declined.

'What you think, Tommy?' McVey did not wait for his Sergeant to answer. 'Reads pretty true to me. Smith in particular. Doubt if she'd be as practised a liar as to carry of a fantasy like this. Identity swap. American hit men. It's like a comic book plot.'

'Bit thin about Cameron. Where does he fit in? Just the boyfriend.?'

McVey shrugged. 'Handy to have him turn up now, but stranger things happen.' He glanced at the chubby figure of Jenkins, thinning hair carefully combed over. 'Don't tell me you didn't notice she's a bit of a blonde bombshell?'

'Oh, I don't doubt they are an item. But did they kill McNeil,' Jenkins hesitated, 'or Ingleby, whoever? and the woman?'

The Inspector took a moment or two before answering. 'Don't see it. Why go together? If he's going to kill them, Cameron goes on his own. Shoots and disappears. You don't have her along as a spectator. Then phone us. And the gun, where's the gun?'

'Tossed from the flat into the Mill Lade. It's big, deep, bottom thick with centuries of silt. Some search that would be and would we even find it?'

McVey chewed for a moment. 'True. Still don't see it. McNeil, or Ingleby pretending to be McNeil is the one who inherits, so why would they kill the golden goose? Doesn't make sense. And according to their statements, Smith was to share in the McNeil money.' He tossed the papers onto his desk. 'My money is on Graham McCluskey.'

'Unusual for him to dirty his hands?'

Who's he got? For a quick clean kill? Nelson? The Wilsons? They're his local muscle, but not for this. He'd needs class for this, would have needed to buy in someone. Not easy in a hurry.'

'What about this mysterious American. Where's he gone?'

'I presume he went back to the States when he shot Ingleby, sorry McNeil. Remember it's this double identity that's caused the trouble.'

'But why hurry? Wouldn't take more than a few days to get him back.'

'You've seen the statements. The US lawyers pulling McCluskey's strings. They threw it at McCluskey's door and for some reason McCluskey couldn't refuse. These murders hinge on that Chicago inheritance and on time pressure before Simpster dies. No, gut instinct. This was a rush job.' He picked up the last of his sandwich, spoke mouth full. 'Right, time to get out there, see what the house to house has brought up. Problem with these modern flats is we don't have the 'stair heid' gossips any more. You got the CCTV for George Street?' Jenkins, hurrying to finish his lunch nodded. 'Good, we should find Cameron's car on that. See if it confirms the time of his drive to the Heritage Mill.' McVey scratched the back of his neck. 'We might be able to see if Smith was with him in the car.' He pushed his chair back and was on the move. 'Christ, Tommy, come on.'

Jenkins brushed debris from his jacket and followed the Inspector along the corridor to the incident room. Constable Tricia Wilson handed him a note as he passed. 'Might be important, Sergeant.' He had a quick read and tapped McVey on the shoulder. 'This confirms the US part of those statements. From McNeil's ex-boss.'

Tricia smiled as McVey said 'Good work.' She sat beside two fellow officers. McVey noted their eyes left him to watch her sit. Couldn't blame them. Tricia Wilson reminded him of a young Catherine Zeta Jones in *The Darling Buds of May*. And she had a natural charm to go with those looks. Good qualities in a detective, people opened up to her. Could either of his two male officers score? Surely Ray Soper didn't have a chance; couldn't see her being smitten by him. God, Soper reminded so much of him at that age and he couldn't pull. Now Jim Townsend, there was a different kettle of fish. Tall, dark and that recent nose break playing football probable made him more handsome. Bit full of himself and thicker than he realised, but he would break a few hearts. Well as long as it wasn't Trish's while they were working on his case.

'Gentlemen. When you've quite finished admiring the scenery.' He saw Jenkin's wince. Damn no doubt that was breaking some bloody PC guide-line, he went on quickly. 'We have good work from Trish with Paul McNeil's boss Miss Irene Hoolihan. I should say ex-boss. Until recently he worked for Yellow Brick Road Estate Agents, in their office opposite the Abbey. He left last week. Resigned on the phone.' McVey referred to Trish's notes. 'He said, I've had a bit of luck. I'll inherit soon from an American uncle. I'm not coming back.

There's nothing on my desk I need. Do what you want with it. So no prior notice. Just that phone call and he didn't go back.'

Soper glanced at the others. 'Bet they loved that.'

'Could say. Irene Hoolihan had to remind him that he had taken keys from the office for a couple of properties he had been selling. He didn't go in. His girlfriend Gerry dropped them off the next day.'

'He didn't want to be seen, H?' suggested Jenkins.

'Thanks, Tommy. That's what I believe. Pass round copies of those statements from Cameron and Smith.' He waited until all had copies. 'Read over later. But note that while we have treated this as shootings of McNeil and Kowalski there is strong probability that the man is actually Colin Ingleby.'

Ray Soper chipped in. 'Wasn't Ingleby the body on the railway line?'

'We thought so, Ray. But now I doubt that. McNeil's ex, Sandra Smith, says that it's McNeil and today's shooting is Ingleby. So does Cameron. And here we have the man we thought was McNeil avoiding his boss. Never went back into the office after he and Gerry Kowalski identified the railway body.'

Jim Townsend looked smug and chipped in. 'The DNA will prove it.'

'You think? These are cousins. But we'll see. Any way I have pathology checking for knee injuries. As I remember Ingleby was a bit of a player in his youth. Tipped for a cap until injury ended that. We'll know for sure soon.'

'What's the point of swapping identity?' asked Jim.

'It's in the reports. Read and digest. But first. Trish get over to Crossroad's and find out what keys McNeil took from the office, maybe there's something we need to follow up on. Why did he keep keys out of the office? That can't be usual practice.

Jim, you're the sports freak. Check I'm right about this sports injury. Follow up on Ingleby and on McNeil finances. Do they owe money? Have they borrowed heavily? And find out who gains from the deaths; if they have wills. We know there's no siblings who gets anything they leave.

'Won't it go back to the parents, H?' A strained silence fell with the question. 'What?'

Jim Townsend looked puzzled as he scanned the room. 'Thought that with no will assets went back to the parents?'

McVey shook his head. 'Christ, Jim, the parents of Ingleby and McNeil were presumed dead in that Indonesian tsunami. Bodies were never found but they were on a sailing holiday in that area, wreckage was recovered from the yacht. Unless you think they have been lying low for years to come back, kill their offspring and scoop the estates?' McVey stared icily. Shit. The problem with Townsend not recognising his intellectual limitations was that he lacked the bloody application to make up for it. 'It's all in the bloody files you're meant to have read.'

Ray, let's go back over all we have on the body on the railway line. Have we missed anything that ties in now? He turned to Jenkins.

'We're going to see McCluskey?'

'We are. We'll have another chat with Shuggie Cameron and Miss Smith. And then, it's bothering me that we didn't find Razor Nelson yesterday. I told Charlie Hodgson it would be no problem' us picking him up for questioning about that CCTV footage. Now we've this. He usually hangs about with Cameron, and used to work for McCluskey. Never mind Charlie's investigation into the death of Sam Browne, does he fit in with this? We need to talk to Nelson. Find out if he knows anything. Where was he early this morning?'

—202—

The bus stop was directly across from the foot of West Brae. McVey had thought of driving over but decided against the hassle of parking and you could overhear things in unguarded conversations between passengers. It always amazed him how indiscrete travellers were, that feeling of anonymity which came out in intimate details or what amounted to confessions. He had made a career enhancing arrest from what he had heard on a train to Johnstone. No such luck today.

As they waited for traffic to clear McVey looked across to Cameron's flat.

'It's well chosen to stay out here, eh, Tommy. Handy for the town centre but beyond most of the CCTV coverage. None of the buildings on this stretch of the West End have cameras. There are the cameras on the traffic lights but they won't show us much. I must have another word with the Council. Whose ward is this again?'

Jenkins took a moment to consider his answer. 'Isn't this Jamieson. Or is it the woman, the one for Town Centre renewal.

'Armstrong. Celia Armstrong.'

'That's it. I think it's her.'

Traffic stopped as a bus held up the flow and both jinked between cars.

'I'll have a word. Celia Armstrong is usually open to our requests. Even one camera covering the junction with Well Street would be useful.'

Jenkins was first to reach the close entrance and pressed the security pad. Cameron answered the buzzer immediately, said 'Come on up Sergeant, Inspector.' before they could speak. On a quick check, McVey could not see any camera covering the door but there had to be one somewhere. Once up the stairs they found the flat door was open and, as Jenkins knocked, Smith met them.

'Go on through. We're in the front.'

The room was clean and tidy. Cameron sat facing the door on a two seater settee and motioned to the arm chair beside the fireplace where the embers of a coal fire glowed. White returned and, when McVey dismissed her offer of tea, snuggled up on the settee. He wondered if she had been crying. She was paler than McVey remembered from the morning and there was a hint of redness round her eyes.

Both looked at him expectantly. He noted that while Cameron seemed totally relaxed there was white skin on the knuckles of the girl's left hand as she griped Cameron's arm, yet her smile did not appear forced. A good actor? Or had she nothing to hide?

'Just a few points from this morning.' He gazed at Smith. 'If you're up to it. It must have been a terrible shock seeing them like that?'

The girl met his gaze. 'Not something I would like to repeat.'

Cameron placed his right hand over hers and they linked fingers. 'We're fine, Inspector. Go ahead.'

'I was reading over your statements from this morning. I'm a little unclear as to when you first met.'

Cameron raised his left arm from Smith's waist to her shoulders and pulled closer. Looked down on her and she looked up. 'Just a week ago wasn't it. In Morrisons.' they both turned their heads towards McVey. 'Hard to believe it's only a week.' He kissed the top of her head. 'But we were meant for each other.' She had returned her gaze to Cameron as he spoke met his eyes. 'Weren't we.'

God, this lovey-dovey stuff was painful to watch but was it real? Was this a relationship of just a week? But everything he knew said that Sandra Smith had been McNeil's girlfriend. If McNeil was the railway line body then this seemed rather convenient timing. Did they kill him? He decided on the direct assault.

'I'm a little confused as to timings. You were Paul McNeil's partner. In your statement you say it is McNeil whose body we found on the railway line on Wednesday morning. And you met Cameron in Morrison's on Wednesday night. Bit quick wouldn't you say.'

'Paul and I… it wasn't working. He was a selfish bastard to be honest. I would have left if I had somewhere to go… and the inheritance.'

'When did you know about this American uncle?'

'Few weeks ago. I wasn't going to leave then. I mean I'd put up with months of him moaning about us not having money. The collapse in his commissions.' She stopped and sat for a moment. McVey waited. 'He began to pushed too hard when selling. It put buyers off. And sellers complained. He was pressing them to cut their price. If there was money coming I deserved a share.'

'So. Let me get this straight. After the fire you and Colin Ingleby went back to your flat, the one you shared with Paul McNeil. You spent the rest of that night in bed with Colin Ingleby. On Wednesday morning you met me and pretended Ingleby was Paul. Why?'

She frowned. 'I just said. For the money. If Paul was dead, no inheritance, obviously.'

McVey smiled. 'But at that point we had not found a body. How did you know McNeil was dead?'

'We thought he died in the fire. We barely got out. Never saw Paul. I still don't understand how he did. And now I think about it, when he did, why didn't he come home?'

'And so on Wednesday morning you, Ingleby and Kowalski all agreed to say that Ingleby was McNeil. Or had you that pre-arranged? Was the fire a convenient coincidence?'

'What! Me in a plot with Gerry Kowalski.' There seemed genuine anger in the voice. 'I wouldn't give…' Smith stopped mid sentence. 'You shouldn't speak of the dead but she was a stuck-up bitch. Colin for some bloody reason was smitten. She nearly blew it when she turned up. Don't you remember Colin cut her off and steered her away from you. The mention of millions was what brought her round.'

McVey had a recollection of Ingleby and Kowalski muttering that first morning he met them at the burnt out restaurant. He had thought it was Kowalski being comforted about the missing Ingleby but it could have been them hatching the plan. It would have required a quick decision by Kowalski if they hadn't discussed it before but then tempted by a few million dollars she could have played along.

'When did you know Paul McNeil was shot?'

'Today.' Shuggie Cameron shook his head and she caught the gesture. 'Oh Sorry, of course. I've lost track of time. Yesterday when I overheard Graham McCluskey threaten Colin and Gerry.'

'None of you knew about an American or the shooting until McCluskey came round?'

'I didn't. Didn't talk to Colin and Gerry much. She was a jealous cow. Didn't like me talking to Colin on my own and I didn't much like talking to her. But I guess they didn't.

I mean she emailed the US lawyers. Would she have done that if she knew? She wasn't that stupid, surely.'

Jenkins had moved round so that he was by the window. 'Did Graham McCluskey say what happened to this American Hit-man? Seems strange to have a professional over and McCluskey come himself to the flat and make threats?'

Sandra Smith began to cry, silently, tears running down her cheeks, held more tightly to Cameron. 'Wasn't it him? The American, this morning.' She shuddered. 'The way those bullets. Between the eyes. Both of them right between the eyes.'

'Come on, McVey. Don't you think that's enough?' Cameron sat forward on the settee. 'Can't you see Sandra's in shock. In a bit of bloody shock myself. Can't you leave this till later?'

McVey pursed his lips. He probably could as Jenkin's question had started a niggle. What had happened to the American? For some reason he made a connection with Charlie Hodgson's unidentified body as White answered. They should find Nelson. Question him about the Sam Browne's overdose. And if Browne was seen on the CCTV at Westerton could it be that the American hadn't gone back but was in fact the body in the burnt out car. It would explain why the US lawyers didn't have anyone to carry out the killings, so that McCluskey was doing their dirty work. 'Ok. We'll leave it there for now. Don't go anywhere. We'll want to talk to you again.'

As he and the sergeant were leaving he stopped and stepped back into the room.

'Seen Razor Nelson recently?'

For a moment Cameron seemed disconcerted. 'No. Why?'

'Just wanted a chat.'

'Not seen him for a day or two. You tried Jimmy's café?'

'Thought you two were close?'

Cameron shrugged. 'I'd try the café.'

The straggle of late afternoon customers in Jimmy's café stirred when Jimmy greeted McVey and Jenkins, his voice louder than was necessary and emphasising their police ranks.

'Inspector McVey. How nice to see you.' he waved desultorily towards Jenkins. 'Afternoon Sergeant Jenkins.'

McVey noted the shifty movement of Robert 'the Grass' as he pushed a carrier bag deeper into a corner. Looked as if Robert had been on one of his light-fingered expeditions to the Central Arcade. Would he get Jenkins to check that before they left? Might? But

Jenkins would not thank him for the paper work. The bag tipped over and some of the contents spilled onto the worn red lino. In the middle of three murder enquiries, it wasn't worth the bother for cheap perfume, a handful of lipsticks, talc, a few bars of chocolate.

McVey pulled a chair across, its legs juddering, pushed its back against the formica top and sat astride. He nodded to Jenkins to occupy Jimmy, began to play with the bowl of sugars and sweeteners.

'Relax Robert, relax. We're looking for bigger fish than you.'

Robert tried to smile but it came out as a nervous twitch. 'Anythin' I can do, Mr McVey, you know that.' He lent closer to McVey. 'You might have asked away from here. You know I'm always happy to help.' He looked round furtively. 'But I've a reputation to protect.'

McVey laughed and patted his arm. 'I wouldn't worry, Robert. What you don't have you can't lose.' Robert looked puzzled but brightened when McVey continued. 'I'm looking for Freddie Nelson. You seen him?'

'Is that it? Lookin' for Razor.' He stopped, frowned. 'Actually now you ask, he's no been around. He an' yon Shuggie Cameron are in and oot o' here most days, but not,' he looked at his watch. 'Noo I think on it must be since Saturday. Saturday breakfast. You ask Jimmy.' Robert half turned towards the counter and saw Jenkins talking to Jimmy. 'Oh. Aye. Right. Aye. Pretty sure he's no' been in since Saturday.'

'But have you seen him around? Or heard anything? Come on Robert.' There was silence as Robert rolled his hands and lifted his eyebrows a couple of times. 'Look Robert, do you want me to pull out the carrier under the table. Just answer the question.'

'He was hangin' around the West End most of Sunday. Near Cameron's flat. Clocked him on my way oot to the town and back. Bloody awful day too. Cold and damp. Thought it a bit strange.'

'You talk to him?'

'Jees, Mr McVey. Not me. Whit? Small talk with Razor Nelson. Yon's too dangerous.'

'So you saw him Sunday? And?'

'Aye well. Monday. He was hangin' aroon again. At least in the mornin',' he looked at his watch again. 'Aye in the mornin'. No later than... ' He shrugged. Canny mind but I dinnae see him in the afternoon.'

'Nothing since Monday morning.'

Robert smiled, gave a thumbs up. 'That's it. Not seen Razor since Monday mornin'.'

He pushed at his empty coffee cup. 'Maybe a wee coffee. Eh, Mr McVey.' Toyed with the saucer. 'You no think?'

'On yer bike.' McVey stood abruptly, the chair almost falling over, then lent back over the table. 'You let me know if you see him around. Right.'

'Of course, Mr McVey. Sure thing.'

'Sergeant.'

Jenkins spoke briefly to Jimmy and joined McVey outside.

'According to Jimmy, Nelson's not been in since Saturday morning, And that's unusual. Jimmy said Shuggie Cameron has also been avoiding the place. Mind you Jimmy's not complaining, says trade picks up when they're not in.'

'That agrees with what Robert said, but Nelson was seen hanging around Shuggie Cameron's place on Sunday and Monday morning.'

'This not being seen since Saturday. Do you think there's any significance in the Sam Browne death? It did look like Razor on that CCTV from the take-a-way.'

'Exactly, Tommy. Bloody certain it's Razor Nelson. And it's a bit of a coincidence that his routine changes. But were does Shuggie

Cameron fit in? And is any of this to do with the McNeil and Ingleby shootings?'

For the umpteenth time Sandra stood at the window and checked along Wellmeadow.

'You absolutely certain McCluskey won't come after me?'

Shuggie rose quickly to put a reassuring arm round her shoulders. 'Yes. Absolutely certain. With Colin dead the claim on the Simpster estate is finished, the Americans are happy. McCluskey has no need to kill you. He's a bastard but not thick. He'll keep as low a profile as he can.'

Sandra drew close. 'You wont leave me though, will you? Not now. I don't want to be on my own.' She shivered. 'Can't get those bloodied pillows from my head. Gerry's head. And to shoot her twice. Why do that? To see her like that.'

'Try to forget it.' Shuggie moved her over to the settee and pulled her down beside him. 'What you need is a change of scenery. Why don't we go away for a few days?'

'Inspector McVey said not to go anywhere.'

'Aye. We'll he can come find us.' Shuggie smiled. 'No. On second thoughts I'll phone the Station and leave him a message. I'll explain you're a bag of nerves about a killer being on the loose and I've taken you to Arran to get away from Paisley.' He dug around in a pile of clippings on the floor beside the settee. 'Here it is. Whiting Bay. The Sandholes Guest House. I'll phone them, get us booked in and let old Scruffy know. He can bloody whistle for us to stay here.'

Sandra's brows pulled down into a frown as Shuggie made the booking with Sandholes Guest House, foot tapping impatiently.

When he hung up and said, 'all sorted, three nights. We've just time to catch the last ferry. If we hurry.' He flinched as she smacked

—210—

his upper arm.

'You bastard. Pretending it is about me being afraid. This isn't about me. Is it? You had this planned. That cutting. You were going to Arran before I said anything, weren't you? Weren't you?'

Shuggie scooped her up onto his knee and laughed. 'I love you when you're angry. It was a bit about you, but yes, should have known I couldn't fool you.' She tried to glower more deeply but his grin disarmed her. Let him kiss her. 'It's your own fault.'

She pretended to have another swipe at him, 'Mine. How is it my own fault?'

'You said I had to deal with Razor. And I think Razor has gone to hide on Arran. We get away from here and we get to hunt for him. See. So I was thinking of you… in both ways.'

CHAPTER THIRTY-TWO

In the Incident Room at Mill Street Police Station, McVey paced between two white boards, one for the body on the railway and the other for today's shootings. He took a marker pen and scored through McNeil on the one for the railway line and wrote Ingleby. He stepped back and scratched the back of his neck. Was it one killer? Could be. But according to Sandra Smith, McCluskey had said the first was down to an anonymous American and, also according to Smith, the second two deaths were likely to be McCluskey. God it would be good to screw McCluskey on them. How much easier life would be if he was able to put McCluskey away for a long time.

He checked his watch. Smiled. Third night that he had not phoned his mother and she was not ringing to check up on him. Now she knew that he was seeing Helen the constant niggling, about being single at his age, seemed to be forgotten. Helen said she would be at the Paper till late but it was after 7.00, surely she would be free by now. He texted. *Yours in an hour. I'll pick up an Indian, bottle of red?* As Helen had been on the killings, he wondered what she had turned up. Perhaps she had found this hit-man. If he existed?

McVey stopped mid stride and swung back to the boards, wrote in a rambling scrawl down the side of the board for Ingleby;

Restaurant Fire—protection? Browne/Nelson/Cameron
Ingleby shot—Tues night/ Wed morning—American?—railway line—Wed Morning Ingleby/McNeil found
Westerton body—Wed evening? Browne?
Browne suicide?—Sat night—Nelson involved?

McNeil/Kowalski Threatened—Tues afternoon—McCluskey
McNeil/Kowalski shot—Tues night/Wed—McCluskey?

He stood back to review what he had written. His phone rang, breaking into the thought that there was a link here and he was missing it.

'Hi Helen. Curry?'

'Can we make it a little later? Something has come up and I need to follow up on it.'

'Sure. I'll make it an hour and a half.'

He knew what was bothering him; this bloody American who shot Ingleby. How had he known he could dump the body on the railway at Arkleston? And why if you wanted a body identified would you drop it in front of a train? What was it with railways? There was this unknown body at Westerton. No-one reported missing. Not a hint as to identify the Westerton body other than Sam Browne might be involved. McVey stopped and stared at what he had written. For a moment he had read American? as being written beside Westerton body. It was just the way he had scrunched against the edge of the board, or was it? Was it a mad idea? The American had disappeared apparently or McCluskey would not have been brought in to it by those lawyers. He picked up red marker pen and wrote at the foot of the board. Phone Charlie Hodgson—could the Westerton death be an American?

'No spicy onions?' Helen had the contents of the carrier spread across the coffee table of her flat on Church Hill. She was popping open take-a-way cartons, speaking, half to herself, as she did so. 'Rice, naan,' then louder. 'Did you hear? No spicy onions?'

Scruffy stood at the window looking out towards the Glennifer

Braes. Out there was a man, well almost certainly a man, who had shot two people in cold blood. He shook his head muttered 'forgot'.

'Naan? Vegetable or garlic?'

'Should be two. I got both. Couldn't remember which you preferred.'

'Don't mind. But the spicy onions. You forgot the onions.'

Scruffy said, 'sorry,' wondered when he could tell her that spicy onions did terrible things to his digestion. She might never share a bed with him again if he had brought them.

'Come on then. Get sat down and tuck in.' Helen spooned rice onto her own and Scruffy's plate as she spoke. 'Don't get stains on that waistcoat.'

He took off the new waistcoat. 'I won't. And thanks again it's…' He struggled to find the words. When she had presented him with a maroon waistcoat and matching tie he had flinched. Visions of colleagues ridicule made him nervous and could he wear it. In fact when he put it on he liked the look and no-one had laughed. '…Well even Tommy Jenkins liked it and that says everything.'

She laughed. 'He could do with someone with clothes sense sorting him out.'

Scruffy tore a strip from a naan, dropped it on his plate and blew on his fingers. 'Jees, that's hot. He's a bit long in the tooth for that.'

Helen took the naan pulled it apart with ease. Gave Scruffy a look, which reminded him of his mother when he let her down, as she shook her head. 'Wimp. That's never hot.' She ran the naan through the gravy, folded neatly and popped it in her mouth. Scruffy was conscious of the debris from his own effort dribbling down his chin, quickly wiped away with the paper towel she passed across the table. Perhaps he was too old a dog for new tricks. But bugger it he would try. Damn if he wanted to be Jenkins in ten years, simply hanging on

—214—

for the pension.

He was aware that Helen had been speaking while he had been lost in the curve of her thigh and a future eating curries and making love. Spluttered as he spoke, mouth half full of chicken. 'Sorry, say that again. American reporter?'

'I knew you weren't listening.'

'You shouldn't have attractive legs.'

She gave him a playful slap. 'Behave. As I was saying... I had to stay on a bit later because an American TV reporter wanted to talk to me. You'd never guess. About the body on the railway.'

Scruffy's mind raced. 'American?'

'Yes. For the third time an American TV reporter.' Helen sounded exasperated, 'Caroline Probert, one of their local stations, not NBC or anything.'

'Local. It wasn't Chicago, was it?'

Helen's look, this time, was of puzzlement. 'Yes. Good guess?'

'Just... something.' He shrugged. 'Sorry, I'll stop interrupting.'

'That's about it actually. She didn't give much away. Just asked if it was right that a body had been found on the railway line in Paisley? Did the police think it was murder?'

'Did she ask anything about the man found in that burnt out car at Westerton Station?'

'Not directly She did mention that she had seen that on the internet. Remember, Scruffy, that was sensational enough to make it onto our national news reports. I got the impression she wanted to do a piece about comparative levels of violence.'

Scruffy puffed out his lips, made indeterminate sounds, 'Perhaps.' He scratched the back of his neck. 'If she comes on again, try to bring up the Westerton killing.' He hesitated then decided to open up. 'Strange she called tonight. See, I had a sudden thought that the

Westerton victim might be American. And now you have a call from the States. She say the name Simpster, Tony Simpster at all.'

'No. I would have remembered that name. Just asked about the railway and any police investigation… What she did ask about was Graham McCluskey. Was it true that he was behind much of the criminal activity in the area. As I said, I think she wanted to compare violence in a city and in a small town.'

'And just happened to pick Paisley to compare with Chicago.'

Helen grinned. 'Paisley partnered with Chicago might look good on the town signs. We both know this place is a bit like the wild west.'

They both laughed but Scruffy could not get the Chicago lawyers, Simpster and that unidentified body, out of his head, until Helen dimmed the lights, placed a glass of red wine in his hand and curled up beside him.

This was how it should be. A jug of wine, a loaf of bread and thou beside me singing in the wilderness. Omar Khayyam had it right. Suddenly the madness of Paisley faded with a kiss.

CHAPTER THIRTY-THREE

It was just after eight in the morning when McVey entered the Incident Room. He was pleased to see Ray Soper in front of the two White Boards. The constable glanced round as McVey entered.

'Morning, Ray.'

'Morning.' Ray pointed to the footnote beneath last night's additions. 'That's interesting, Inspector. You think the dead man at Westerton is American. The Westerton case isn't ours. Is it?'

'H, Ray. Call me, H. No, it's not ours. Should be Dumbarton but Glasgow have taken it because of… lets say implications. But I was running over things last night and there are mutual participants. I have a hunch there may be an overlap with our man on the Railway line. And now we have yesterday's killings to add.'

'I wanted a word… ' Soper found it difficult not to address his superior officer as Inspector or Sir, but McVey's smile as he hesitated encouraged, 'H.' He tapped the board now headed McNeil/Railway. 'Sandra Smith. I decided to follow up on McNeil's relationship with Smith. She lost her job the day the body was found. And it was over a row with Sam Browne.'

'She knew him? What connection?'

'Make-up, Sir.' Ray Soper corrected himself under McVey's quick glance, 'H. She was working on that film they're making about Cyrano de Bergerac. Seems Browne was a bit of an arse with the women and she took revenge by doctoring the prosthetic nose. Any way Browne had her fired.'

'And he's dead.' McVey scratched the back of his neck. 'And

her boyfriend is dead. And she said that she only hung on for this inheritance. But if he was dead she wouldn't get anything?'

Soper looked smug. 'Ah but there's more. According to a colleagues in make up at the film set, Sandra Smith will inherit from McNeil. So I wondered was there ever this mysterious American? Could Cameron and Smith have killed McNeil for the money?'

'So there's a will. Unusual at his age. Who wanted that?'

'I wondered that. But again, according to the girls in wardrobe and make-up it was signed months before the American inheritance and at a time when he had little assets. In fact it seems McNeil got into arrears on his mortgage. It was when they were… Madly in love… That was,' Roper peered at his notebook. 'That last bit is from Gail Liddel, about sixteen, H, and a romantic. Smith had some savings and bailed him out. They both made wills at the same time leaving everything to each other. Sort of long term commitment.'

McVey scratched his neck. Took the marker from the foot of the board and put a question mark against Sandra Smith. Wrote 'inherits'. 'It's a thought, Ray. Good work. We'll see what Jim found. If there is a will? Shuggie Cameron and Smith? They're certainly close now. So when did that start?'

He paced over to the window. Perhaps he had gone off on a tangent. But would anyone make up an American killer coming to Paisley? If you're making up a story would you go for a film plot? Perhaps you would if you worked in the industry as Sandra Smith did. He returned to board. Soper had moved over to the coffee machine but came to join him.

'My hunch is that there is a killer from America. Probably Chicago. But let's keep an open mind. Ask around. Were Cameron and Smith an item before McNeil was killed? Shuggie's an easy man to spot and Smith, with her looks; surely someone would have seen them together. They're hardly inconspicuous.' A gurgling from the coffee machine in the corner of the room caught his attention. 'Good man. Milk, two sugars.' As Soper crossed to the mugs, McVey shouted after him. 'Milk, only one sugar… no make it a sweetener. I'll be in my office, bring it through.'

As McVey sipped his coffee he missed the sugar. Missed more the sticky bun he usually enjoyed. Missed the break to have a fag. Thought of Helen hardened his resolve.

It was 9.30 before McVey finished his telephone conversation with Charlie Hodgson. As he returned to the Incident Room, he noted Jim Townsend and Trish Bonnar chatting by the coffee machine; Ray Soper typed away at his desk; Tommy Jenkins pretended to be absorbed in his notes as he caught McVey out of the corner of his eye. McVey tapped the boards.

'Updates, team. Ray, have you said about your theory?'

They listened as Soper ran through his interviews with Sandra's Smith's colleagues and his thought that there might be no American; Smith and Cameron killed McNeil for the money.

'Thoughts, people?' Asked McVey but followed up before anyone could answer. He had noted the panic on Jim Townsend's face when Ray said McNeil and Smith had wills. 'Jim. This will. You were on finances. Found this will, did you?'

'Not as yet. I'll get on it today.' McVey raised his eyebrows in silent question. Townsend took the hint. 'Ah. Finances. After the tsunami deaths of their parents, Ingleby and McNeil both received payouts. It's how Ingleby bought the restaurant. That may have been no blessing as it was going bust. The recession blew it and he had borrowed to revamp the business as Gerry's. Seems he was hoping to attract a younger crowd. But never achieved it with the way Gerry's looked? Deluded. Not retro and not… ' Jenkins struggled for a term.

McVey cut in. 'Thank you Egon Ronay. We get the picture it was doomed.' He held up a hand stopping any further comments. 'What about McNeil?'

'From what I can gather he used his inheritance as a deposit on that flat. Bit flash. A spender was how everyone described him. Proper Del Boy, even had the fake Rolex.' Townsend looked round the room for a reaction, got none and continued. 'But word was that he had problems with money, with the ups and downs of the property market.' Townsend nodded to Soper. 'So I can see him tapping his girlfriend.'

'But you've not found a will?' Townsend shook his head. 'Today. Right.' McVey turned to Bonnar. 'Trish?'

'Confirm what Ray says about McNeil's money worries. His boss at Yellow Brick Road Estate Agents said that his flash approach did not suit all clients. Not been doing well on the sales recently. Interestingly those keys he kept out of the office, H, one set was for McCluskey's penthouse. Seems he was obsessed with having a flat like that and met McCluskey a few times when they were trying to get a sale.'

'So when did he have the keys?'

'Not returned until they were asked for and that was after he resigned.'

'After the fire?'

'Yes.' Bonnar flicked back through her notes. 'He resigned on the Thursday of that week. Phoned as soon as the office opened. Irene Hoolihan commented on it. As if he'd been waiting for the dot of 9.00. She almost didn't recognise his voice but thought it was the prospect of wealth. He was talking of this huge legacy he would have. Gerry Kowalski handed back the keys on Thursday.'

McVey began to wander the room and the others sat waiting. Jenkins chipped in

'Significant that the penthouse has been refurbished. Top to bottom, you said, H.'

'Significant. Dam right. But I thought it was because of McCluskey. But if McNeil had a key. Could Smith have got it… or Ingleby… I've always thought that the refurb so soon after we found the railway body was suspicious. Bloody sure someone died in that flat but is there evidence after all that work?' He stood silent for a few moments.

'Trish and Ray, find the builders. I believe it was the Wilson brothers. Anything you can get. And Ray, good theory about the killing but there is an American. Not to say Smith and or Cameron didn't kill McNeil but Inspector Hodgson confirmed to me that my thoughts on this were right. They traced the shoes their victim was wearing. One of the few things to survive the fire and they were an unusual brand. Turns out that they are Don C Sneakers, only available in Chicago. So likely that he was working for Geland Shuster and Liebermann.' He let the moment of success linger. 'Jim, find the will. Tommy, you and I have will have another chat with Graham McCluskey.'

Arran was bathed in morning sun. In the bay window of Sandholes Guest House, Shuggie looked across the breakfast table as Elsie Fairhurst placed a Full Scottish Breakfast before Sandra. When Elsie Fairhurst said full, it was meant, for there were two robust sausages, black pudding, tomato, generous portion of mushrooms, and a slice of fried bread. Sandra smiled her thanks. Shuggie marvelled at her appetite but was glad her nervousness of yesterday was under control. Indeed, as soon as they drove off the ferry he had sensed her relax and last night she had, for the most part, slept soundly in his arms.

However, when she woke him with her whimper in the early hours it had taken a few minutes to reassure her that he would always be there, before she regained her composure and got back to sleep. Now seated at breakfast, Sandra was calmer but he realised his world of casual violence was alien to her. She had seen the reality and it frightened her. Alien and yet here they were in Arran hunting Razor. She wanted him to find and deal with Razor.

He supposed it made sense. Razor's next attempt to kill him might succeed and she would be left alone. And the violence would be hidden from her. He would make sure of that. She did not have to see the outcome.

She looked over to him as Elsie put a plate with two poached eggs on toast at his place.

'You sure that's all you want?' She swung the knife over her plate. 'This looks delicious.'

'I'm fine with this.'

Elsie gave a small shake of the head. 'It wouldn't take a minute for me to fry some bacon. Or what about a nice sausage. They're local, you know. Lovely.'

'No thanks. I'm happy with the eggs.' He burst a yolk and watched it soak into the toast. 'Are there any houses with a byre in the village, Elsie?'

The question stopped Elsie on her way out to the kitchen. She stood frowning. 'My and that's a strange question.'

Shuggie had been worrying since he got out of bed as to how they were to find Razor. It had seemed a good idea yesterday when Sandra was so uptight to get away but now they were here he could see no way to achieve it. Arran was much bigger than he had recalled.

It wasn't likely that Razor would fall into their hands by chance. They could hardly go round describing Razor and asking if he had been seen. Supposing they were lucky, that would drop them right in the frame if anything happened. Records of the car coming on and off the island would place them at the scene. There would be witnesses as to their questions. He doubted if many men would forget having seen Sandra. She sort of stuck in your head. Now his first attempt at a casual enquiry had raised confusion and Elsie Fairhurst would remember it. Inwardly, he cursed his clumsiness.

'A byre? Are you into farming?'

Shuggie put a fork loaded with toast and egg in his mouth. It gained him time. Swallowed. 'I think it's too many programmes on TV. Those self-build and fantasy homes. Sandra and I though there might be byres.' He tapped Sandra's leg with his foot, raised his eyebrows a little in supplication for support. 'Didn't we? Byres could be the next thing after all those barn conversions. We wondered if they might be cheap being on an island.' He tapped Sandra's leg again.

'Oh, yes. Byres.' Sandra nodded her head. A bit overdone he thought, but at least she had understood what he wanted. 'There anything on the go?'

Elsie pondered for a moment. 'Can't think you'd find anything in Whiting Bay itself but there must be on the island. Above here at Kings Cross and on towards Lamlash. There's out by Kildonan and Lagg. But wouldn't you be better to look on the internet?'

Shuggie grasped the escape. 'Yes. Of course. And we will when we get back. Just wanted to see the island first. See where we like. Just an idea if there was anything near here.' He pointed out the window to the view down to the beach. 'This is a lovely spot.'

'There's houses in the village for sale. You will see the signs. But byres. I'm the wrong woman. Sorry.'

Shuggie changed the subject. 'Lovely eggs. I can never do poached. These are... lovely.' Tapped Sandra's leg.

'These local sausages are good. Perhaps we could get some to take home?'

'Congrieve's in Lamlash. A good number of my guest do.' Elsie chuckled as said, 'I should ask for commission.' She left them to their food.

'Thanks.' Shuggie whispered. 'I'll explain later but we take the few days break and forget about finding Razor.' He saw Sandra scowl. 'It's her reaction. We can't go around asking questions.' He froze as a door creaked. 'I will explain when were on our own.' said in a louder voice. 'So today I think we go up to Lochranza and the distillery. Never mind taking sausages home, a couple of bottles of malt sounds good to me.'

The road north from Whiting Bay was quiet and they had time to take in the views down to Holy Isle and beyond, especially as the first few miles were in strained silence. Sandra had not taken well to the suspension of the search for Razor. How was she to cope with the fear that one day she would find Shuggie in a blood-soaked bed? But, by the time they left Lamlash behind and were dropping down to Brodick, she was mollified and recognised the sense in Shuggie's concerns.

At the foot of the hill was the junction where the pier entrance met the main road. Two policemen were chatting on the corner and seemed to stop to watched them drive past. Sandra breathed out noisily.

Shuggie checked his speed. 'It's OK.'

'You sure? They gave us a long hard look.'

'It's what policemen do. Watch cars. Watch people. They had no interest in us.'

He drove a short distance and then pulled into a parking space by the promenade, banged the steering wheel.

'Bloody fool!'

'What?' Sandra spun round to look back to the pier. 'Are they following us?

What is it?'

'Shuggie shook his head. Put a hand on her knee. 'Sorry. It's not them it's me.

Damn and blast. This, I'll go to Arran and track Razor down. No need. I could have done it in Paisley.'

Sandra sat quietly, waiting. 'It's the police.' Shuggie sighed. 'It's me just realised.

Razor's cousin is a sergeant in the police.'

Sandra shrugged shook her head. 'So?'

'Razor's not on Facebook or anything like that. But his cousin's family, they've no reason to hide. I know some of their names. I'll lay odds they have Facebook or Instagram, some social media presence I can find.'

'Oh, Bloody whoopey doo! And?'

'Razor relative's. Same Granny. The Granny with house on Arran. I bet you I can find that house on the computer.'

She sat for a moment, lent over and kissed him. 'You cleaver man.' Tapped the steering wheel. 'Right. Let's get buying. I want Arran Aromatics. So we stop there, then your Distillery.'

In the en-suite bathroom at his Loch Lomond house Graham McCluskey could see the water of the Loch while he lay in the bath. He turned off the jacuzzi jets and slipped beneath the water. The sound system looped back to Sain Saens 'Dance Macabre' as he broke the surface. It suited his mood. He should be tired but had given up on sleep for the moment. It was good to have been back on the streets. It had been a while since he'd done his own clearing up. All the hours of practice in the basement shooting range had paid off. The woman sitting up caught in the glare of his torch, totally blinded and shot before she could raise her hand to shield her eyes. The surprise on Colin Ingleby's face turning to shock in the split second before he died.

He pressed the intercom.

'Mrs Lightfoot. Bacon. Eggs, fried, on black pudding. Ten minutes. Coffee.'

Perhaps now was the time to eliminate another problem. Razor had bottled it. He should deal with Cameron himself. But today was for business not pleasure. He had to show his face in Barrhead. Either the guys were getting slack or they were screwing him. Take was down for the last two weeks. Scum. No doubt when they knew Jennifer was in hospital they thought he would be distracted. Pure luck that he'd said to meet this afternoon. By that time news of the shootings would have spread. He could use it as a reminder of what happened to those who got it wrong. That he was watching and... No outright threats. Not yet. Jennifer always told him it was what was unsaid that carried the biggest fear.

He pressed the intercom again. 'Fried bread, Mrs Lightfoot. I have an appetite.'

It was time he thought about expansion. This side of the river, Clydebank, Helensburgh. Oban, Jennifer would like Oban. He could talk it over with her tonight. Somewhere with some nice shops, jewellers, high class places. Yes, expansion. Get Jennifer to plan the strategy, she'd enjoy that and it would stop her dwelling on the fear of cancer coming back.

Would stop him too. Pity you can't shoot it. Burst into a bedroom and hit it right between the eyes. One shot and gone. He pulled on his dressing gown and padded out to the decking above the swimming pool. Mrs Lightfoot was waiting with the breakfast tray.

CHAPTER THIRTY-FOUR

Lochranza basked in sunshine. Shuggie and Sandra sat outside at a picnic bench at the Sandwich Station watching the queue waiting for the ferry to Clonaig. At least Sandra was watching, for Shuggie was immersed in a search of the internet.

They had stopped at Arran Distillery and in the pick-up were three bottles of malt carefully packed among the soaps and lotions from Arran Aromatics. It was all Shuggie could do to contain his impatience as she had browsed soaps, perfumes and candles but he had to admit that the temptations of the distillery had similarly diverted him from tracking down Razor's hide-away. He had thought that they would get a coffee and sandwich at the Distillery Café but Casks Café had been buzzing. Outside a coach disgorged another group of visitors for a tour who chattered and photographed, as they poured through into the visitor centre. Shuggie abandoned the idea of spending further time. He wanted to be able to concentrate. The Sandwich Station was ideal, with enough going on to absorb Sandra and stop her asking, every few minutes, how his search was going.

He sat back and pushed the tablet across the wooden boards towards Sandra.

'Got it. Rosie Nelson. Razor's niece. See these on Instagram.'

Sandra scrolled as he pointed. 'So. Photos of a dog?'

'Read the comments. Corrie at High Corrie. See.' Shuggie lent across spun the screen so that they both could see. 'See. Here. Great Great Grannies Heilan' Hame.' He came round and typed. 'Facebook. Look at the post about last summer. That's it. We've found the house.

God, drove past Corrie on the way here. Remember the village by the sea. You commented on the houses on the landward side of the road with the washing in little gardens on the shore side. Said it was quaint.'

'But that was just back there.' She pointed vaguely. 'In that village? What five miles away?'

'Bit more but it is near. And it's not that place down on the shore. There's a little cluster of cottages on the slopes of Goatfell.' He clicked again. See Google Maps. Between the village on the shore and where the stream flows down from the mountain. See it?'

Sandra nodded. 'So what now? We go get him?'

Shuggie closed the apps and took back the tablet. He shook his head. 'No. remember what I said earlier. We've been seen. Here. On the island. I didn't check but probable CCTV at the Distillery. At that shopping complex at Arran Aromatics. There will be on the pier at Brodick. We enjoy being touristS. We leave tomorrow.'

'But... '

'Don't worry. Once we're officially back in Paisley, I am coming back. But this time I sail from Largs.' He saw the puzzled look on Sandra's face. 'Mate with a motor cruiser.' He gestured to the cruisers moored in Lochranza Bay. 'Moor around here. Fix Razor and sail home. No-one will ever know I was here.'

She grinned. 'I see that, I think? You can do it.' Half a statement half a question.

Shuggie did not reply but took a bite of sandwich and as they both sat staring out over the pale blue of the water, listening to the lap of the sea, he raised his cup to her and she responded, so that they clinked cups in a silent toast.

It was warm on the decking of his house and Graham McCluskey was asleep after the night's exertions and the big breakfast. He jerked awake, senses tingling at the sound of footsteps. The Bullfinches, that he was watching when sleep overtook him, flew off with this intrusion. McCluskey relaxed when he saw it was Jackson approaching carrying his Ipad but stiffened when he saw the demeanour. Jackson did not usually look so grim.

'It's the Columbians, Boss. Granny's seriously ill.' he held out the tablet as McCluskey shook himself fully awake. Grabbed it.

'What do you mean. Seriously ill?' McCluskey tried to focus on the screen. 'Shit man. Where?'

Jackson jabbed a finger against a Facebook post. 'There.'

McCluskey slumped in the lounger. Threw his head back then refocused on the screen. Read aloud. 'To let all friends know that granny is seriously ill.' He stopped and looked at Jackson. 'Jesus Christ, this is serious. The Columbians don't cry wolf and if they say Granny's ill we… ' Jackson tilted his head and gestured to keep reading. 'To all grandchildren we repeat she has a health emergency… and it could be terminal…' McCluskey was stunned into a brief silence, broken by 'Fuckin' hell, Jackson. What? Fuckin' terminal'

'That post has just gone up. I brought it at once. But I did have a quick look as I brought it out.' He reached for the Ipad and McCluskey surrendered it to him. Watched him tap.

'I think it must be this. Chicago police raid' Jackson passed it back.

McCluskey read. Flicked forward and back for moments before standing to walk back and forth. After several passes he stopped before Jackson. 'Geland Shuster and Liebermann, raided and papers seized. That could be terminal. And after last night could not be at a worse time.'

'Last night, Boss?'

'Forget it. Just a problem I solved for them. But if their offices are… ' He began to pace, stopped again before Jackson. 'I get out now. See where we are when this settles. Perhaps Liebermann is ring-fenced? Get the emergency bag put it in the car. You know the plan. Book me on a flight to Georgetown in Guyana; anything you can get leaving as soon as possible, but anything you can get. I'll speak to Mrs Lightfoot, now, about the boys.' McCluskey hesitated. 'You drive me to the airport. We stop on the way at the Hospital. I need to see Jennifer before I go.' he checked his watch. 'Can you do that in forty-five minutes?'

'Boss.' Jackson lifted a hand in acquiescence.

'Car in forty five minutes. Remember you don't know where I've gone.' He put an arm on Jackson's shoulder. 'Sorry didn't need to say that, did I. Nor this… but I will. Make sure Jennifer is OK. Right. Thanks. I'll text Jennifer so she's prepared for this.'

He took a last look at the loch. Texted to Jennifer. *Columbine's Granny in difficulty. Have to rush. Will visit before I go to her. XXX.* Muttered to himself, 'Thought they were meant to be shit-hot lawyers. Jesus, how long have the police been watching them? If there are recordings of telephone calls, I'm fucked.'

He took a last look over the waters glinting in the afternoon sun. How long before he could return? Could he ever return? Should he contact the boys? No. Time to speak to them was when he was safe in Guyana. And Jennifer would be home soon. With their Mum and Mrs Lightfoot, they would be fine. Damn it. Would they miss him? His musings were cut short by Jackson returning.

'Boss. I've booked a flight to London. Check-in opens in two hours. I'm afraid it is ten hour wait before the ongoing flight to Georgetown in the early hours of tomorrow morning, but it was best I could do.'

'Fine. It's out of here today, so that's fine.' McCluskey tapped his arm reassuringly. 'Keep alert. Bugger knows what this will bring, if the Chicago police have all the trails. There will be bastards trying to cut in, if they sense any weakness. Tell them I'll be back and any insubordination will be dealt with.'

Jackson laughed, a long slow rumble. McCluskey was taken aback at first for Jackson rarely smiled never mind laughed, then smiled. 'You'll enjoy telling them that.'

'I like to see fear, Boss.' Jackson replied. 'That's why I work for you.'

The two men stood looking into each others faces, wide grins. McCluskey felt settled for the first time since he had read the Columbian's post. Jackson was right. He enjoyed the threat, enjoyed retribution. He would be back and stronger. He broke the moment.

'Case in the car?' Jackson nodded. 'Right. Quick chat with Mrs Lightfoot on way out and were off'

It was not long before they were speeding towards the Erskine Bridge. As they exited the roundabout for Balloch, McCluskey caught sight of Inspector McVey's maroon Rover heading in the opposite direction, pointed it out to Jackson.

'Scruffy McVey. Lay odds he's heading to see me. I wish him luck with Mrs Lightfoot.'

CHAPTER THIRTY-FIVE

Inspector Charlie Hodgson settled in the low chair by the café window. From there he could keep an eye on the street corner by Mill Street Police Station and would see Sergeant Jenkins signal that the others were ready. It would be good to get a few moments alone with Scruffy. He saw his colleague, Inspector Hamilton McVey point to a Danish pastry and shouted over to the counter. 'Not for me , H, just the coffee.'

McVey swung round. 'You on a diet, Charlie? Surely not.' He gestured to the cakes. 'Tempt you?'

Charlie, noticing that Scruffy was thinner than before, consoled himself with the thought that he was succumbing, as it was simpler but, in truth, he had seen the cake appearing on Scruffy's plate. 'Aye. Go on.'

Scruffy joined him at the table and the waitress followed with the tray carrying two Americanos and the pastries. Hodgson was struck by the difference in Scruffy since they last met. Not only had he lost weight, the waistcoat and tie were a sartorial venture which Charlie did not expect. The hair was neat. The shirt had been ironed. Rumours of this change had reached him in Glasgow and there was talk of a woman behind it all. After all the years of Scruffy being single, and with a mother like Scruffy's, Charlie Hodgson had scoffed at the idea; until now.

'So it's true then?'

Scruffy looked puzzled for a moment, eased the material where his trouser stretched over his knees, then remembered the question he had laughed off as they entered; 'Will I meet her?'

'Oh. The rumours, yes they're true. Helen, her name's Helen.' Scruffy dropped a sugar cube into his cup and stirred. 'And yes, you will meet her. Not today of course, bit busy for that.' He played with the dissolving cube. Hodgson had the feeling that Scruffy was debating whether to say more. 'And we wouldn't want her around for this. She's a reporter you see. On the local. But a story like this would give her a scoop for one of the Nationals.'

'By God you pick them, H. No pillow talk then. Tossing and turning last night. Big day ahead. We're not going to find trails of TV crew and press speeding with us over the Erskine Bridge.'

McVey made a show of checking his watch. 'At this moment I expect she will be at Heritage Mill getting reactions to the Forensics search at McCluskey's flat.'

Hodgson raised an eyebrow, gave a low chuckle.

'It's not like that, Charlie. I said nothing but you know Forensics are not inconspicuous when they descend. With Heritage Mill being next to Morrisons car park there were numerous telephone calls to her paper. This is the big story at the moment so she was sent to follow up on them.'

Hodgson half bit, half tore off, a piece pastry and chewed thoughtfully. 'Any news from Forensics?'

'Early days but 'Woody Moffat… '

Hodgson spluttered on coffee and pastry. 'Is old Woody still on the go? Well, if there's anything, he'll find it.'

'…Too true. He has already. Amazing. Isn't it. They think they've eliminated all trace but it's bloody hard,' McVey tapped the table after 'bloody hard' and grinned at his unintended joke. 'Bloody hard to do that. Woody says there are traces of blood at the entrance to the flats, in the lift and at the door of McCluskey's penthouse. His guess is that it happened when they moved the body. Likely that someone died in the flat or the body was taken there.'

'You think it's my man, Hunter Dunbar. Will he get blood type, DNA?'

'Woody? I think he'd get DNA from a stone. My money is on it being blood from McNeil. Pity we missed McCluskey on Friday, I would love to have him in the interview room explaining this.'

'Never mind the interview room. Wouldn't you want to see his face when we descend on that mansion of his on Loch Lomond and start to pull it apart? God, I'm looking forward to this afternoon. The stuff from the Chicago Police raid on the lawyers, it's pure gold. From it we should be able to find enough to put McCluskey away on drugs charges for a long time. Not often we get to solve five murders and bust a drug ring in one go.'

McVey smiled thinly. 'Solved? We don't know who killed the American. Can we prove who killed McNeil, Browne, Ingleby, and Kowalski?'

'Find Freddy Razor Nelson, H. He's the key in my case. He links Browne to Dunbar. That will hopefully get me my killer and give us evidence on the others. Then we have the lot. Five murders and a drug ring. Good day's work. Promotion even.' He smiled across the table. 'Good way to start a marriage, Eh?'

McVey smiled back and shook his head in amusement. 'I'll get you Razor. We've traced him on a bus to Largs. He's holed up somewhere down the coast. I'm sure. Give us time we'll get him. The drugs? Razor's small fry. And yes we have the Chicago evidence, but my guess is Jackson will step up and take the rap. Faithful retainer and all that crap. Loyalty amongst thieves. Probably say that McCluskey didn't know half of it. But you're right about the masses of info from Chicago. I've Trish up there,' McVey nodded to across the road to the Police Station, 'ploughing through it all, and they must have ripped Geland Shuster and Liebermann apart. She's highlighting everything that mentions McCluskey.' McVey sighed, long, wearily. 'If we ever get him back. He disappeared when he reached Guyana.'

Charlie Hodgson leaned forward and shook a finger. 'Ah! But we've destroyed his operation.' Saw McVey's look. 'Well, we will today.'

McVey scratched the back of his neck as he sighed again. 'Not sure Charlie. I hear Jennifer McCluskey came home at the weekend. The king may be dead but long live the Queen? Hard as nails that one, I tell you.' He drained his cup. 'But there will be a very, very rich girl in this town, whose partner might rock that particular boat.' He paused for effect. 'Hugh Cameron. He's shacked up with McNeil's ex. Indeed they would be in the frame for that killing it it wasn't for the confirmation of the US involvement. With Simpster's death she comes into money. If she sticks with Cameron, he will have access to the sort of funds to blow this town wide open.'

'How does she get Simpster's millions?'

'McNeil had a will. They were keeping Simpster on ice until they could get rid of McNeil. From what I hear staff at the Chicago Care Home have admitted Simpster died days after admittance and pathology will confirm it. If he was dead before Dunbar killed McNeil. McNeil inherits and Smith inherits from him. Unless we can get Cameron on something from all this, he will be bloody rich, bloody powerful. You know there's no love lost between him and Jennifer McCluskey.'

'Razor Nelson was his sidekick, H. Find him and you can put Cameron away. I need him to figure out the Westerlands killing and Sam Browne's overdose. We need Razor Nelson. He's the key for me.'

CHAPTER THIRTY-SIX

The Firth of Clyde lay like a mirror. The motor yacht, Death Leopard, cut effortlessly out from Largs Marina and set course for Arran. With full cockpit canopies raised, all that the observers on the pontoons could make out was a cheery wave from two people on board. The thirty-one foot Bayliner picked up speed, the V of her wash spreading outwards.

'Do you like the name?' Asked Shuggie. He glanced over to the navigator's seat on the port side of the cockpit, saw Sandra wrinkle her nose. 'It's Pete's sense of humour. He used to be in the marines. And, if you're borrowing a friend's boat for this trip, might as well have death in the name.' Sandra stayed silent. 'You've not become squeamish about this, have you? I did say you could stay behind.' He was pleased to see a faint smile

'Squeamish? About Razor you mean. Shit no. Let's get it done and we can put this behind us. She smiled more now. 'I was worried I would be sea sick.' She swung her legs out from the chair. Long luscious, rising to pale blue shorts, a sun yellow blouse, Shuggie tore his eyes away to check their progress. Ahead two fishing boats needed his attention, flying the signal that they had nets out. He altered course to the west, closer towards Bute, in a wide sweep, then returned his gaze to Sandra and smiled. 'But you're OK?'

Sandra dropped down from her perch to stand beside him at the wheel. Her arm went round his waist and she stretched up to peck his cheek. 'OK. It's bloody brilliant. Wish I done this years ago. I feel as if we're flying.'

Shuggie gestured to the consul. 'Actually in a way we are. At this speed we're skimming the surface.'

'How fast?'

'On the gauge.' He pointed, 'there. I'm not pushing her but we're cruising at about twenty-five, twenty-six knots. Pretty close to thirty miles an hour. I've had to detour round those prawn fishermen but we'll be at Arran within the hour.'

Sandra left him at the helm and went below. He could hear her exploring and her exclamations of surprise at the luxury below. He shouted down the companionway. 'You could buy one you know. In fact you could buy much plusher than this.' Her blonde head appeared at the foot of the steps.

'What?' She shook her head a little, hair kissing her cheeks. 'I could buy this did you say?'

'One like it. Or better. You can have anything you want, now.'

A frown flicked over her face. 'I told you. I won't believe it. Not until the lawyers write.'

'Well the American ones won't. They're in jail. But its true. You saw it on the computer. They don't know precisely when Simpster died, but have fixed a date range and it's certain Paul died after that. So he will inherit... then you will inherit. You're rich, Sandra.'

'I hope. But no plans. Let's not start making plans. Not yet.' She shrugged. 'Coffee. I've found all we need. There's even choccy biccies.'

Shuggie pushed the throttles a little wider, joyed in the surge of power. 'Yes, please. Coffee.' He shouted after, as she disappeared. 'And a biscuit.'

It seemed little time till they approached Lochranza. Shuggie was pleased to see there was a mooring a distance from two already occupied. He watched Sandra sway her way to the bow, boat hook presented to the sky like some medieval knight. He marvelled at her balance and she proved to have a good eye, lifting the line on her first attempt. He watched her joy as she gave a jig on the bow.

'Careful,' he shouted, 'don't go overboard.' He thought he saw movement in one of the yachts and regretted drawing attention. Held a finger to his lips and stepped quickly back into the shadows of the canopy. When Sandra joined him, she helped to lower the tender into the water and attach the line to the stern ready for his departure, both rather subdued, knowing what lay ahead. Ripples whispered against the boat hull and it seemed as if the RIB was talking back as it swung gently at the end of its rope. In his head Shuggie thought the boat said death, death, death.

The cabin was comfortable. They had brought a selection from the Deli for an evening meal but neither was hungry. They sat together and nibbled at cold meat and salad until dusk began to fall.

'Time I was away.' he said.

She kissed him, soft and long. 'Take care.' As he pulled on a dark jumper she reached for his hand, held it. 'Don't go. We can leave Scotland. Leave Razor far behind. If I have money then the world… anywhere in the world. We can find a safe place.' Shuggie shook his head and releasing his hand from her grasp, went out to the bathing platform, pulled in the RIB. They stood together in the half light. Sandra put her hand on his arm as he stepped over into the tender. 'I know I made you promise. Forget that. I don't care if Razor is alive. I care you're alive. Stay. For me.'

Shuggie pulled the little outboard to life and spun the boat so that he could reach Sandra. Let his hand fall softly on her calf, caressed it. 'I'm afraid I can't. This isn't about my promise to you, or about him trying to kill me or about the money. This is about a fire years ago.' He blew a kiss as the engine revved. 'This is about Mel.'

'Come back,' she whispered.

It was an evening where the eye was drawn to Goatfell and the sun dying. The clear sky of earlier was now crossed with trails of stratos cloud, edged blood-red.

As he skimmed south Shuggie barely gave the scene a glance. Images of childhood, day trips and holidays, crowded his mind. Mel laughing, Mel splashing him with icy water. Those long summer days lying in the sand. Perhaps Sandholes Guest House had been a mistake. Happy memories of Mel in teenage pomp, on the beech at Whiting Bay, seemed so fresh. He felt such a longing to see her again. A mad desire to forget about Razor, forget today and to keep heading south and when he had passed Brodick and Lamlash, time would have reversed. At the water's edge in Whiting Bay, Mel would be waiting, in bright yellow bikini, centre of her teenage world. Shuggie blinked tears from his eyes and wiped his cheeks. Laughed to himself. If Sandra saw him, her strong man,, crying for a ghost.

As evening faded into night the dark mass of the island spread over his path. He throttled back, killing speed and reducing the wind-chill. On his starboard he could see the sandy beech at Sannox and two miles ahead the lights of Corrie.

In a few moments he skirted the small harbour and made shore where a bank of trees obscured the view from the road. In a house, back towards the village, a Friday night party was in full swing. Shuggie raised a grateful head to heaven for their throbbing dance music must have concealed his arrival. RIB safely hidden in the shadow of the trees, he made his way up the track into the hills.

Nine cottages formed the clachan of High Corrie. From the photographs posted by Razor's niece, Shuggie felt as if he knew the place well. Lights shone in three of houses. The one to his right must be the Mitchell's, elderly, like their dog, fortunately a very deaf old dog. Further right was Jeff… something. Wrote crime books.

Should have read some of those. Learnt how to do it. Ahead would be Mrs Ford. Thought she would be turned in by now. Mind you old folk, funny hours. But no lights in the cottage beyond. Razor sitting in the dark? Or out? Or gone elsewhere? Not here? Shuggie began to panic. Planning he had been so certain this was the place he had never considered he could be wrong.

He moved quietly between the houses. Froze, as he avoided the spill of yellow from Mrs Ford's. From inside came voices and he recognised the gravel tones of Razor Nelson, carefully edged into a position where he could see in. Razor and the old lady were sitting by an open hearth, bottle of whisky on the low table between them. The two faces cast with deep shadows by flickering flames reminded Shuggie of an etching for 'The Cottar's Saturday Night'. He dropped back into the darkness at Razor's cottage. He tried the door. It was unlocked. Through the open door he could see into the main room. A fire glowed feebly in the hearth. Shuggie went in, lifted a wooden chair and placed it behind the door. Anyone entering could not see him until they were over by the fireplace. He put two bottles of whisky on the floor by the chair. Found glasses in a cupboard and left two on the mantle-piece. From his jacket he brought a roll of cloth. In the moonlight it was just possible to see the glint of gunmetal as he unwrapped the pistol taken from Hunter Dunbar. Now he was ready.

It was about an hour before Shuggie heard the door of Mrs Ford's cottage open and the farewells of a rather drunk Razor and Mrs Ford's cheery 'Take care, Freddie.' The veil of cloud had cleared. The moon was high and full. There was sufficient light for crossing the short distance between the houses and for Razor to navigate the small hall. Shutting the outside door Razor stretched round the jam into the main room and put on the central light. He stepped over to the hearth, lifted the poker and enlivened the embers before tossing on a log from the waiting pile. As he stood to watch flames lick over the bark. He saw a movement in the mirror over the mantle-piece. Spun round to see the figure sitting behind the door.

'Shit, Big Man.' The beginning of a lunge to attack was broken by the sight of the gun. 'Shit. Nae need for that, Big Man. Is there?' He hung on one foot, swayed and dropped into the armchair by the fire. Shuggie could see the mind racing, fighting the fog of alcohol, fighting shock, the body tensed for a shot. 'Dinnae do it, Big Man.' Razor shook his head sharply, trying to jerk sense into a spinning world. 'Christ. It wis yon McCluskey, you ken. I wis on orders. I'd nae choice, man.'

Shuggie let him stew. Sat quietly for a time. 'We've always choices, Razor. You and me. Sometimes we make bad choices.' He took one bottle from the floor rolled it across to Razor. 'Tonight we drink to choices, eh. We'll have a drink for old times. You and me. Pour us a couple of good ones. Glasses behind you.'

Razor took the bottle. As he poured Shuggie sighed and tapped the gun. 'Don't even twitch. We're going to have a few drinks but if you try anything... Put my glass on the floor, half way between us, then sit back very still.'

Razor did as told and sat back in the chair. Shuggie noted how the movements were more controlled as the adrenaline took effect. 'A toast. To absent friends. To McCluskey.'

Razor hesitated, saw the movement of the gun and downed his glass.

'Yes, McCluskey. He's gone. Finally the police have caught up with him.'

'Whit? He's in jail?'

'Not yet. But he's legged it. Left the country. So, no him to run to now.'

Shuggie saw Razor sag, without thinking reach for the bottle then stop. 'On you go. Have another. Another toast.' He raised his glass, having barely touched the first. 'To Sam Browne. The boss who wasn't. May liars be punished and justice be served.'

Razor tossed his back. 'It wis McCluskey.' The voice was shaking. He raised a hand, pleading with Shuggie. 'I telt ye. I dinnae like it but McCluskey said Browne was to be the Boss. Who was I tae argue?'

Razor needed little encouragement to pour more whisky. As Shuggie left him in little doubt that the police were closing in, Razor became maudlin in his entreaties to Shuggie for help; swore unending loyalty if he would. The second bottle of whisky was opened. The log added to the fire began to sink into ash. It was time to go.

'Time for a walk, Razor.'

The gun was no longer necessary. Razor was falling into a stupor. As Shuggie walked over to where Razor sat he put the second bottle from the floor into the poacher's pocket of his jacket. Putting an arm round Razor he hoiked him from the chair and ushered him outside. The houses lay in darkness beneath thin cloud, which shone with silver, as Shuggie guided Razor onto the path towards the summit of Goatfell. Razor muttered and cursed as he was dragged higher. There was a point when crossing the style at the deer fence, Shuggie lost all control of him and he rolled feet away down hill. At last they reached the falls. A few days dry weather had reduced the flow and the spectacle but for Shuggie all was worth the climb.

He perched Razor by the bank and searching round with his hand found a brick-sized stone. Razor never saw the blow and in his state may not have felt it. His body crumpled from the bank and followed the rock into the foam. It caught on the bed of the burn.

Shuggie took the near empty bottle from his pocket. Remembered a picnic and Mel. Began to cry. 'I did toughen up, Mel. I did.' He lifted the bottle. 'Here's to you, Mel.' He drank, threw the bottle to break beside Razor's body. 'You'd have loved Sandra, Mel.' He wiped the tears. 'Perhaps I can.'

MORE CRIME FROM RYMOUR BOOKS

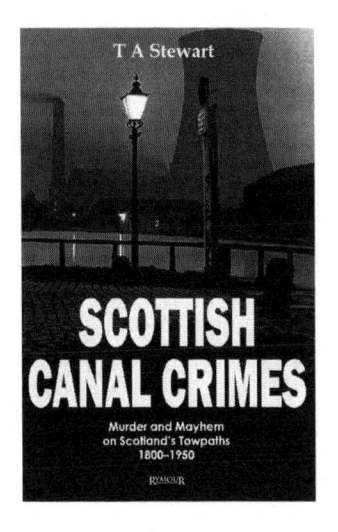

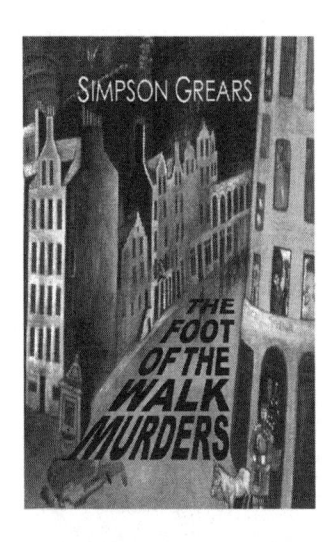

https://www.rymour.co.uk